The Safe Room

The Safe Room

Barbara Shapiro

Five Star • Waterville, Maine

Quote from *The Keepers of the House*
by Shirley Ann Grau (copyright 1964 by Shirley Ann Grau)
used with permission from JCA Literary Agency.

This novel is a work of fiction. Names, characters, places, and incidents are either the product of the author's imagination, or, if real, used fictitiously.

Five Star First Edition Mystery Series.

Published in 2002 in conjunction with Tekno Books and Ed Gorman.

Set in 11 pt. Plantin by Minnie B. Raven.

Printed in the United States on permanent paper.

Library of Congress Cataloging-in-Publication Data

Shapiro, Barbara A., 1951–
The safe room / Barbara Shapiro.
p. cm.—(Five Star first edition mystery series)
ISBN 0-7862-3012-6 (hc : alk. paper)
1. Lexington (Mass.)—Fiction. 2. Fugitive slaves—Fiction. 3. Underground railroad—Fiction.
4. Abolitionists—Family relationships—Fiction.
I. Title. II. Series.
PS3569.H3385 S24 2002
813′.54—dc21 2001058592

To all those who have been forced to flee their homes
in search of freedom

"It is as if their lives left a weaving of invisible threads in the air of this house . . . and I stumbled and fell into them."

— Shirley Ann Grau, *The Keepers of the House*

ACKNOWLEDGMENTS

And the names remain surprisingly the same. Thanks to my first readers: Jan Brogan, Thomas Engles and Floyd Kemske. Thanks to my second readers: Diane Bonavist, Deborah Crombie, Scott Fleishman, Gary Goshgarian, Tamar Hosansky, Pat Sparling, Vicki Steifel and Donna Stein. Thanks to my agent, Nancy Yost, my publisher, Ed Gorman and my editor, Mary Smith. And, as always, thanks to Dan, Robin and Scott.

CHAPTER ONE

A single, sharp sound woke me. I sat up in bed, disoriented, askew, and struggled to listen through the fog that hangs between sleep and waking. But all I could hear were the whispered sighs and creaks of Gram's old house struggling through the night, nothing as sharp and clear as the noise that had torn away my sleep. Had I dreamed it? I lay back and closed my eyes, thinking of all those who'd lived and died within these walls: seven generations of Hardens, whom I counted in the night the way insomniacs count sheep.

I had gotten as far as Colonel Stanton Harden, when I heard it again. A faint rasping, a grating, as if something, or someone, was scraping metal against metal, a manacle against stone. Digging? The noise rose from deep within the house, yet at the same time, it came from outside. From all around.

I crawled from bed and looked into the yard. It was hooded in shadow, and as the wind played through the trees, the streaks of darkness shifted and deepened and assumed odd and alien shape. No one was there. I opened my bedroom door and peered into the murky hallway. A stair riser creaked, the aging furnace rumbled its protest against the chill, but as I strained toward the scraping, I could hear nothing. No one was there.

In the morning, my bedroom was filled with the brilliant light of early May, and the phantoms of the night had departed to wherever it is phantoms go when the sun is out. The brilliance of a New England spring was powerful enough to banish even the most resilient of ghosts, and by the time I climbed into my car and headed for work, I had forgotten all about the strange sounds that had haunted me in the darkness.

Although I was twenty-seven, I was only a bit more than a year into my first real job—waitressing and substitute teaching didn't seem to qualify, although they had felt real enough at the time—and I still secretly reveled in the idea of being a part of the "grown-up" world of commuting and carrying an unpaid balance on my credit card. Of course, my mother and my cousin Beth, both of whom were committed to curing what they considered my protracted adolescence, would have claimed I was far from grown-up.

Hadn't I broken off an engagement to the "perfect man"—perfect, that is, except for the fact that I caught him cheating on me two months before the wedding? ("Everyone should be allowed one mistake," my mother had explained to me. "Especially someone as brilliant and good-looking as Richie.") Hadn't I wasted years getting a master's degree in a discipline as frivolous as sociology? And wasn't this proven by the fact that I was currently underpaid and underemployed as a part-time do-gooder with no chance of advancement? Not to mention that I lived with my grandmother. It was a wonder I could drag myself out of bed in the morning.

Still, there I was, up and out and actually enjoying my drive to work, which I liked to think of as a ten-mile trip across the social class system of America. I started from the modest, three-bedroom-two-and-a-half-bath colonials of Lexington, proceeded past the expansive lawns and mansions of Belmont Hill, and dipped into a corner of Cambridge jammed with teeth-gnashing rotaries, used-car dealerships and loud signs announcing appliance sales. Then I headed east on Memorial Drive, the impeccable grounds of Harvard University lining both sides of the Charles River, and across the BU Bridge, past some of Boston's toniest townhouses. But soon the well-kept boulevards melted into a grimy sameness of garbage-filled streets and unpainted, tired structures, and I was in a place where the blocks were gap-toothed with the flattened, charred remains of futile turf wars—and grass only grew where it shouldn't. An introductory sociology course in forty-five minutes or less, depending on traffic.

That morning, when I reached the run-down intersection of Centre and Washington Streets, there was something about the angle of the shadows that flashed me back to the morning of my first job interview at SafeHaven. I had somehow lost my bearings, but I hadn't been scared driving in aimless circles around sagging porches crawling with children and three-legged furniture. I had been excited. It was so exotic, so exhilarating: the obscenities scrawled on the walls, the rusted cars haphazardly resting on their tireless rims, the bored stares of the mothers, the vacant stares of the addicts. This was real life, this was where real things happened.

A year later, as I swung a well-practiced U-turn and parked in front of a tattered gray house, I knew all too much about the real things that happened in real life.

Two signs were mounted on the house's porch railing. One sign, scrawled in barely legible Magic Marker, read: "R. M. Masdea, DDS, No Appointment Necessary," and the other, neatly lettered, said: "SafeHaven." I peered through the grimy window of Dr. Masdea's mean little office and felt a rush of sympathy for those who had to let that awful man touch their teeth. It was an easy bet he overcharged too. I pushed the buzzer under the "SH."

"It's Lee," I yelled into the intercom.

When no answering buzz released the door, I hit the button again. Things were always breaking down at SafeHaven, both physically and emotionally, and we often functioned like a MASH unit, rushing from one crisis to another, focusing on whichever one appeared to loom largest at the moment. "Triage mentality," Kiah, the program director, called it; and it was an apt description, for whatever the big problem of the day was, invariably, a new crisis would arise to push it to the back burner, where it heated up and boiled into the next day's crisis, which pushed that day's crisis to the back burner, where it heated up . . . It's the nature of cycles to keep cycling, and SafeHaven had yet to find a way to beat them. But we kept trying.

A wary brown eye filled the broken peephole, then there was a grunt and the door swung inward. "Lee," Joy said with a scowl. "Damn button's busted again. Pain in the butt. Every time somebody comes, I gotta get up and let 'em in myself. Then the phone rings and the door goes again and I can't get a damn thing done. Kiah says we can't fix it 'til the next check comes from the feds. Pain in the butt," she muttered as she walked down the narrow hallway to her office. "Fucking pain in the butt."

I followed Joy to her desk. She sat down and her frown deepened. "We're running out of everything and Kiah says she's gonna have to turn clients away—even if they're in a real bad way."

Joy had only been on the job for a few months and hadn't yet caught on to the rhythm of life in an inner-city drug program. For once, I felt as if I was the insider, one of the in-crowd, rather than the outsider I knew myself to be.

In many ways, I was in a foreign land, a place with different customs, different rules, even a different language—and as hard as I tried, as long as I stayed, I would always speak with an accent.

I leaned over and gave Joy's ample shoulders a squeeze. "Kiah's never turned away a woman who needed her, and she's not going to start now. I'm finishing up the report, and they're going to give us the money for next year—I promise." I only hoped the god of procurement at Health and Human Services was listening.

"You don't think we're gonna have to close down?"

"No way." I raised my arms and clenched my fists. "Super researcher to the rescue: in search of truth, justice and a speedy buck!"

Kiah stuck her head out of the door of her office. "Truth, justice and a speedy buck?" She walked over and gave me a hug; she was tall and thin and moved with the willowy grace of a ballet dancer. "Thanks for coming in today, girlfriend."

It was officially my day off, but "officially" didn't count for much at SafeHaven—one of the many things I liked about working there. Kiah was another. She was a remarkable woman: tough and confident and extremely competent, but softened, and made even more remarkable by an amazing ability to get inside a person's head and understand—truly understand—why she did the things she did.

I shrugged, slightly embarrassed by my pleasure at Kiah's gratitude and her use of the word "girlfriend." In the year we'd been working together, she and I had evolved an odd kind of friendship—one that contained mutual respect and affection, but also a touch of distance, a wariness of circumstance we couldn't quite overcome: I left at the end of the day, and she did not.

"You didn't leave your grandmother home alone holding the bag, did you?" Kiah rubbed the heel of her hand against her cheekbone, a habitual gesture of both exhaustion and determination. Kiah's skin was a gleaming ebony that I'd always admired; when I once mentioned this, she told me her mother cried at its darkness when she was born. Now she said, "I wouldn't want to be accused of standing in the way of Tubman Park."

Not only would Kiah never be accused of standing in the way of Tubman Park, she was the reason I was involved with it—or more accurately, why my grandmother was involved with it. I lived with Gram in a house built by my great-great-great-great grandfather, Colonel Stanton Harden. He had been an ardent abolitionist and Civil War hero, and the house had been a station on the Underground Railroad—and that was the connection to Kiah. Kiah was a board member for the new Harriet Tubman Network to Freedom National Park, which, when it was completed, would connect hundreds of Underground Railroad sites into a six-hundred-mile-long park—actually, more of a six-hundred-mile-long archipelago. According to the *Boston Globe*, the Park would revive the spirit and history of the Underground Railroad "from the fraying edges of national memory."

"I'm bringing Trina back with me to help when I'm done here," I said. "Want to come give us a hand?" When I had first told Kiah about the history of Harden House, she immediately arranged to meet Gram and get a tour. Before I knew it, Gram, my cousin Beth and I were overseeing the house's designation as part of the Park. It was an ongoing joke that Kiah was responsible for the mammoth workload this had created—as well as the mammoth obsession that drove my grandmother.

"Don't I wish I could." Kiah waved her hand in the direction of her cluttered office. "Everything's pretty much on schedule?"

I shrugged. "I guess I'll find out soon. We're meeting with the contractor this afternoon."

"And your report?"

"The budget'll be ready for the accountant before I leave—if everything checks out with her, it can go out tomorrow." A large part of SafeHaven's money came from research-demonstration grants awarded by the federal government, and the next year's funding was dependent on the quality of the previous year's report. I could feel the weight of this responsibility lying heavy across my shoulders. I told Kiah I'd better get to it, and left.

Although I was officially a research assistant, no one at SafeHaven was slotted into a single job description. In my sixteen months on staff, I'd been a therapist, employment counselor, baby-sitter, carpenter, chauffeur and secretary—just to name a few. I did whatever I could, relishing the idea that although I might be working a "real" job, I wasn't working a "straight" one. Pantyhose were not my thing.

As I headed to the back stairs that led to my tiny attic office, I couldn't resist poking my head in the living room. Another reason I liked working at SafeHaven was that it was part of my job to mind other people's business—and I'm a nosy person by nature. I waved to Jayce, who was washing windows, and to Darla, who was mopping the floor. Jayce gave me a sad, sweet smile, but Darla ignored me. Darla was in the "week two funk." She was sure to come around after she had worked through her "week three fury." Either that or she'd leave.

I stopped outside the dining room, which doubled as a therapy room when it wasn't meal time, and watched morning group through the clear spot at the top of the etched-glass panel in the door. When the heavy wood-frame doors were closed, it was hard to hear what was being said—which was why the dining room was a good site for therapy sessions—but it was possible to see what was going on if you pushed your eye to the tiny piece of unclouded glass. Often, seeing was enough to know all.

A dozen women were sitting around the long scarred table: eleven clients and one counselor, Ruth Thompson, the head of treatment and a reformed addict like most of the staff. (SafeHaven was a grass-roots, community-based type of place, and I was almost singular in both the paleness of my skin and the lack of drug or alcohol abuse in my history.) I knew all the women, liked some and disliked others. I looked more closely when I saw that Trina Collins was sitting next to Ruth.

Although impartiality was the watchword at SafeHaven, it was impossible for individual staff to respond equally to all clients. After all, SafeHaven was all about connections between people, and chemistry was a big part of connection. Right from the start, Trina had sparked something in me, and it wasn't just the notoriety of her case, or the unfairness with which she had been portrayed in the media. Nothing made what she did justifiable, but right and wrong weren't as clear-cut as they appeared on TV. The first time I saw Trina—excluding the nightly news—she had been sitting in the shabby armchair in Kiah's office, shell-shocked, her handsome face dimmed by all she had been through. She was so skinny her jeans had been fastened around her waist with a shoelace.

Now, as I watched her lean over the table, full of good health and resolve, her face stern but her eyes warm, I felt a swell of pride. She was speaking earnestly to Shirleen, who sat across from her. Trina had come a long way since that first day, and although all the hard work had been hers, I liked to imagine that my friendship had been of some assistance. And although she still had much farther to go, and more battles to fight than either she or I might care to think about, I believed that Trina was going to be one of the few to break out of the cycle. Kiah wasn't as certain.

I turned from the window and climbed the stairs. Even if my mother and Beth thought I was wasting my time, my great-great-great-great grandfather, the Colonel, would be proud of what I was doing.

"Bitch!"

Trina took the abuse, sitting quietly, knowing that though nine of ten times it wouldn't make a bit of difference, there was that one of ten that just might. This was what she needed to do. To make it up to Hendrika for what she had done to her. To stay out of prison. To stay alive.

"Chill," Trina finally said to Shirleen, knowing it wasn't personal, but feeling like it was. "It might be hard to hear, Shirleen, but you gotta look at what came down. You need to get Willie back and you don't want what happened to Willie to—"

"I never did nothing bad to my baby!" Shirleen screamed. "I took care of him from the day he was born. My baby loves me!"

" 'Course he loves you," Trina said. "You're his mama. But that ain't always enough."

Shirleen glared at Trina, and Trina understood the other woman's anger as if it were her own. She had been exactly where Shirleen was. In that same seat. Shirleen was bullshit at the cop who bagged her instead of Thatch, the asshole dealer who deserved more time in the hold than he could serve in ten lifetimes. Shirleen was bullshit at the skanky sister from Children's Services who took Willie away. And Shirleen was bullshit at the judge who ordered her here. But mostly Shirleen was bullshit at Shirleen.

"Puttin' on airs," Shirleen muttered. "Ms. Trina Collins and her fuckin' straight fuckin' airs."

Trina glanced over at Ruth, hoping she'd run interference, but Ruth just sat there like some round, peaceful Buddha doll, all calm and serene-like. So Trina conjured up the sweet, tiny face of her lost little girl and tried again. "Drinking while you was pregnant was bad for him," she said. "Willie had a bad time—a really tough time. All those weeks in that preemie ward hooked up to all that shit. And now that you're pregnant again you gotta think about—"

"Who the hell are you to tell me what I got to do?" Shirleen demanded. "To tell me all the bad shit I did? At least my baby's still alive!"

I headed home to Lexington with Trina in the passenger seat beside me. Trina wasn't the first woman I'd brought home on SafeHaven Furlough—part-time work during the last phase of treatment—but she was the first success. Kiah claimed Gram and I were too trusting, that it was hard for white folks to understand, that we tended to go overboard in whatever direction we chose. And after what happened with Anet, I guess I'd have to admit Kiah had a point—but that didn't mean the point was valid in every case.

Trina had been working for my grandmother for almost a month, officially as a secretary, but she was a good sport, and did pretty much whatever Gram needed. And my grandmother needed lots of assistance—not because she was old or infirm, actually nothing could have been further from the truth, but because of the incredible amount of work that had to be done before Harden House could become part of

Tubman Park: schedules and renovations and deadlines and contractors and inspections and paperwork and paperwork and more paperwork. Although Gram had been indifferent to family history before meeting Kiah, now the Park was her prevailing preoccupation, her passion, surpassing even her zeal for tennis. Unfortunately, Gram's organizational skills did not compare to her backhand—which was where Trina came in: Despite Trina's lack of formal education, or maybe because of it, she was a whiz at organization.

To my grandmother's credit, she had taken out a rehab loan and found a company named Preservations to do the necessary renovations—although calling Preservations a company was a bit of a stretch. Preservations was really Michael Ennen, a nice guy who was long on good looks and charm, but short on experience. Gram was convinced that his two years of architecture at Harvard (he had dropped out), two more studying history at BU (he had dropped out), and a dozen summers spent working carpentry jobs with his father made him the perfect contractor for Harden House. His work had to be completed before the US Park Service would certify the house as an official "station" in the Park, and I worried that Michael's charm wasn't going to carry as much weight with the inspectors as it did with Gram.

"Is Michael going to be there?" Trina asked, as if reading my mind.

"Did you ever notice how neat he is all the time? How can a real contractor have such clean fingernails?"

"The man likes to take care of himself."

"I bet he spends more time getting ready for a date than I do."

"Check it out."

"I don't think so."

"Suit yourself." Trina shrugged. "But remember: a piece of a man is better than no man at all."

"You're so full of shit," I said. "You think I'm going to believe you think a piece of Lionnel is better than no man at all?" One of the first real conversations Trina and I ever had was about Richie and Lionnel. She had told me how Lionnel got her hooked on him and then on heroin, and how he took a powder as soon as he found out she was pregnant. I told her how I had discovered Richie in bed with one of his graduate students—Richie was a real, live rocket scientist, at MIT, no less—two days after I mailed out the wedding invitations. "Guess a man doesn't need to be black to be a shit," Trina had said, and we had solemnly promised we'd help each other to stay away from handsome men. Trina was not holding up her end of the bargain.

Trina grinned. "I admit Lionnel's a sleazy, slimy, rotten dog, but the man has his uses."

I stepped on the accelerator, passed an old Chevy on the right, and zipped under a light as it went from yellow to red—all right, so it was completely red, but the two cars behind me went through it too. The successful Boston driver is the one who knows which risks to take.

"I saw you with Ruth in group today," I said, changing the subject. "You seemed like you were doing real well."

Her smile disappeared and she turned away. "You must've been doing your spying early on."

"Oh?" I waited a good couple of seconds, then said "oh?" again. When Trina continued to stare out the window, I switched the radio to a rap station I knew she liked and didn't say anymore. It wasn't easy. No one has ever accused me of being reticent, but over a year at SafeHaven had taught me to hold my tongue. I kept quiet for an entire song.

Trina watched the rowers out for crew practice on the Charles. Her shoulder-length braids were gathered in a tattered ribbon, and her neck was exposed; it was so innocent, so vulnerable, such a heart-breaking creamy brown. Trina was twenty-three, but looked seventeen, maybe younger. As we crossed the BU Bridge, she turned and followed the path of a sleek boat full of college girls, racing toward Boston Harbor, its oars disappearing then rising from the dark water. A place she'd never been. A life she'd never had.

Yet, weren't they more alike than they were different? Trina and those girls? Trina and me? We all wanted the same things: a comfortable existence, health, love, peace, safety. Trina was smart and beautiful and had everything going for her except the facts of her birth and every day of her life. Unfortunately, we got what we deserved even less often than we got what we wanted.

"Shirleen can be a real bitch," I said, meaning it. Shirleen had attitude taller than the Prudential Tower. She once told me to fuck off after I offered to help her set the table.

Trina turned from the window and looked at me sadly. "Oh, Shirleen's not so bad. She just wants that baby back so much that she's all twisted around by it—that and the guilt."

The expression on Trina's face reminded me of the first time she had told me about Hendrika's death. She claimed she had felt the spirit of her child rise and wrap itself around her, full of love and forgiveness. Trina said Hendrika came to her often, at daybreak, the hour of her birth.

"Do you still feel like Hendrika's with you?"

"Sure," Trina said. "The dead don't ever leave."

CHAPTER TWO

August 28, 1858

Today is my seventeenth birthday, and Papa has given me this diary as a gift to commemorate the day. Though I have often wished for just such a chronicle, I find it difficult to feel gladness as my dear Mama is not here with me. Mama passed on in the spring, on March twenty-one, one hundred and sixty days ago. I know Mama is with our Lord, in a happier place, but still, I am sad. Papa says if I read my Bible, the words of our Lord shall provide the comfort I seek. I read, I do, or try my best to do so, but comfort eludes me. Papa does not understand me as Mama did, but he is a man and has many important things to which he must turn his attention.

Still, I have much hope for the future. I have two beaus, or rather, two boys with whom I would consider keeping company. One is called Lewis Campbell, of the Connecticut Campbells, and the other is Wendell Parker, whose family was among the earliest settlers of Lexington, way back when it was still named Cambridge Farms. Lewis is quite handsome and took three dances on my card last year at the Buffrum-Chase Christmas Ball, but he resides in Hartford, a day's journey from Lexington. Although Wendell could not, in truth, be described as handsome, he has a kind soul and his home is just across the Common from Harden House, which is where we live.

Dear diary, please excuse my rudeness, as I have not yet introduced myself or my family. I am Sarah Abigail Harden, daughter of Stanton Elijah Harden and Charlotte Margaret Harden, nee Abbott, late, of Lexington, Massachusetts. I also have one brother, Caleb Lloyd Harden, born in 1842, one year after I.

Papa is a famous man. He is known throughout the Commonwealth for the strength of his religious and moral convictions as well as his speeches against the sins of slavery. He has many enemies and takes far too many risks to help runaway Negroes, and I am often concerned for his safety. But Papa says he is doing God's work, and that the Lord protects his own. I, of course, do not question Papa, but nonetheless, I cannot but wonder how the Lord can maintain vigil on all of those who claim to be his own.

September 3, 1858

I received a letter from Lewis Campbell today by the afternoon post! Nancy Southwick had stopped for tea, and the two of us did giggle so over the contents of the correspondence. Lewis spoke briefly of his studies and his father's business plans, then said that his thoughts were already turning to Christmas and the Buffrum-Chase Ball. He added that he hoped he would have the pleasure of dancing with me again, and he signed the letter, "yours very truly." Nancy claims that this is a sure sign he has marriage on his mind!

I admit, I do admire him greatly, and his family would be acceptable, yet I am not certain I wish to be such a distance from Papa and Harden House. Nor, as Nancy remarked, do I wish to be separated from my dear friend Nancy Southwick. Wendell Parker does not cut nearly so fine a figure as Lewis, but he is of mild temperament, and Papa does admire his moral leanings. Nancy tells me Mr. Elijah Parker, Wendell's father, left him a parcel of land in his will, and that Wendell intends to build himself a grand house. I do confess it would be quite wonderful to be mistress of a great house, out from under the thumb of the dreadful Mrs. Harrington, and, truth be told, a bit more removed from Papa, whose piousness, at times, can be trying.

September 15, 1858

We went to a gala dinner party this evening at the home of William Lloyd Garrison of Boston. He is the publisher of The Liberator, *and the most famous abolitionist in the entire United States! Everyone knows of the mock gallows that were built outside his house by the anti-abolitionists and how, while he was jailed for opinions printed in* The Liberator, *he wrote, "I am in prison for denouncing slavery in a free country!" He and Papa are grand friends.*

Although there was much talk of the great injustices of the Fugitive Slave Act of 1850 and the "conspiracy of silence" perpetrated by those who prosper from exploiting the Negro, the party was most enjoyable. There were twenty in attendance for dinner including Lawrence Cabot Adams and Mr. and Mrs. Chas. Thayer Perkins. There were cold oysters and oyster pate and three kinds of wine. I was seated next to Wendell Parker whose talk was more lively than usual, although I dare say it was a few too many glasses of Roman punch which loosened his tongue. Papa would not agree with my assessment as he is most taken with Wendell due to his strong opinions against slavery.

I know that the conditions of the Negro in the Southern states are deplorable and wish with all my heart that those in bondage might soon be free, but I also wish that the men would not have taken so much time in the discussion of this matter in what otherwise was a lovely and gracious evening.

October 10, 1858

Just as I have feared, Papa was almost caught today helping a runaway slave. As the sun set, he arrived home with Dr. Howe and Mr. Weston Chapman, all three breathless and covered with leaves, but unharmed. As I wiped the dirt from Papa's cheeks, he instructed me to remain close-lipped about the comings and goings at Harden House. He said we must always be on our guard against those "respectable citizens" who seek to undo the good we are trying to do. So I have decided to lock away this diary within the back drawers of my chiffonier until it is safe for these words to be read.

Despite my misgivings, it is true that I am most proud of Papa, who is doing God's work by providing safe passage for those who seek freedom from the subjugation of slavery. He always leaves a light glowing in the front parlor window, a back door ajar, and keeps an ear pressed to the grapevine dispatch. He feeds, conceals, then helps the refugees along their way. He is watched by our neighbors, threatened by the authorities, and sometimes betrayed by his friends. But Papa says that the laws of God must take precedence over the laws of man. He is a very wise and brave man.

Neither Caleb nor Papa is ever afraid, and I venture to guess that were dear Mama still alive, she would have no fear either, but I am only seventeen and a girl. Nancy Southwick whispers that the house of Papa's friend, Professor Samuel Hillard, was stoned and that the professor is no longer allowed to teach at Harvard College. She also said a man named Lovejoy was killed and another's hand was branded with the same horrid instrument they use to mark ownership of cows. "SS" they burned into his skin. "SS" for Slave Stealer. What if such things should befall Papa or Caleb?

October 24, 1858

In consequence of Papa's near arrest a fortnight ago, Papa and Caleb and Wendell Parker are constructing a secret room in which to conceal the fugitives. Although Wendell is two years older than Caleb (one year older than I), they have been friends since they were small boys. Wendell's father was an abolitionist too, but he died of consumption last year, and it has been left to Wendell to carry on for him. Wendell is usually silent, but I must admit that it is nice to have someone about Harden House besides Caleb and Papa and Mrs. Harrington, whose only conversation is of the torment of her gout and the weight of her unfinished tasks.

The men do all their work at night, in bits and pieces, and hide hammers and wooden planks in the bottom of the carriage to be brought into the house under cover of darkness. I am most impressed with their cleverness. They are building a door with concealed hinges that opens into a space no one would ever suspect is there! It is behind the landing of the staircase, between the east and west parlors. It is most exciting!

But I must say no more, as these days there are many bounty hunters about, and Mr. Harrison Gray Otis spoke of Papa at one of his Whig meetings, calling him a "d—abolitionist" and a "curse and a contagion" to the good people of Lexington. Papa has never pretended to be anyone save the abolitionist he is, but being named by Mr. Otis will make it increasingly difficult for him to carry on. He has oft been watched before, now he will be watched always.

It's difficult to know whom to trust. Papa was most surprised when Mrs. Lucretia Child did loudly click her knitting needles last Sunday when Reverend Lyman declared in his sermon that "those men who speak against slavery speak against the Union." Mr. Child's family hails from Kentucky, and he is quite vocal about his proslavery beliefs. Although Papa was encouraged by Mrs. Child's act of defiance in so public a place, he found it distressing to hear such sentiments spoken of from the pulpit of our little church.

Papa reminds me that despite the words of the reverend, I must never question the righteousness of our mission. He nods gravely and pushes his spectacles up on the bridge of his nose, a gesture I always equate with his compassion and humanity. I nod in return, but do not reveal my true thoughts. I do not tell him it is not righteousness that I question, but safety. Is it so very wrong to desire the safety of the ones I love most dearly?

As I write these words I see that I must open my heart and drive away my fears, for what else do the poor fugitives desire but the safety of those they hold most dear?

October 25, 1858

There is a family coming, a mother and her little girl, and the safe room is not near to ready! Papa got word last night from a station master in Hartford, Connecticut. God and weather permitting, a young woman named Rachel will arrive with her baby, Chloe, just before dawn tomorrow. They have come all the way from the Carolinas.

Papa, Caleb and Wendell hurry as much as they are able, and even I have been pressed into assistance. Although I recognize the seriousness of the work, and the many dangers it poses for the poor fugitives, as well as for my own family, I cannot help but be exhilarated by partaking in activities beyond keeping my receipt book and overseeing the cleaning and cooking of the peevish Mrs. Harrington.

Although I would not admit it to anyone but you, dear diary, I have always felt myself to be a bit apart from Nancy Southwick and Cousin Lizzie and even dear Mama. They are well-satisfied with the activities of embroidery and handwork, entertaining and visiting, with ensuring the housekeeper has properly laundered the linens and that the children are clean. Although I do desire to be wife, mother and mistress of a fine home, I sometimes find myself also desiring more, although what "more" is, I know not.

It is enough for me today to feel of so much use, to God and to my fellow human beings, for today I do more than just pull the ropes and handle the ribbons of our small household.

This morning I went out to the carriage, as if in search of a missing hat. Papa instructed me to place three pieces of wood inside my gray cloak, and then walk nonchalantly back into the house. I did just as he asked, pretending that losing my bonnet was the most vexing event of my day. Wendell told me I was very clever, and I could feel my face flush with pleasure at his praise. Caleb whispered that Wendell is sweet on me, and appeared surprised when I calmly acknowledged the truth of his observation. Men can be so foolish.

As Papa, Wendell and Caleb work on the safe room, my job is to keep watch for slavers and bounty hunters and those nasty, prying persons who wish the Negro to remain within the chains of slavery. As a good Christian woman, I try to have compassion for all souls, for all ways of thinking, but I cannot understand why anyone would wish to see another human being in bondage.

October 26, 1858

Rachel and Chloe have arrived safely! The mother is weak and quite sickly, but the child, a little girl of about two, is chubby and healthy and a very happy sort. It appears Chloe's father was a white man, but mother and daughter don't seem to notice any difference between them. Papa says that is because there is none. The soul has no color. Neither do the ties of family.

It breaks my heart to think that there are so many men about, maybe some as close as the apple orchards behind our house, who desire to tear this little family apart. Harriet Exeter told me bounty hunters take babes from their mothers' breasts, then sell the little tykes down river. In almost all of these occurrences, mother and child never see one another again. Harriet also told me there are many children whose skin is far lighter in color than that of their mothers. Another great abomination of slavery, but one of which we rarely speak.

Rachel rests on the trundle under the bed in my room. Her fever is high, and she has no interest in taking any sustenance. When I tell her she must, for her little girl's sake, she gamely attempts to swallow the soup. Often, it comes up again.

Mrs. Harrington is not happy with our guests. She prefers to pretend that they are not present and to thwart any efforts I might offer on their behalf. When I requested that she put up a quart of split peas to soak overnight so that Rachel and Chloe might have the hearty sustenance of winter pea soup, she claimed there were no peas among the provisions. I was certain there were at least two quarts of peas in the canning cupboard, and told her as much. But when I went into the cellar to retrieve them, I found there were none and was forced to admit she was right. Mrs. Harrington smiled for the first time since Rachel and Chloe's arrival.

October 27, 1858 (morning)

Papa says we must find a way for Rachel and Chloe to leave tonight. Bills have been posted at the depot with their description and the offer of a large reward. It is also reported that Mr. Child (the one from Kentucky) has told Mr. Harrison Gray Otis that the fugitives are in Lexington. We cannot fathom how Mr. Child came upon this information, but we do know if fugitives are believed to be in Lexington, it will also be believed that they are at Harden House.

But Rachel is far too ill to travel and the safe room is not yet complete!

October 27, 1858 (afternoon)

As if there were not troubles enough in our little household, another fugitive has arrived at our door. He comes to us with tales of near capture and is dragging a broken leg. Until Dr. Miller can tend to his leg, which is very nasty indeed, this man is no more prepared to travel than Rachel. It is a wonder he was able to elude the slavers and make it here. Papa says it is a sign that God is with us. Despite her claims of deep piousness, Mrs. Harrington is extremely vexed.

Wendell and Caleb found the man in the barn. Papa says he's really just a boy, barely twenty, but he looks twenty-five to me. His name is Silas Person, and he hails all the way from Louisiana. It is easy to see from the manner in which he handles his pain, that he is a strong and brave man. He is also very handsome, but his smile is so sad. He too had a white father.

Wendell and Caleb work on the safe room as much as they dare, and often Wendell takes tea with me in the late afternoon. He is a nice enough boy, but I cannot in all truth say I am much taken with him. I wish Mama were here to advise me. Is it necessary to be taken with a man to become his wife? I feel in my heart that it is, but think that it may not be. Nancy reminds me of the goodness of Wendell's soul and the fine house he shall build for his bride. I wonder what Mama would counsel.

Every day, Papa takes a stroll about town to show that he is not occupied with anything more than acquiring a good cigar. I do my featherstitching and tend to our patients as best as I am able. I play with little Chloe, who is the delight of my day. I also keep watch. For unless we find a place to hide our three guests, they will not be guests for long. And we shall be in jail.

October 27, 1858 (evening)

Mr. Silas Person (Papa says I should refer to him as such) is a most remarkable man. Although it is evident to any who might see that the condition of his leg causes him great pain, he never utters a word of complaint. He plays with Chloe and makes her laugh so that I am free to nurse Rachel. I pray that Dr. Miller will arrive soon, as I fear infection will set in.

Mr. Person can also read! I came upon him with his head in one of Caleb's books, and he confessed that Master William, the eldest son of his master, had taught him when he was just a child. His master knew of it, but never spoke of it, as it is illegal in the South for a Negro to read. The master turned a blind eye to all of this and gave Silas free roam of his library. Mr. Person has read many of our great authors: Hawthorne and Franklin and Thoreau. Even Mrs. Stowe! I dare say he is far better read than I. Perhaps better read even than Caleb or Wendell Parker.

Mr. Person's job on the plantation was to be a companion to Master William. In the morning, Mr. Person would work alongside the other house slaves, but in the afternoon, when Master William had finished with his tutor, Mr. Person and Master William would go fishing and hunting and sometimes even drink corn liquor together. Every afternoon, Master William would teach Mr. Person what he learned from his tutor that morning, and now Mr. Person is as educated as any fine gentleman. It is jarring to hear him talk though, for he speaks with the long vowels that bring to mind the speech of the Southern anti-abolitionists.

October 28, 1858 (morning)

News has just arrived that Mr. Alexander Lyman, the constable of Concord, has organized a party of men to patrol the forests of Lexington and Concord in search of runaway slaves. Mr. Lyman claims the Fugitive Slave Act decrees it to be every man's patriotic duty to support slavery, and that those who do not are criminals as common as any thief. He told Mr. Weston Chace that he is coming this way, that he knows all too well what Papa is "up to," and that he will put Stanton Harden down "by fair means if I can, by foul if I must." He has dogs with him.

Papa says he does not care about Mr. Lyman's blustering, that he is not afraid because he is in the right. When I asked Wendell what he thought of Mr. Lyman's threats, he told me not to worry my pretty head over such things, assuring me that many strong and wise men were on their side and that neither Papa nor I had anything to fear. But I was not comforted by his words and admitted as much to Mr. Silas Person. To my surprise, Mr. Person said Mr. Lyman and his like are to be feared, but that they can also be beaten.

After Dr. Miller set his leg, Mr. Person hobbled down the stairs to help Wendell and Caleb finish the safe room. I do not know how he has the strength, but Wendell says he has been of great assistance. And Lord knows Wendell and Caleb need all the assistance they can muster, for Mr. Lyman and his men are certain to be here any moment, and neither Rachel nor Silas is near able to travel.

October 28, 1858 (afternoon)

Mrs. Lucretia Child has just arrived at our back door with the news we have been most dreading: Mr. Lyman is at Charles Phillips' farm, just a short ride from us, and he is headed our way! He told Mrs. Phillips he knows for certain that Rachel and Chloe are here, and that he would be willing to stake his life that the slave from Louisiana, the one they have been tracking since Providence, Rhode Island, is also being harbored under our roof, in defiance of the laws of the Commonwealth of Massachusetts and the United States of America. He claims he shall return "the property to its rightful owners" and "punish all those who believe they are above the law."

I imagine I hear the barking of dogs as we hurry our guests into the safe room. The hidden panel still needs another coat of paint, and I cannot imagine how anyone will be fooled. When everyone is concealed, Papa and Caleb settle in the west parlor, and Mrs. Harrington takes the seat across from me in the east parlor, her face as cold as a January night.

Our darning needles click in the heavy silence, although I mend nothing.

CHAPTER THREE

Grandma Clara liked to describe herself as a "knee-jerk liberal whose knees don't jerk as well as they used to," but her razor-sharp tennis game belied her words—at least the part about her physical condition. And although she also liked to think she wasn't the grandmother type—she was a terrible cook, wouldn't be caught dead knitting and was captain of the senior women's team at her tennis club—there were certain emotions that even the least grandmotherly of grandmothers couldn't escape. And worrying about my love life was one of Gram's. I was guessing thoughts of that nature were mingling with her annoyance at my tardiness as she waited with Beth and Michael for Trina and me to get home.

"So what's the problem with Michael Ennen?" Gram had asked just that morning, raising a single eyebrow. (As kids, Beth and I used to spend hours in front of my mirror trying to imitate that gesture; Beth finally got it, but I was never able to isolate one eyebrow from the other.) I tried to explain about women not needing a man to define them anymore, about it being the twenty-first century and all, but Gram would have none of it. "Some things don't change," she declared. "And a man who is nice to his sick mother will be nice to his wife." I had rolled my eyes.

The squeal of my tires interrupted my thoughts. I was taking the exit off Route 2 a bit too fast, and I hadn't put air in the tires since I had bought the car from Richie over a year ago.

"Hey," Trina shouted as we fish-tailed slightly in the curve. "Just 'cause I said the dead are still hanging out doesn't mean I'm ready to be one of them."

"You really believe all that stuff?" I asked as I drove more slowly toward Lexington Center.

"Stuff?" Trina's smile was amused. She was clearly baiting me.

But I wanted to hear her answer, so I said, "You know, heaven and hell and life after death—that stuff."

"I'm not all that sure about the heaven and hell piece, but yeah, shit, there's got to be an afterlife."

"Why?"

"Look around you, girl—at you, me, the trees. Wouldn't you say the fact that we're alive at all, that all this shit is here, is much weirder than thinkin' we'll stay that way?"

I knew her argument didn't really make sense, but still, I couldn't immediately come up with a repudiation. I shrugged.

"Plus," Trina said. "There's got to be more to it than this."

That argument made more sense—especially from her point of view. I drove through Lexington Center as fast as I dared. There were these damn crosswalks every half-block, and the law in Massachusetts—which was ignored in Boston, but upheld in Lexington—was that a vehicle must stop for a pedestrian in a crosswalk. Another difference between Boston and Lexington was that the cops in Lexington were far less busy than their big city compatriots—and I had a fistful of crosswalk violations to prove it.

It was almost four when Trina and I pulled up to Harden House. "Harden House" may sound stuffy and pompous, but that was what we'd called it since I was a kid—and the things learned in childhood are not easily undone. Gram was my mother's mother, and that side of the family had been blue-blood since the beginning of time. My father's family, on the other hand, was New York Jewish, coming up the hard way through the garment district and City College. As there hadn't been a glimmer of dissent among my mother's relatives when she brought a Jew into the clan, the use of a proper name for a house seems a forgivable transgression.

In defiance of the pretension of its name, Harden House was rather small and sat close to the road. But it was also beautifully proportioned and classic in design: the consummate black-shuttered, white colonial farmhouse, complete with attached barn and red front door—although crying out for a new coat of paint. At one time, there were acres of land, cows and corn and even a small apple orchard, but over the years the land had been sold off bit by bit, and now the property was similar in size to the quarter-acre lots that abutted it.

The Hardens were big on lineage and principle, but short on business savvy, and it was sheer inertia that had kept the house in the family for so long. Local prosperity and the quality of Lexington's school system had increased its value. Michael estimated that, after the renovations and including the furniture—mostly quality pieces the Colonel had imported from France before the Civil War, and no one had bothered to sell or give away—the whole shebang was worth well into seven figures. Although Gram thought Michael could do no wrong, on this point she was sure he was in error. "That's ridiculous," she told him. "Bad plumbing, a rotting barn and eight crumbling rooms can't be worth a million dollars." "It's authentic," Michael had assured her. "Authenticity and walking distance to Lexington Center are worth a lot."

When Trina and I came through the back door, Beth and Michael were sitting at the kitchen table drinking iced tea. Gram was leaning against the counter, a carton of milk at her elbow, still in her tennis clothes. She looked pointedly at the clock over my head.

"Sorry," I said.

Gram hugged Trina. "I'm in the middle of *Having Our Say*. Great recommendation. Those Delany sisters are amazing—feisty and smart and so embracing of life despite everything. Bessie and Sadie—vinegar and molasses—I love it. What a perspective they've got, 101 and 103, like living through multiple lifetimes. It makes even me feel young."

Trina smiled happily. "Figured you'd like it. *Jackie By Josie*'s cool."

I was surprised to hear that Trina and Gram were swapping books: the few times I'd offered Trina a book, she'd refused politely. I had figured she didn't like to read. "*Jackie By Josie*?" I asked Gram. "Isn't that about some woman infatuated with Jackie Kennedy?"

"I also gave her *Le Divorce* and a new novella I just read called *The Underachiever's Diary*."

"Aren't those a bit frivolous?"

Gram frowned at me.

I reached into the refrigerator for the pitcher of iced tea, poured a glass for myself and one for Trina. "Sorry we're late," I said to Gram again. "I got stuck at work."

"Held captive by WaifHaven?" Beth grinned at Trina. "Present company excluded, of course."

Although Beth had a huge heart when it came to her friends and family—she was always making surprise parties, finding the perfect gift, and was the first to drop everything and get to the hospital in any emergency—she was basically a snob. It wasn't that she was especially prejudiced, or had an aversion to any particular minority, it was just that Beth was very Beth-centered, and poor, black, drug addicts were not part of Beth's world—despite her own past struggles with prescription diet pills.

Trina and Gram ignored Beth, continuing their conversation, but I said, "If only there was a haven for the intolerant."

Beth turned to Michael. "Lee was always the smart one in the family. Maybe one of these days she'll get herself a real job."

Gram raised an eyebrow. "Interesting comment from a woman whose 'real' job is golf and decorating."

"You forgot shopping," I said.

Beth laughed merrily and waved her manicured fingernails at me. She was unabashedly into things: expensive cars, jewelry, furniture, even her golf clubs were embossed with some fancy-schmancy designer's logo. "My obsession with image over content," she called it, adding that it was a damn good thing her husband Russ had taken her advice and sold his software company to Microsoft for stock instead of cash—and then, against all logic, gone back to school to become a dentist. This observation was inevitably followed by a boisterous, bubbling and contagious peal of laughter. Beth was an astounding mass of contradictions: pretentious and a bit ostentatious, but better with a drill and a wire-stripper than any man I knew; overweight and bullying as a child, but svelte and strong and a true friend now; nosy and opinionated, but charming and funny and unfailingly self-aware. She was the older sister my mother had never given me—for both good and ill.

"You're just jealous of my impeccable taste," Beth said.

I had no response. Beth's words were true, and we both knew it. I'd always envied her unique style, her flair, and especially the way she carried it off, looking so put together without appearing to have tried. Being around Beth always made me wish I had made that hair appointment or bought those great shoes or noticed the stain on the collar of my blouse before I left the house.

Michael carefully inspected the clipboard in his hand, all lanky and loose-limbed as he flipped the pages, clearly uncomfortable with our affectionate-antagonistic banter.

I felt sorry for him. "You don't have any sisters, do you?"

"Good guess." His smile was boyish and appealing, and I noticed one of his front teeth was chipped. "Two brothers."

I felt a flush climbing my cheeks and made a rather clumsy, puffed-up production of taking a sip of iced tea. I didn't look at Trina.

"I have to show Beth and Trina something upstairs," Gram said to Michael. "Why don't you and Lee get started, and we'll catch up with you later?" She smiled sweetly at me.

"What do you have to show them?" I asked suspiciously.

Michael jumped from his chair before Gram could answer. "Sounds good," he said to Gram. "The inspection's next Monday, and we've got to make a decision about filling the hole in the foundation—fast." He turned to me and his dimples flashed. "Want to start with the cellar? I'll show you what I've done to shore up the safe room."

"The cellar?" I hated the cellar. It was small and mean and dark, and the clammy smell of long-dead animals rose from the dirt floor like cold fog off a swamp. The ceiling was low and lit by bare bulbs spaced so far apart that the walls were draped in shadow. Knee-high mounds of dirt pimpled the hard-packed ground, and despite a few half-hearted attempts, no one seemed to be able to figure out where they had come from. "How about we start somewhere else?"

"Beware of the woman with the iron teeth!" Beth taunted in the same sing-song voice she had used to torment me when we were kids. She raised her hands in front of her face and transformed her long, blood-red fingernails into menacing claws. Her eyes gleamed with the gloating pleasure I remembered all too well.

I stuck out my tongue at her. The woman with the iron teeth was the mistress of the cellar, the evil witch of my youth, the antagonist of my dreams. According to Beth and her brother Tommy, the woman with the iron teeth lived in the tunnel behind the small root cellar, and she loved to eat little girls whose first names began with "L."

My mother maintained it was Beth and Tommy—and the woman with the iron teeth—who were responsible for my childhood nightmares and sleepwalking, but I'd always been afraid I'd inherited the crazy Harden gene. This gene had caused at least one Harden woman in every generation to experience a "breakdown" in which she heard voices, saw people who weren't there and spent a lot of time wandering around the house talking to the walls. "Dotty" Aunt Hortense, as she was affectionately known in the family, had walked off the roof after a particularly spirited encounter with no one. As of yet, none of my female cousins had been committed, and as far as I knew, none were even on Prozac.

"Stop it, both of you," Gram said, shaking her head. "I swear, Beth, sometimes you act just like that mean little girl you used to be." Then she turned her exasperated gaze to me. "And you can't possibly still think there's anything down there that will harm you."

Once, when I was about eight, I had seen a huge rat in the cellar, and now the hairs on the back of my neck rose at the memory of that disgusting tail disappearing into the fieldstone foundation. I rubbed my arms and avoided Gram's eyes.

Beth grinned wickedly. "Michael will protect you," she said. Then she grabbed Gram and Trina by the hands and pulled them from the kitchen.

Trina was annoyed, but she let Beth drag her into the dining room anyway. She knew the cousin didn't do well with contradiction, and it didn't seem worth it to start up all that squawking. But as soon as she could, she yanked her arm from the spiky grasp, though she had to admit the cousin's fingernails were awesome: long and square and painted a dark, sparkly red. Trina pulled herself to a stop in front of the fireplace and stared at the carved mantelpiece, not wanting Clara to see how pissed off she was.

The fireplace was nearly as tall as she was, and before she realized what she was doing, she reached out and touched it. Behind the bricks, between the chimney and the stairs, was a secret place with no windows and a hidden door. A safe room from the Underground Railroad days. The entrance was on the other side. You got to it from the landing of the stairs in the front of the house.

The first day Trina had come to Harden House, Lee showed her a panel in the wall halfway up the stairway and told her to push it. Lee didn't tell her why, and Trina didn't want to do it, but Lee promised she'd be glad if she did. Trina needed the SafeHaven furlough gig to work out, so she swallowed her suspicions and gave the panel a shove. It fell away, and she stared into a deep, narrow slice of space no one would ever have guessed existed. It looked empty down there, but Trina knew it wasn't. It was tight, dark and smelled bad, and there was something struggling inside those walls. Whatever, or whoever it was, tugged at her soul.

When Lee described how the house had once been a station on the Underground Railroad, how whole families had crowded into that hot room with no air, Trina understood who was tugging at her: it was all those folks who had come before. Her ancestors. Trina had never cared much about politics or all that black pride shit the sisters and brothers were always spouting, but she liked thinking about the ones who had had the guts to fight back. That was when she felt proud to be black. Right then and there, she had jumped into the safe room. Just like that. She was hoping to get closer to the ones who made her feel proud, but once she was in there, it wasn't pride or closeness she felt, it was the pain of remembering.

The safe room was way too much like that closet he had put her in: smelly and cramped, with a ceiling you couldn't see but could guess was full of spiders and other scary creatures. It was after he finally let her out of the closet that she stopped going to school and nobody noticed. She never understood that. How could nobody notice? Didn't the school call or something?

Standing in the safe room, Trina had felt all those men and women, little children too. Scared and brave. Beat down and hopeful. They were there. Here. Feeling them, thinking about what they'd been through, made her even more certain about getting her own life turned around, even more determined to make it up to Hendrika. Hendrika hadn't done any more to deserve being dead than any of the lost souls hanging around in that tight little room.

Beth poked Trina in the side, bringing her back to the

present. "Pretty subtle of Gram, huh?" Beth said. "She wants to show us something upstairs. Ha!"

Trina dropped her hand from the fireplace. The cousin was one of those white folks who figured if they were touchy and friendly, it'd prove they weren't prejudiced. She didn't answer.

But Clara did. "One of the advantages of being old is that you don't have to be subtle—you're forthright and direct and everyone's so impressed when you 'speak your mind.' " She rolled her eyes at Trina. "Can you imagine what Beth's going to be like when she hits sixty-five?"

Trina tried to smile because she liked Clara, but she just couldn't believe Clara wasn't seeing what was right in front of her face. Like the cousin ever said what she was really thinking. That girl would say and do anything that would get her her own way. "Kind of scary," Trina said, meaning it, but not in the way Clara thought. Trina didn't have any interest in the likes of the cousin. The cousin's world would never be any wider than what she saw.

"Now, what can I show you upstairs that you could possibly have any interest in?" Clara winked at Trina. "Let's go up to my bedroom—I'm sure you're just dying to see the new dress I bought for Karen's wedding."

"I'm interested," Beth said. "Where'd you get it?"

Clara didn't answer. She just went into the hall. "It wasn't your interest I was concerned with," she told the cousin.

Trina followed Clara up the stairs, trying not to laugh. Clara wasn't like most white folks—who either ignored you or sucked up to you because you were black—Clara just treated everyone the same. Like, for example, the cousin had never offered Trina a book, probably because she didn't think Trina could read, and though Lee offered her books all the time, the books were always about some down-and-out black person or some other shit-on group, like American Indians or women in Afghanistan. But Clara gave Trina books just because she'd read them and liked them, and figured if she liked them, Trina might too. Last week, Clara had asked Trina to suggest a book for her to read. It didn't take nearly as much energy to be around Clara as it took to be around most white folks.

The stairway was real narrow, turned on itself twice, and ended in a small landing. Trina had never been up this way before; she'd only come up the back stairs one time when Clara asked her to fetch some papers from the bedroom. At each side of the landing was a bedroom, and Trina knew there were these two smaller bedrooms too, but the only way to get to them was by going up the back stairs or by walking through one of the front bedrooms. The house was smaller than it looked from the outside, and the way the rooms were set up wasn't too practical. Trina winced at what she was thinking. Like she knew anything about houses and what made them practical.

Trina followed Beth into Clara's room because she didn't know what else to do. It was nice in there. Lots of windows and a painted floor with these small rugs that looked as if some little kid had made them. Clara picked up a stack of books from a chair and told Trina to sit down in it. The cousin frowned and sat on the edge of the bed.

"As long as we're here, I might as well show you the dress," Clara said. She pulled a black dress from the closet. It didn't look like much.

Beth stood up to feel the fabric, and Trina tried to look interested, but she wasn't. The furniture was all real old, and some of it looked like it was ready to fall apart, but she could see it was quality. Antiques. The kind they auctioned off for thousands of dollars to people who already had too much furniture. Trina thought about morning group at SafeHaven. No one in that room ever had too much furniture.

Trina noticed a small dressing table in the corner she hadn't seen the first time she was in the bedroom. On the top, in the middle of a mess of brushes and powders and perfume bottles, was a jewelry box. The bottom drawer was pulled open, and a bracelet was laying half in and half out of it. It was a beautiful thing, sparkling in the sun. Must be real diamonds. And emeralds. It was so little, couldn't weigh more than a bit, but it had to be worth a fortune. A year's rent. Maybe more.

Trina looked at the bracelet and thought about morning group again, about how none of those sisters would ever have enough furniture or a year's rent. She wondered what the chances were, even if she managed to stay clean and keep herself out of prison, that she would have enough furniture or a year's rent.

When Trina looked up, the cousin was staring at her.

The entrance to the cellar was under the back stairs; it had been dug at the time of the kitchen addition, an afterthought judging from the steepness of the wobbly risers and the narrowness of the top of the stairway—only children could descend facing forward; for adults, sideways was the only way down. The original house had been just five rooms: dining room/kitchen and two parlors on the first floor, two bedrooms up. A full kitchen and two rear bedrooms were added sometime around the turn of the nineteenth century. No one seemed to know how access to the cellar was gained before the addition. I didn't care much. I hadn't been down there once in the year I'd been living with Gram.

Michael pressed the latch of the cellar door, but the door stuck. He kicked the bottom panel; the door lurched forward and a musty odor blew into my face. The cellar smelled just as it always had: of dampness and mold and all sorts of things dead and decaying. The rat's skeleton was probably somewhere under the stairs—or worse, his living descendants. I took an instinctive step backward. Michael cupped my elbow and smiled indulgently, as one would at a child who's afraid to go down the playground slide.

I pointedly withdrew my arm from his grasp. "I know there's no such thing as the woman with the iron teeth."

His smile widened. "I'm relieved to hear that."

I started down the stairs, lifting my chin and turning my shoulders with a false bravado that was probably just as telling as my hesitation. But I didn't swagger for long: after the cramp of the top two steps, the wall dropped away, and there was no railing and little light. I slowed and pressed my hand to the damp fieldstones to keep my balance. I didn't know what was worse, touching the slime-covered stones or falling headlong into the gloom.

Michael snapped on his large flashlight and focused the beam on the rickety stairs. The light helped, but it also emphasized the creepiness. I took a deep breath and slowly made my way down to the hard-packed dirt floor. When I got there, I turned, crossed my arms, and looked up. "Coming?" I asked.

The cellar was actually two cellars: the one under the original house (the "old cellar" was what we had called it as kids) and the one under the kitchen (the "new cellar"). Both had low ceilings and dirt floors—and bugs and spiders and rats and, for all I knew, snakes. The cellars were connected by a tall and narrow hole cut through the old fieldstone foundation.

I forced a smile as Michael came down the stairs. "The safe room's above the back of the old cellar, isn't it?" Of course I knew it was, but I was hoping that somehow the house's architecture had been rearranged since the last time I had looked. I really hated the old cellar.

"Yup." He nodded toward the opening. "Shall I lead the way?" he asked gallantly. "Or is it ladies first?" If he'd been wearing a hat, I'm sure he would have removed it and placed it over his heart.

I thought of Gram, Beth and Trina, two floors above in the sunlight, probably giggling about me at this very moment. It was thrilling to be able to provide everyone with such amusement. Michael waited patiently, and the annoying twinkle in his eye reminded me of Richie.

To get into the old cellar, you have to bow your head, twist your shoulders and step up, all at the same time. I flawlessly executed this maneuver, and, although it was darker and mustier and nastier—and was the actual home of the woman with the iron teeth—once I crossed the threshold, I felt better for my blustering. The old cellar was maybe thirty by thirty, a perfect square, just as the original house had been. It, too, was divided into two parts, split down the middle by the foundation of the fireplace above. We were under the dining room. My head barely cleared the ceiling. Michael was hunched over.

He let his flashlight play over the room, illuminating the serpentine cracks that broke through the mortar and the spider webs holding fast to every corner. A sawhorse. Some bulky construction equipment. A jumble of old cartons lying amidst puddles of standing water. Neatly stacked piles of lumber. More tools. Michael's light lingered over a particularly fierce-looking tool, a gun-like device, which rested on a belt ribbed with very long, very pointy nails. "Maybe you can use the nail gun to protect you from the woman with the iron teeth," he said with a reckless wave of his light. "Or there's always the portable drill."

I brushed imaginary dirt from the front of my jeans, and moved a step closer to the flashlight.

Michael grinned. "Want to take a look?" When I didn't answer, he motioned for me to follow him over the uneven ground. "The problem is that the floor of the safe room's rotting and unstable. Lots of those heavy old beams were never properly supported, and they didn't meet the Park Service specs." He waved at a dozen concrete piers uniformly jutting from the dirt floor. "These footers are for the new support members."

I tried to look interested.

He pointed above his head. "See the light coming through those cracks? That's from the safe room."

Although I knew the cracks were a bad sign—and that they were going to cost my grandmother a lot of money—it was still good to see the sun. I imagined the air smelled fresher. I kept my eyes on the light.

"I'm going to replace a bunch of the rotted joists in the ceiling," Michael explained, "and when the metal support members are set on these piers, it should be just fine."

I wasn't much interested in support members and rotting joists. "What's the deal with the foundation?"

Michael pointed his flashlight at the rough rectangle chiseled through the foundation on the east side of the house; it was about five feet high, ten feet wide and a couple of feet deep. The mysterious piles of dirt grew all around it, and behind it, on its back wall, an opening had been dug out of the dirt.

"Did you ever hear anything about slaves being hidden down here?" Michael asked.

"It's an old root cellar. Gram calls it the 'root closet.' She says she remembers shelves in there when she was a girl."

"But what about the tunnel behind it?"

I wasn't going to tell him that the collapsed tunnel in back of the root closet was the home of the woman with the iron teeth. I pressed the toe of my sneaker into one of the dirt piles, and wondered what Beth and Gram were doing. They had been playing their game long enough.

"It's very unstable—dangerously unstable." Michael waved his flashlight over the entrance of the tunnel. "But interesting. Someone went to a lot of trouble to get through there."

"You think this could have something to do with the Underground Railroad?"

"That's what I was thinking. So I checked it out. Did a little digging inside yesterday. Paced it out outside. But I didn't come up with much. The tunnel starts to collapse about five feet back and the rock gets solid a few feet beyond that." He swung his light up to the ceiling. "It runs under the front yard, heads toward the road, which doesn't make any sense if it was used for running slaves. What would have been the point of digging a tunnel in that direction? Where were they trying to get to?"

"Maybe it wasn't always the front yard? Maybe the road wasn't always so close?"

He looked pleased with my question. "I took a look at some of the old plot plans. One was dated 1841. That road was there then."

"Still . . ."

"I know it's not as romantic as you might like it to be, but my guess is that this hasn't got anything to do with runaway slaves—someone just started to make your root closet larger and never got to finish the job."

I didn't like his tone or his wording—it's not as romantic as you (read: female) might like—and I inched a bit closer to the opening. The tunnel was three feet above the ground and a couple of feet around. The far wall was a mess of rocks and twigs and fallen dirt. It smelled bad. "Why would anyone want a root cellar that deep?"

"A ten-by-ten root cellar wasn't all that uncommon," Michael said as if he were some kind of root cellar expert. He picked up a shovel and knocked it against the edge of the rectangle. "And this front end could go any time. It's a real hazard," he added as if he were some kind of engineering expert.

I knelt down and looked more closely. A few pebbles fell in front of me. What did Michael know? He wasn't a historian any more than he was an engineer. History surrounded this house, was a part of its very fiber, its every post and beam. How could he be so sure fugitive slaves hadn't been hidden here? Hadn't escaped through here?

"I'd been hoping to match the fieldstone and patch it right," Michael said, "but I haven't been able to find the right stone, and the Park Service won't pass us unless the foundation's completely sealed. I know it's anachronistic, but I think we should go with concrete."

I rocked back on my haunches. What kind of contractor used a word like "anachronistic"? "I thought you were so into the 'correctness' of historic preservation—wasn't it you who told Gram you were going to restore the house, not renovate it?"

"If I believed this was an actual Underground Railroad tunnel, I'd say to hold off, but getting the house into the Park means a lot to your grandmother, and I don't think we're losing much here to do that for her."

"How can you be so sure?"

"I can't," Michael said reasonably, "and that's why I'm presenting the options. You can double-check my take on the tunnel or I can get the concrete guys out here and keep us on schedule for the inspection. But I've got to fill the tunnel first to buttress it before the concrete's poured, so someone's got to decide pretty quick which way you want to go."

I wondered if Gram and Beth were ever going to get down here, and listened for their footsteps. I didn't hear anything, so I peered into the dark hole. It pulled me and repelled me. "You want to fill it with dirt?"

"That would be the cheapest."

I poked my head in a bit farther.

Michael lowered his voice ominously and said, "Don't go any closer or the woman with the iron teeth will get you!"

I threw a glance over my shoulder. "Did you know I skydive?"

"Really?"

I had actually only gone skydiving once—and it had scared the shit out of me—but I was annoyed by the surprise in Michael's voice and the disbelief on his face. I turned back to the hole, took a deep breath and crawled into the tunnel on all fours.

"What are you doing?"

"Double-checking your take."

Another pebble pinged to the dirt in front of me, and I was suddenly reminded of rats and spiders and the possibility of snakes. Jumping from an airplane was terrifying, but at least it was full of air and light and space. The only thing crawling into this tunnel and skydiving had in common was the terrifying part.

I heard a low rumble and sensed that the air had become thicker, somehow dirtier. Then the walls began to tremble, to shiver and dissolve around me. Dirt skidded down the side of my face, along my back, over my legs. Rocks. Dirt. More dirt. I tried to push backward, to free myself, but before I was able to move, an even more powerful wave of dirt crashed over me, pinning me flat on my stomach. I was covered by dirt, surrounded by dirt, smothered by dirt.

It was as if the weight of the house, along with its burden of its inhabitants and history, was falling down on me, crushing me with its power.

CHAPTER FOUR

October 29, 1858

I am filled with gladness as I write that we are all unharmed and Harden House is secure. Papa was magnificent and so too was the safe room. Everyone played his or her part to perfection, and even little Chloe, usually such a bright whirling dervish of noise, knew to be still when the Whigs were about. Although in the past I have sometimes questioned Papa's piousness, in this instance, the Lord did indeed protect the just and the righteous.

As Mrs. Child had warned, Mr. Alexander Lyman, constable of Concord, arrived with two men and three dogs. It was my job to act as hostess, to offer the gentlemen cakes and a light repast. When I did so, Mr. Lyman was curt, almost rude. He waved his hand dismissively and demanded to speak with my father. I had never before seen the two men with him, although they appeared to be of a rough sort. Neither of them said a word.

Papa walked down the stairs, pushing his spectacles to the bridge of his nose, as serene as if there were no fugitives hidden behind the wall at his back, and I trembled at his courage. "Mr. Lyman, Sir," Papa said, extending his hand in greeting. "Welcome to you and your companions."

It was obvious Mr. Lyman was taken aback by Papa's cordiality, for he coughed and blustered and finally managed to sputter a few words about nigger runaways and danger to young girls.

"I very much appreciate your concern, Alexander," Papa said. "We have seen no runaways, but now that you are here with your companions and your dogs, I'd be in your debt if you would take a moment and look over the premises for us."

The two men remained in the yard with the dogs as Mr. Lyman docilely followed Papa through the house. I returned to the east parlor and once again took up my darning. Papa made sure that Mr. Lyman was out of the house within minutes. The Whigs remained on the property until nightfall, but of course, they found nothing.

It brought joy to my heart to see Mr. Alexander Lyman so vexed.

November 3, 1858

Rachel and Chloe took their leave today, and I cried as I bid good-bye to that sweet child. I fear so much for her safety, but Papa reminds me that they have already traveled the most difficult portion of their journey and that the Lord is with them. It isn't that I don't believe him, or think the Lord would fail to watch over a poor mother and her child; it is just that there is so much evil in this world that I wonder how the Lord can keep track of it all.

Papa tells me more dutiful reading of my Bible shall shore up my faith and end this confusion. It is my determination to do just that. I shall also pray daily for their safe passage.

November 4, 1858

Papa says that my dear friend, Nancy Southwick, may not come to visit! He says it is far too dangerous for anyone who is not acquainted with our endeavors to call, and that I shall content myself with my chores and prayers and the company of Caleb and Wendell and himself. He is so concerned with the needs of others, but fails to understand the needs of his own daughter.

As I look upon my last sentence, I am filled with shame. I know Papa is right, that there are needs far greater than mine, but I do so long for the conversation of Nancy and a few mo-

ments of light laughter amidst all this passion and seriousness. Wendell is nice enough, but the more time I spend with him, the more dull he becomes. Lewis Campbell cuts a much more dashing figure and his conversation is always lively, but I am beginning to fear that Papa is so preoccupied with his activities that he may not wish to go to Connecticut for Christmas, and that I may never see Lewis again. Then I remind myself that even though Papa is completely engrossed in his abolitionist endeavors—and rightly so—he is well aware that visiting cousin Lizzie and Aunt Elizabeth, Mama's sister, will mean much to me this year, my first Christmas without Mama.

I wonder why it is my family who must carry this burden. I shall be very glad when it is over.

November 5, 1858

Now that I may do no entertaining, I have many empty hours to fill. I sit in my Boston rocker with my needlepoint and listen to Mrs. Harrington lament until I believe I shall go mad. Nothing appears to please this sour woman. Papa's activities least of all.

When Mrs. Harrington is not at my elbow, I slip away from the house and visit Mr. Silas Person in the barn. He tells me of his journeys. Although his eyes flame with fierceness as he describes his travails, I think he must be a very kind man, for I have the notion that he is telling me these tales to distract me from my own melancholy. When I was speaking of Chloe, of my worries for her safety, Mr. Person told me that the laughter of a free child is the purest sound on this great earth.

"The worst part about being a slave isn't weariness of the arms or the legs," he said, "it's the hopelessness of the soul."

November 6, 1858

I was correct in guessing that Mr. Person had a white man for a father. "I am a 'quadroon,' " he explained as he pitched hay this afternoon. I sat at the foot of the stack watching him. "A person who has one Negro grandparent."

I didn't quite know how to respond. I was embarrassed by this frank discussion of his parentage, but I was also intrigued.

Mr. Person must have sensed my discomfort, for he said gently, "Things are lots different in Louisiana." He cleared his throat and all gentleness left his voice. "My daddy was the master of the plantation, and my mama was sired by the master before him. The Southern whites think they own Negroes the same as they own any animal."

"Oh, no," I cried, unable to believe that any man who was as well spoken as Mr. Person could ever be considered an animal by another man.

He didn't answer me. He went back to pitching hay, and I sat in silence, embarrassed by my naiveté, not knowing what to say, whether to apologize, how to leave. I watched the ripple of his muscles as the pitchfork hit the hay then lifted it. I was mesmerized by his concentration, the power with which he approached his task. Who could think this man was anything other than a man?

"I had a wife," he said suddenly. "Her name was Ozella. She was pretty and sweet as the berries we picked in springtime. Her hair was long and dark and I used to comb it for her every night." He leaned on his pitchfork and his eyes gazed beyond me, into the past. He looked so sad, so weary. Then he came back, and his eyes connected with mine. "Her hair was thick and straight. A lot like yours."

I felt a warm flush spreading up my cheeks, and I touched the hair gathered at the nape of my neck. "What happened to her?"

"Died in childbirth."

"And the baby?"

"Don't know," Silas said, his eyes gleaming with unshed tears. "I heard it was a boy."

Before I could respond, Wendell burst into the barn. "What are you doing in here, Sarah?" he demanded. "Why are you sitting in the hay? You'll catch your death of cold." He reached out his hand to me. I took it and allowed myself to be drawn to my feet.

"I was talking with Mr. Person," I explained, brushing hay from my skirt, embarrassed for Wendell, but not quite sure why. "He was telling me about his wife."

Wendell nodded curtly to Mr. Person, then lead me from the barn. "It isn't proper for a woman of your station to converse alone with a Negro," he scolded as we walked to the house.

"The poor man is lonely," I explained. "His wife just died."

"That's unfortunate," Wendell said, "but it makes no difference to you."

I did not argue nor resist, being a proper young lady, but I was most annoyed. Wendell Parker is neither my father nor my brother—and he surely is not my husband, nor even my betrothed—and therefore he has no warrant to instruct me on what is proper or improper behavior.

November 7, 1858

All of Mr. Person's stories are extremely painful, and I now understand why he so rarely smiles, although when he does, his smile lightens my heart. Mr. Person was sixteen years of age when he and his three brothers were sold away from their mother and the plantation on which they had been raised. They were shackled together and forced to walk from Vicksburg to Jackson, Mississippi, along with four hundred other slaves. As the eldest brother, Mr. Person watched over the little ones. The roads were alternately dusty and muddy and everyone was chained together without sufficient food or drink. If one fell over or was pulled into a stream, all the others would follow.

Mr. Person managed to keep his brothers alive, and the four boys were sold in Jackson, then marched in chains to a plantation north of New Orleans. The boys never saw their mother again.

Mr. Person is scarred by the horrid events of his life, and I do not blame him for his bitterness, yet I want so badly for him to understand that we are not all like those he had known. "All white men and woman are not so cruel," I told him. "Many of us are kind."

"I cannot wait around for those who might be kind," he said, his voice as hard and unyielding as iron. "It's safer not to trust anyone."

How could he not see that my heart was pure, that Papa and Caleb and Wendell and I were truly on his side? I think I might have cried right there in the barn if Silas had not smiled at me just then, telling me with the warmth in his eyes that perhaps he did know me to be of a different sort.

November 8, 1858

Dr. Miller came today and examined Mr. Person. When he was finished, he announced that Silas would not be able to travel for at least three more weeks. Silas said nothing, but the hardness in his eyes said everything. I worry that he will leave before he is able.

November 9, 1858

Just as I had feared, Papa says we cannot go to Connecticut for Christmas! We have gone to Hartford for the holidays since I was a small child, and Papa knows I longed to visit with Aunt Elizabeth this year more than ever before. He knows how desperately I miss Mama, and now I shall not be able to dance with Lewis Campbell! Papa says it is more important for him to be here for Mr. Person and the other fugitives than to "gorge himself on roast turkey."

Sometimes I wonder if "St. Papa" makes too much of his own importance.

November 10, 1858

Mr. Silas Person is still with us, and today he told me more of his travels. His journey from Louisiana to Lexington is a most miraculous story of his courage and perseverance, as well as the story of an enslaved people fighting for the freedom that is rightfully theirs. For as Mr. Person reminded me, the Negro slaves were not brought here from Africa; Negroes were brought here and then turned into slaves.

One of the most amazing things he told me was about quilts. Yes, quilts. But these are very special quilts, almost magical, for Negro women design them full of secret symbols which show when it is time to escape and where it is safe to go. It is a Morse Code of stitches and knots. Pictures to tell of a particular action. Is this not immensely clever? A communication that cannot be overheard or ever washed away! Mr. Person said it was made all the better because the messages were hidden in plain sight.

And the quilts have such wonderful names: Monkey Wrench and Wagon Wheel and Shoofly and Flying Geese and Tumbling Boxes! Each with its own secret message. Mr. Person knew it was time to gather his tools when the Monkey Wrench quilt was hung from the porch of Aunt Zella's quarters. When the quilt was changed to Wagon Wheel, he packed his things, and when he saw Tumbling Boxes waving from the railing, he made his escape. He says many others are following in his footsteps.

Quilts helped him along his way also: one was a map that could only be seen when it was turned to its reverse side, and another was a pattern of arrows which showed him which way to go! We up North so often think that it is only we who are helping the Negro, that without us, they would forever be slaves. Mr. Person's stories remind me that the Negro is fighting for his own freedom, and has been doing just that for a long time.

Most often though, Mr. Person had no one to aid him on his lonely and dangerous journey. After escaping the plantation, he slipped into a bayou and passed three days and two nights by himself in the branches of a tree at the heart of a snake-infested swamp. Then he made his way to New Orleans.

In New Orleans, he jumped into the hold of a steamer and hid amongst the cargo. Silas knew that every boat heading north on the Mississippi was met by police and checked for runaway slaves, so when the steamer reached Kentucky he walked calmly onto the pier and began unloading containers from the ship. The police believed him to be hired help and paid him no mind.

From there he traveled along the Maysville Road to Ohio, hiding in barns and backyard pits, eating wild blueberries, and when he was lucky, finding a kindly Negro cook who would spare him a bit of food. He went hungry for days and slept where he was able: in fields, along riverbanks and one night, in a coffin! He went from safe house to safe house, traveling usually by foot, but once in the secret compartment of a double-bottomed hay wagon.

He was harbored and aided by "Midnight Marauders," the conductors of this extraordinary association we call the Underground Railroad. What is it that makes one man so wondrously selfless and another so evil? Silas was being chased by bounty hunters in the forests west of Concord when he fell and broke his leg. He managed to elude them, then limped all the way here. When I told him he was indeed a brave man, he claimed bravery had nothing to do with it. "I am risking nothing," he said. "Without freedom, I have nothing."

Silas' conversation is far more interesting than that of Wendell Parker. Perhaps even more interesting than Lewis Campbell's.

November 11, 1858

Now I know why Silas has not left Harden House. He confessed to me today that his brothers are also following the quilts. They have escaped the plantation, and it is Silas' mission to blaze the trail to freedom for his family. He heard through the grapevine dispatch that at least one of them made it to Red Oak, Ohio. I told him I would pray for their successful journey.

His eyes got that hard gleam, and he said, "Prayers are not nearly enough."

I was frightened by the intensity of his anger. "I can do more than just pray," I stammered. "I can talk to Papa, and he and his friends on the Vigilance Committee will make sure your brothers are safe." When he didn't say anything, I added, "They can do it. They will." But Silas still said nothing.

November 13, 1858 (morning)

I am ashamed of writing of "St. Papa" the other day. Papa is truly a wise and noble man, and I am but a small and selfish girl. When I told Papa of the plight of Silas and his three brothers, Papa pushed his spectacles up on his nose and immediately went to meet with Wendell's uncle, Theodore Parker, and the Vigilance Committee. He told them the story, and all who were present, including Mr. William Lloyd Garrison, vowed to help.

As Silas is unable to travel, the idea is that his brothers shall be brought to him, then they shall all go on to Canada together. Mr. Parker and Mr. Garrison will take advantage of their many connections to get word to Silas' brothers that they are to come to Boston. I told Papa about the Negro women who sew the secret quilts, and he was delighted with this intelligence. He said the quilts might be a valuable aid in leading the brothers to Lexington and helping many other runaway slaves.

As Harden House is under almost constant surveillance by

Mr. Lyman and his Whigs, a safe way must be secured for the boys to escape from here. Papa suggested that a secret tunnel be dug from Mama's canning cupboard in the cellar to the abandoned well in the eastern woods. He said Caleb and Wendell could do the work. Silas' brothers will hide in the barn or carriage house—using the safe room when necessary—until Silas is ready to travel, then all will escape through the tunnel to the well, where members of the Vigilance Committee will be waiting. The Committee will lead them north to freedom, while anyone watching the house shall see nothing.

Is this not a brilliant scheme?

November 13, 1858 (afternoon)

After lunch, I begged Papa to allow me to tell Silas the wonderful news. Mrs. Harrington's frown was so deep that it appeared to be permanently gouged into her face, but Papa ignored her and said that I could. I wish it had not been necessary to apprise Mrs. Harrington of our schemes. I trust her even less than I value her company.

I, too, ignored her and raced out to the barn. When I found Silas pitching hay, I was suddenly shy and blurted out a silly question about the red flannel sack he wore around his neck. But Silas did not think it was silly—he never thinks my questions silly—and he told me the sack was a charm bag, sometimes called a "Mojo" or the "Hand," and that he wore it to bring him good luck.

"It must be working!" I cried. "It's good luck that I've come to tell you of." But when I described the plan, rather than the smile of pleasure I longed to see cross his face, Silas' eyes grew hard and his mouth narrowed.

"You can tell your brother and his friend not to bother," he declared, his voice full of fierceness. "I will dig the tunnel myself."

I stepped back, confused and I admit, a bit hurt, by his unexpected anger. Then he reached out and touched my hand, and my entire body flared with his passion. I looked into his eyes and understood that I had been mistaken: it wasn't anger Silas was feeling, it was determination. His fight to bring his family to freedom would be deterred by no man. And I would do everything in my power to make his dream come true.

CHAPTER FIVE

It turned out that I wasn't crushed by the weight of the house or its history. After some furious and, according to Beth and Gram, very impressive digging, Michael pulled me from the tunnel with nothing more serious than a bruised ego. But as I stood under the shower, letting the water pound the dirt from every surface and cavity of my body, I kept thinking about all that filthy, wet, spider-ridden dirt collapsing on my head, filling my nose, my mouth. All that dirt burying me, smothering me, bringing to life every nightmare I'd ever had of darkness and ghosts and death in close places.

There was a banging on the bathroom door. "The dirt's already flowing into Boston Harbor," Beth yelled. "You've been in there for almost an hour—it's all gone, believe me. You're as clean as you'll ever be."

"Bye," I said, hoping she would go away, but instead she came into the steamy room and settled herself on the closed toilet seat. Beth had little tolerance for delayed gratification and even less for someone else's agenda.

"Michael sent me up to make sure you're okay," she continued. "He's taking Trina back to WaifHaven, and he brought a bunch of cartons up from the cellar—he said it'd make it easier for you in case you didn't want to go back down there again." She pulled back the shower curtain and raised one eyebrow at me. "I think someone's sweet on you."

I yanked the curtain out of her hand and jerked it closed.

"Butt out," I said, but I was pleased. "I acted like an asshole."

"Men love assholes in distress."

"How about some privacy here?"

"Hey, you've got to look at the upside of this," Beth said. "Maybe your childhood fears have finally been realized, and now you don't have to worry about them anymore."

I peered around the edge of the shower curtain. "What are you talking about?"

"Destiny, precognition, predetermination." Beth rubbed her palms together and her eyes gleamed. "Maybe when you were a kid, your subconscious guessed that someday you'd be buried down in the cellar, and that's why you were always so afraid of the place."

"Yeah, right." I stuck my head back under the running water. "It was all my subconscious's fault—it had nothing to do with you and Tommy."

"Whatever." The door clicked shut.

Although Beth's theory on the origins of my claustrophobia was a bit over the top—and didn't jibe with my childhood memories—I kind of liked it. And when I turned off the water, I actually felt lighter, freer. As if I had faced the worst of my fears and survived. As if I didn't have anything to be afraid of anymore.

When I got downstairs, Michael and Trina were gone, and Beth and Gram were sitting on the old Victorian sofa in the kitchen, surrounded by the cartons Michael had brought up from the cellar.

"Feeling better?" Gram asked.

I leaned over and kissed her. "Much." I nodded toward the carton in front of her. "Anything interesting?"

"Less than you might think." Gram reached into the box and pulled out a handful of moldy children's clothes. One of the things I loved most about Gram was how she didn't fuss: I said I was fine, and she was going to take me at my word. "Storing things in a damp cellar isn't the smartest thing I've ever done," she added.

"It's all wrecked?"

"Most of it."

"Do you want me to call this disposal company I used the last time we moved?" Beth asked. "They come pick up all your stuff and chuck it for you."

Beth was almost single-handedly responsible for the surge in the service sector in the greater Boston area. She was a marvel at finding people to do every and any chore. Need someone to tint a skylight? Fight with the insurance company about an erroneous bill? Drop off dry-cleaning? Beth knew who could do it for you. But it wouldn't be cheap.

Gram frowned at her. "I don't think that will be necessary, Beth. Lee and I can handle this ourselves, if you're too busy. Michael wants the cellar cleaned out as soon as we can do it so that he can start grading the floor."

Beth slumped into the sofa. "That isn't what I meant."

Gram didn't say anything. She dropped the moldy clothes back into the carton and pulled another one toward her.

Gram could be awfully hard on Beth. She disliked what she viewed as Beth's sense of entitlement, and even when I reminded her of Beth's unentitled and extremely unhappy childhood as the awkward, overweight only daughter of my always perfectly turned-out Aunt Rhoda, Gram would have none of it. "Beth doesn't think the rules apply to her," Gram would tell me. "A job wouldn't hurt."

I knelt down across from Beth and pulled a small metal object from the carton closest to me. I dumped it into her hand. "What do you think this could be?" It was cone shaped, plated in mother-of-pearl and about the size of a child's fist.

Beth put the small end to her lips and blew out. "Not a megaphone," she said.

Gram laughed and held out her hand. Another impressive thing about Gram was that she didn't hold a grudge. "I think that must have belonged to one of the great Harden philatelists. It's a magnifier for studying stamps."

"I thought they were abolitionists, not philatelists," Beth said with a grin. She doesn't hold a grudge either.

"The Colonel was actually both." Gram pressed the magnifier between her hands, a faraway look in her eye. "The Colonel's grandson, Ulysses Harden, collected stamps too, and so did his son, Elijah, my father. Your Uncle Joe has the collection." Uncle Joe was Gram's brother.

"Must be worth a fortune," Beth said.

Gram raised an eyebrow at me.

I crossed my legs and leaned back against the rounded arm of the arched sofa. I rubbed the dark velvet with my knuckle, as I had loved to do as a child; the touch of the soft fabric and the smell of the old dust filled me with longing for times that could never be again. "Did you ever hear anything about another safe room in the cellar?" I asked Gram.

"You mean the tunnel you climbed into today?"

"Could it have been? Or maybe some kind of underground escape route?"

"I suppose it's possible," Gram said, "but I doubt it. My guess is some ancestor started to make the root closet into a real root cellar, but never finished."

"That was Michael's guess."

"That Michael's a smart young man."

I ignored her comment. "So if Ulysses Harden was the Colonel's grandson, then—"

"Don't think we didn't notice the change of subject," Beth interrupted.

"—who was Ulysses' father?" I continued.

"Sarah was his mother," Gram said slowly. "The Colonel's daughter. And I think the story was something about her going out to Ohio with her husband and then moving back to Massachusetts when the husband died. Ulysses must have been just a boy."

"But then why was his name Harden?" I asked. "Wouldn't he have had his father's last name?"

"The husband must have been a cousin," Gram said. "They often did that then. If I hadn't been so damn quick to give those cartons to Nancy, maybe we'd be able to find out his name."

"What cartons?"

Gram waved her hand impatiently. "Oh, my friend Nancy Winsten—you remember her? She works at the library?—well, anyway, she was all hot to trot over some old letters and receipt books I found in the attic, and she begged me to donate them to the library's Lexington Room collection. She was very persuasive, said that they'd have their own shelf or something. 'The Harden Papers.' I didn't have time to go through it all, and there didn't seem to be anything all that sexy in there, so I gave in. Now, of course, with Tubman Park and all, I wish I hadn't. Do you suppose I could ask for them back?"

Beth was still on the previous topic. "Maybe Sarah's husband wasn't a cousin," she said. "Maybe his death was such a devastating blow to her that she couldn't bear to even hear his name, so when she came back home, she changed their last name back to Harden so she wouldn't be reminded of her lost love."

Although Beth's theory was, once again, a bit over the top, it too had its appeal. "Sarah never married again?" I asked Gram. "She didn't have any other children?"

"I've never heard about anyone in that generation except for Ulysses, although Sarah did have a younger brother, Caleb." Gram stood. "You know, there's a picture of Sarah around here somewhere." She went into the east parlor and returned with a small framed daguerreotype. She handed it to me. Beth pressed close. "I'd guess she was probably in her mid-twenties in that picture," Gram told us. "Pretty little thing."

"She looks like she's forty," Beth said.

I didn't say anything; I was staring at Sarah, lost in the softness of her large, intelligent eyes. It was impossible to tell from the picture what color they had been, but it was obvious, even from this stiff portrait, that they held compassion, perhaps touched with a bit of pain.

"She looks like you, Lee," Beth said.

"I don't think so," I said, studying the sepia-tone in my hand. Sarah was beautiful, with high cheekbones and a small perfect mouth. And even though it was only a head shot, it was apparent that she had been much more petite than I. "Not even close."

"Look, Gram," Beth persisted, "doesn't Lee look like Sarah? Around the eyes?"

Gram took the daguerreotype and scrutinized it. "I suppose," she said dubiously. "Maybe a little." Then she returned it to its place in the parlor.

When she came back into the kitchen, I asked, "So all

the Hardens are descended from Sarah?"

"I'm sure there are lots of others, but we've lost touch. Sarah's our direct ancestor—or the direct ancestor of all the Hardens we know. The eldest child of the eldest child, heir to Harden House."

I rested my chin on my knees and ran my knuckle over the velvet. "Politically correct from day one." Although Harden House was inherited by the eldest child (to keep it intact and in the family), it was passed down without regard to sex—and that was very forward-thinking in the nineteenth century. Most of the twentieth too. "Sometimes I feel closer to who we were than who we are."

"You mean like to all those old crazy ladies?" Beth asked. "To what's-her-name? Dotty Aunt Hortense?"

"I'm sure that's not what Lee's referring to," Gram said.

I gave Beth the cross-fingered "shut up" signal from our childhood; she loved to bait Gram, who was a real sweetie but didn't have much of a sense of humor. "No," I said, "I mean the abolitionists and feminists and civil rights advocates. Sometimes I feel like I'm out on a limb by myself politically. No one seems to think like me anymore—even Kiah Wilkinson thinks I'm too liberal."

"And who would know better?" Beth asked.

Beth and her husband were active in the local Republican party, and Russ would tell anyone who would listen—when he wasn't glued to his computer buying and selling his stocks and bonds—that Ronald Reagan was the best president we'd ever had.

"You're not alone," Gram assured me. "I think like you."

I patted her arm. "Kiah thinks you're too liberal, too."

It was true that I often felt more connected to the past than to the present: to Gram, who as a young girl worked to promote the use of birth control; to her mother, Elizabeth Bigelow, one of the first suffragettes, and her father Elijah Harden, who served three terms in the House of Representatives; to Ulysses, a state senator who helped settle thousands of freed slaves in Massachusetts; to Colonel Stanton Harden, a Civil War hero and a moving force among Boston abolitionists.

"Sarah Harden was very involved in liberal causes," Gram said. "If I remember correctly, she was instrumental in starting the first Negro college in Massachusetts. And helping black orphanages."

"Hey," Beth said. "It's the new millennium. Tempus fugit. No point in mooning over all the unfair things that went on in the dark ages."

"What about the unfair things that go on today?" Gram asked.

"There're lots more opportunities than there used to be," Beth said.

"Not as many as you might think," I said.

"Look at your friend Trina," Beth said. "She's a perfect example. After all that awful stuff—being so addicted and killing her baby and all that publicity—with the help of our tax dollars, she's had the opportunity to get herself off drugs, she's working and now she's got a chance to change."

"Yeah, Trina's had lots of opportunity," I grumbled. "Being born into poverty, shunted from one foster home to another, abused, never knowing how long she'd stay, how she'd be treated." It annoyed me to hear Beth use Trina's success to substantiate her hard-hearted views. "Trina's always wanted to be a singer. Did you know that?" I asked. "Did you know that she has a beautiful voice, that she used to sneak into clubs when she was a little kid? She once told me that after she sang, everyone would clap, and that that was the only time anyone ever noticed she was there."

Gram put her hand on my knee, both to silence and console me. "Trina didn't kill her baby," she told Beth. "That's why the charges were dropped—even the judge knew it wasn't right to put the blame on her like that."

The truth was that the charges hadn't been dropped; Trina had accepted a plea bargain which reduced the indictment from second-degree murder to involuntary manslaughter. But I didn't bother to correct Gram. The exact details of the situation didn't matter. What mattered was that Trina had been a multiple victim: a victim of an overzealous DA up for reelection, of a local news media focused on a crack war that erupted the same week Hendrika was born, of some very bad decisions and of even worse luck. Sure, she shouldered some of the responsibility, some of the blame, but there was so much she had had no ability to control.

"Maybe it wasn't technically her fault," Beth argued, "but you've got to admit, she had a hand in it—or an arm, as the case may be."

Trina's daughter, Hendrika, had died because the placenta she needed for nourishment was damaged by her mother's heroin use. She was born two months premature and very sick; she lived one week. That one week with her dying child had been enough to break Trina's heart—and to turn her around. Trina was filled with remorse and was doing all that she could to create a new life for herself—and not just because her plea bargain stipulated that failure at SafeHaven meant a prison term. She was doing it because she had been changed by all she had lost. "I'm gonna have another little girl someday," Trina had told me. "And I'm gonna name her Hendrika too, but she's gonna be healthy and strong and go to college."

"It's not as simple as you make it sound," I snapped at Beth.

Beth raised an eyebrow. "Maybe it is."

Gram cleared her throat, indicating that this conversation was over. "I'm glad to hear that you're not enamored of history, Beth."

"You are?"

"It's good to live in the present, to appreciate the moment. To be here, now, not to spend too much time dwelling on what was," Gram said.

Beth and I both looked at her warily. "True," I said slowly, "but somehow that doesn't sound like you."

"I have something to tell you girls—actually to ask you." Gram sat up straight and looked us each in the eye for a long moment. "Although this affects Beth most directly, I think it might upset Lee more."

"Are you all right?" I demanded. "Are you sick?"

"No, dear," she said, giving my shoulder a squeeze. "Not to worry. I'm just fine. This isn't about me, it's about the house."

"Harden House?" Beth asked. She was the eldest child of the eldest child and expected to inherit it. Her mother had died five years ago.

I held my breath, afraid I knew what was coming, although I couldn't understand why I would be upset about Gram leaving the house to me.

Gram placed her hands in her lap. "I'm thinking of breaking with family tradition."

Beth's eyes filled with tears. "You're going to give the house to Lee?" she wailed. "Is this because I'm a Republican?"

"This doesn't have anything to do with politics," Gram

said, smiling, "and I'm not giving the house to Lee. I'm going to give it, and all the furnishings, to the Lexington Historical Society. I've been talking with them about the process."

We were both speechless.

"I know it isn't necessary, but I wanted to discuss this with you girls before anything's finalized." Gram turned to me. "How do you feel about this? What do you think?"

"I, ah, I guess it's just hard to imagine Harden House not being in the family, not being there for the grandchildren like it was for all of us . . ." I said slowly.

"But now it will be there for the grandchildren," Gram explained. "This is the way to make sure it always will."

"You think I'd sell it?" Beth cried. "Why do you always—"

"It's not just you, Beth," Gram said. "That's why I'm not leaving it to any of the grandchildren. The house is a big burden, a big expense, and someone's going to need to, or want to, sell it someday."

Beth and I looked at each other. There didn't seem to be much more to say.

"It's your house, Gram," Beth finally said, tears streaming down her cheeks. "You should do what you want with it."

I nodded and rubbed my knuckle against the soft velvet of the sofa, wondering where all my memories would live.

Trina went right upstairs after Michael dropped her off. She sat on her cot in the dorm. The dorm was one large room that had been made by taking the walls out between three smaller rooms. Some of the inside boards still showed through on one side. It was ugly and was stuffed with way too many beds that a bunch of white ladies had decided they didn't want anymore. It was neat as an army barracks except for the few "personal items" you were allowed to keep on your table. Most of the tables were full of Bibles and baby pictures and chipped china Virgin Marys.

But Trina's table was empty. The only picture she had of Hendrika was one that was in the newspaper, and it showed Hendrika all tiny and limp and hooked up to a shitload of machines that were way bigger than she was. Trina didn't like to look at the picture, but she couldn't throw it away either.

No one but Trina was up there in the middle of the day because she was a senior and had special privileges no one else had. There were four steps at SafeHaven: freshman, sophomore, junior and senior. But nobody thought they were in school. You got promoted if you didn't screw up for an entire month, but there were so many rules hardly anyone could do that so most sisters stayed freshmen 'til they'd done their time or the insurance ran out. Then they'd go back and try again. But there was no going back for Trina. If she fucked up, there was only prison.

Trina picked at a bare spot on the blanket, thinking that she didn't know who she was anymore. She wasn't like she used to be before Hendrika, not like those burn-outs in the 'hood, and she sure wasn't like the folks she saw from the window of Lee's car walking to work or going out to lunch or racing their fancy boats in the river. But she couldn't relate to anyone at SafeHaven either. Was she still Trina Collins? Was Trina Collins still her?

She flashed on Lionnel. Smart, sexy, rich Lionnel. She loved him and hated him all at the same time. He called to her, but she turned away. The Big H called to her, but she sang real loud so she couldn't hear its sugary, skaggy voice. She saw Clara's shiny bracelet hanging from the open drawer of the jewelry box. It called to her, too.

But she wasn't gonna go to the bracelet, and she wasn't gonna go to the junk, and she didn't have to answer to Lionnel any more. She owed it to Hendrika to say no to the temptation, to give it a real try. And as much as Trina hated this place, she was sure prison was way worse.

Before Beth left, she slipped me a small bottle of sleeping pills. "They're good," she said. "Very short-acting." When I protested that I didn't want them, and that she had no business with them either, she explained that these were nothing like the sleeping pills she had accidentally overdosed on when she was wired on too many diet pills.

"These are really mild," she assured me. "A whole different chemical thing. And if you take two, you won't have any dreams."

Not dreaming seemed like a good idea, so I swallowed two of the little orange pills before I got into bed, then I read until I was so tired my chin dropped to my chest. But Beth was wrong. I did dream. Twice.

In the first dream, I was sitting in the east parlor playing Scrabble—a game I detest—when I heard a deep rumble. I tried to run, but I was glued to my chair in that annoying paralysis of dreams. Helpless, I watched through the window as dirt poured over the house. The dirt rose quickly, then burst through the panes, ripping the frames from the walls and sending an avalanche of earth exploding toward me. I tried to scream, but dirt filled my mouth. It was burying me, crushing me. Then I heard the muffled sound of digging. It was distant, but forceful. "Michael!" I yelled, and woke myself up.

I was in bed, and my damp T-shirt was stuck to my

back. Moonlight shone through the windows. The house was still. I lay back against the pillow and closed my eyes, childishly pleased that my subconscious was stronger than Beth's pills. It was akin to the inflated pride I felt when I was a kid and the doctors said only boys walked in their sleep, but I was a girl and I was famous—or infamous—for my sleepwalking.

Then I heard it. The sound of scraping, of metal against metal, of manacle against stone. Digging. Just like the night before.

For a moment I was pinned by fear. Did this mean I had inherited the gene? Was I hearing voices like Dotty Aunt Hortense? Would I soon begin to see people who didn't exist? To talk to walls? Walk off rooftops? No, I might be a twenty-seven-year-old adolescent, but I wasn't crazy.

Relieved and emboldened, I climbed out of bed and went into the hallway. I listened, but there was nothing. Then it started again. Louder. More insistent. It was coming from the cellar. I glanced at Gram's closed door and then through the spiky balustrades descending below me. I wasn't crazy, I reminded myself. The heating system might be broken. I headed down.

The kitchen was shadowy, the appliances grotesque and monstrous in the moonlight; the curved sofa looked like a cougar, hunched and ready to pounce. I opened the cellar door and went down the stairs. The digging was closer, the sound more intense. I imagined I smelled sweat, a man's sweat, the musk of hard toil.

I stopped at the bottom of the stairs, motionless, transfixed. It was coming from the old cellar. I crossed the hard-packed floor to the rough door in the foundation, captivated by the noise and terrified by it, drawn by the odor and repelled by it. I stepped across the threshold. The old cellar was dark, as always, and yet I could see clearly, as if the damp fieldstones glowed with their own internal light, an icy glow as horrid and unforgiving as the scene it illuminated.

A black man stood in front of the root closet. He was light-skinned, his shoulders massive, and he held a shovel in his hands. He was turned away from me, rhythmically, furiously, frantically, pulling dirt from the tunnel. The muscles of his naked back were slick with sweat and rippled as he worked. He had a crude cast on his left leg, which rose from ankle to knee, but it did not impede his progress. A pile of dirt grew at his feet. There was a passion, a rage, to his movements.

I gasped, and as I did, the man lowered his shovel and began to turn his powerful neck toward me. I knew I didn't want to see his face, but understood the confrontation was inevitable. I stood frozen, filled with the terrified fascination of dread. But as he completed his turn, right at the moment when his eyes would have met mine, he wavered, grew translucent, and then he was gone.

CHAPTER SIX

I hadn't walked in my sleep for fifteen years, but there I was, barefoot and wearing only a T-shirt, cowering on the cellar floor.

There was no man with a shovel, no woman with iron teeth; there was just me: alone, cold and scared. I pushed myself from the hard-packed dirt and raced up the cellar steps, through the shadowy kitchen and parlor, up the main staircase and into my bedroom. I jumped into bed and pulled the covers over my head, just as I had as a kid when I woke up someplace I shouldn't be.

Although my mother had always blamed Beth and her brother Tommy for my sleepwalking—I once overheard my mother telling my father that Beth was a little brat—the truth is that it started way before Beth came up with the woman with the iron teeth. I was so young when I first began finding myself in strange places in the middle of the night that I thought it was normal; I just assumed everyone woke up in the cedar closet or under the living room couch. It wasn't until my parents started erecting gates and taking me to doctors that I realized I was unusual. The doctors weren't able to do anything about my nocturnal wanderings, but the gates and locked doors kept me safe until puberty changed some hormonal or electrical imbalance in my brain—at least that was the theory at the time—and my sleepwalking stopped.

Until now.

I pulled the blanket down to my chin and peered into the

gloom, wondering if this was indeed verification that I was the member of my generation to inherit the Dotty Aunt Hortense gene. The first rays of dawn were just beginning to give substance to the room, nudging at the shadows and my imaginary demons. I glumly watched the furniture define itself, growing into a bureau, a chair, a desk, and wondered if I'd soon begin talking to them. Then, as the sunlight hit my face, I closed my eyes and fell into a deep sleep.

When the phone rang, it felt as if no time had passed, but the clock on my end table said it was almost nine. Gram had been on the tennis court for over an hour, and my nightmare was distant and unreal, drifting into that blessed amnesic fog of yesterday's dreams.

The voice was deep and gravelly and sounded as if it belonged to an old man. It took me a moment to place it. Michael. "Sorry to wake you," he said.

"You didn't," I lied.

"Don't you have to go into work today?"

I felt hung over and rubbed my forehead. "Tuesday," I said. "I'm, ah, I'm not going in until after lunch." The accountant was reviewing the budget section of my report, and I couldn't do anything more until it had been approved. "What's up?"

"Is the dirt there yet?"

I saw the pile of dirt growing at the feet of the man in my dream, and the details of the nightmare sprang full-formed from the fog. I could hear the scrape of the shovel against the rock. I could taste the metallic bite of my fear. "Dirt?" I croaked.

"Lexington Sand and Gravel was supposed to deliver a load of dirt first thing this morning. To use to fill the tunnel." Michael sounded exhausted. "Is it there?"

"I don't know," I said, relieved we were talking about real dirt, but unnerved by the nightmare images assaulting me. "Maybe Gram let them in. I'm still in bed."

"I thought I didn't wake you?"

"I'm awake," I said quickly, "I just haven't gotten up yet."

Michael cleared his throat. "I'm afraid I have some bad news." His sigh was long and deep. "My mom's in the hospital."

I sat up. I knew Michael's mom had a heart condition, and this sounded bad. "Is she okay?"

"Pretty sick. She's stable for the moment, but in the ICU hooked up to more machines than you'd think possible. The doctors say the next week will tell the tale."

"Her heart?"

"Yeah."

"Is there anything I can do to help you?"

He forced a chuckle, but he sounded more tired than amused. "Fill in the tunnel?"

"Forget the tunnel. Forget the house."

"If that foundation isn't cemented over when the Park Service comes, we're not going to pass the inspection."

"We'll live."

"No." His voice was tight with stubbornness. "My crew's tied up on another job 'til the twentieth, and I promised your grandmother I'd do it myself to make sure we didn't miss the opening of the Park."

"She'll live. The house'll get in on Phase Two."

"I won't let her down," he insisted.

Kiah, a woman who had seen more than her fair share of trouble, once told me that in the midst of a crisis, people often feel so helpless that they grab onto seemingly inconsequential things and insist on seeing them through. "It's all about control," Kiah had explained. "And it's real important to let folks hold on to their illusions." It seemed as if Michael needed his illusions.

"We'll do it," I said.

"Do what?"

"Beth and I will fill the tunnel." It seemed like the right thing to do under the circumstances.

"You think?"

"Beth's really strong—she's at the gym a minimum of two hours a day—and she's a lot better at all kinds of construction then you'd guess from looking at her. I can be her assistant." To prove my sincerity, I climbed out of bed and, with the portable phone pressed to my ear, headed downstairs to check on the delivery, jabbering to Michael so he'd stay on the line.

The cellar was damp and shadowy, as usual, and a large pile of dirt was standing a few yards from the tunnel opening. When I told Michael the dirt had arrived, he explained what needed be done. It was pretty basic: fill in the tunnel and the rear part of the root closet so that the hole in the foundation would have a solid back when it was filled with concrete. Basic, but not without jeopardy for a grown woman who couldn't let go of her childhood fears. I kept Michael on the phone until I got back upstairs.

Beth and Trina walked in just as I was pouring myself a cup of coffee. Gram had a tennis match she thought might run over, so she had asked Beth to meet Trina at the Alewife T Station. She needed Trina all day to get the paperwork completed for the inspection. I told them about Michael's mother and the offer I had made.

Beth paced the kitchen nervously as I talked. When I finished, she tapped a fingernail on the counter and bit the cuticle of another. "How about I call Ryan?" she offered.

"You know, that handyman I use? Maybe he could squeeze us in."

"Today?" I was pretty skeptical.

Beth reached for the phone. "Never know 'til you try."

But for once, Beth's service network failed her, and so did the yellow pages. The downside of a strong economic upturn is that everyone's busy.

"I'll help," Trina offered.

"Help with what?" Gram came through the back door and headed straight for the fridge. She grabbed the milk and poured herself a large glass; Gram was a big believer in milk and drank at least a half gallon a day. I went through my explanation again. Gram polished off the milk and shot Beth an annoyed glance.

"I never said I wouldn't do it," Beth said defensively. "Remember how I fixed that electrical short? And I don't pump iron every day for nothing." She raised her arms and clenched her fists. Her biceps were damned impressive, and she was a whiz with a blown fuse.

"I'll help too," Gram offered. "Lord knows, I'm no good at paperwork."

"No way," I said.

"Don't kid yourself, Lee." Gram jabbed her finger in my gut. "I'm in far better shape than you are—probably with stronger and healthier bones." A dig about my refusal to drink milk.

Although Gram's words were more than likely true, she was still sixty-nine, and I wasn't going to let her shovel dirt. "There are only two shovels, Gram," I said, hoping that this was the case, or at least that it wouldn't be known not to be. "How about you and Trina deal with all that paper, while Beth and I get started in the cellar?" I wasn't any more thrilled with this plan than Gram was, but I forced a smile.

"I don't have to be at work for a couple of hours yet, and Beth and I can get a lot done before I have to leave."

Gram grumbled about Trina being able to do a better job without her, and Beth grumbled about wearing the wrong clothes.

"Come on," I coaxed. "It'll really help Michael."

"Far be it from me to stand in the way of romance," Gram said, but she didn't look happy.

Beth raised one eyebrow and smirked. I ignored them and went upstairs to get Beth a T-shirt and jeans.

When I came back down with the clothes, Beth, in her predictable-unpredictable way, went gung-ho on the project. She dragged me into the cellar and barked instructions as if she'd been a building contractor her whole life—or a drill sergeant.

"Those jerks left this pile of dirt too far from the tunnel opening," she grumbled. "We're going to have to move it. You start shoveling while I check out the situation." She paced across the old cellar, stepping around puddles and tools, mumbling about uneven footings and electrical hook ups. "And they haven't even wired the sump pump yet. How the hell do they expect to get all this water out of here without a pump?" She walked to the far wall of the new cellar and back again, then circled the rooms poking at walls and floors. She finally stopped in the spot where the man in my dream had stood. She picked up one of the shovels.

"Is it too much coffee or are you taking diet pills again?" I asked.

"This was your idea, not mine," Beth reminded me. "And anyway, your fears have all been realized. Remember? Now that you've survived being buried alive, you've got nothing left to be afraid of."

"What about the woman with the iron teeth?"

Beth's grin was demonic as she handed the shovel to me. "Except for her, of course."

The air felt oddly thick, edgy and electrified, like the atmosphere right before a thunderstorm, and I didn't like it. But I stuck the shovel into the dirt.

"You're doing it wrong," Beth reprimanded me, grabbing the shovel from my hands. "Bend your knees or you'll screw up your back and we'll never get this finished." Then she demonstrated the proper shoveling technique three times. Her frenetic enthusiasm was scary.

I spent the next couple of hours breathing dust and letting Beth boss me around. I tried not to think about my dream, but the longer I was down there, the more clearly I remembered the rippling muscles of the man's back, the intensity of his efforts, the anger in the swing of his arms.

When Trina came down to tell us she had made lunch, I dropped my shovel so fast, both she and Beth laughed. But I didn't care: I was out of there.

When I pulled up to SafeHaven, Kiah was standing in front of the house talking to a tall, extremely handsome black man. He was in his mid-twenties and dressed in a well-tailored conservative suit. As I was parking the car, he turned away from me, and the fabric of his jacket tightened across his broad shoulders, hinting at the toned muscles underneath. If it wasn't for the way he was waving his arms and the steely look in Kiah's eyes, I would have guessed he was the latest neighborhood success story. Instead, I guessed he was someone's boyfriend.

I got out of the car and walked toward the house. I nodded to Kiah, and as I pressed into the hedge to squeeze around them, the man began a slow turn toward me. For a moment, I was once again in my dream, my feet rooted to the ground, terror licking at my stomach. Then he stepped aside, bowed slightly and smiled. A jolt shot through me that was equal measures of fear and sexual attraction. I felt flustered and foolish. "Sorry," I mumbled. Another man who was clearly too handsome for his own good.

"Lionnel Matthias." Kiah waved at Lionnel, then pointed to me. "Lee Seymour." Although her face was set in a polite expression, I knew from the snap of her wrist that she was annoyed.

"Lee," he said slowly, his voice caressing my name, then his smile broadened and his eyes latched onto mine; he oozed sex appeal with an irresistible hint of danger. He held onto my hand. "I've heard about you from Trina."

So this was Trina's Lionnel. He was even better looking than she had said. And scarier. I took a step back, but I was unable to look away.

Lionnel released my hand and nodded toward Kiah. "My buddy Kiah and me were just shooting the breeze. Telling each other lies."

"Lionnel's leaving," Kiah said. "We're done here."

Lionnel cocked his head to the left and said, "For now." Then he touched the brim of a non-existent hat and sauntered down the street. A man in control of his world. I watched him until he turned the corner.

"Wow," I said as we headed up the stairs.

"You know how some men get more attractive after you've known them a while?" Kiah asked. "Well that man just gets uglier."

"Couldn't get much prettier."

"As a very wise white man once said, 'Pretty is as pretty does.' "

I figured Kiah must be really irked if she was quoting Forrest Gump. Maya Angelou was more her style. "Was he looking for Trina?"

Kiah leaned against the doorjamb of her office. "I didn't see anyone here looking for anyone."

Again I was surprised. Honesty was one of Kiah's prime directives. "One hell of a fine-looking ghost."

She snorted in derision. "I don't think this is the first time he's been sniffing around."

"Has she seen him?" Trina's probation agreement stipulated that she could not "consort" with known felons; if she were caught talking to Lionnel—a known felon at least a dozen times over—it could mean prison.

"Not that I know of, but I've got a bad feeling."

"Trina's been doing great. She's clean, working hard, doing a terrific job for Gram."

"It's not that simple, Lee."

"Maybe it is," I insisted.

Kiah didn't answer.

"Why don't I talk to her and see if I can find out if anything's going on?" I offered. "She's at the house now. I can give it a try when I get back."

Kiah pursed her lips in her there's-no-way-a-white-person-can-understand expression.

That look always pissed me off. "If you don't think anyone can break out of this, why do you bother?"

"I didn't say I don't think anyone can break out," Kiah corrected me stiffly. "I just said I had a bad feeling about Trina." She walked into her office, picked up a folder from her desk and handed it to me. "Budget's all set." Then she smiled, apparently forgiving me for being white. "Good job."

I took the file, pleased, despite my annoyance. "Just let

me do a final read-through, then I'll give it to Joy to copy. After you sign the cover letter, she can drop the whole package at the post office on her way home." I raised my hand for a high-five. "It's out of here!"

Kiah slapped my hand. "One down."

Great, I thought as I climbed the stairs to my office. I was going to be finished in an hour, and although I could find plenty to do here, I couldn't in all good conscience leave Beth on her own for the afternoon. My budget was approved and my report finished, but all this good news meant was that I was going to have to go back down into that damn cellar.

When I got home, there was a note from Beth propped up on the kitchen table. She had forgotten that her son Zach had a baseball game. She had to pick him up from school and drop him off at the field, but she'd be back by 3:30.

I went into the west parlor, which Gram used as an office, and was pleased to see that Trina was there by herself. She was sitting at the large oak desk that had belonged to Elijah Harden, Ulysses' son and my great-grandfather. In the family lexicon, Elijah was "the Congressman" the way Stanton was "the Colonel." I dropped into one of the worn leather wing chairs that faced the desk and stretched my legs out in front of me. "Hey," I said casually, hoping I was setting the right tone for a girl-to-girl heart-to-heart.

"Hey." Trina didn't look up from the long form she was filling out. Her braids fell in a ripple of ringlets around her face, and her velvety skin was pulled taut over her stunning cheekbones. She and Lionnel must have made one terrific looking couple.

I was wondering if Lionnel was good in bed, but I asked, "Where's Gram?"

"Upstairs, I think."

"How're you doing?"

"Okay."

"Making a dent?"

"I guess." Trina glanced at the clock on the wall, then returned her gaze to the papers in front of her.

"You think we'll get everything done in time for the inspection?"

Trina scratched her head with the back of her pen, still not meeting my eye. "Does anyone really care about all this paper?"

"Probably not."

Trina's eyes finally connected with mine, but her smile was fleeting.

"Bureaucrats have to keep themselves employed."

She grunted.

I cleared my throat. It was as if Trina sensed I wanted to talk to her about a touchy subject, and I didn't know how to broach it without coming on as the righteous white person she sometimes thought I was. I wished I had never told Kiah I'd have this conversation.

Trina tapped the edge of the desk with the pen.

I rubbed the toe of my sneaker into the faded Oriental rug. "So everything's cool?"

She shrugged.

"You're almost there. Don't let anything screw you up now."

Trina's eyes clouded briefly with the resignation of old age, the hard-earned knowledge that things were what they were, not what we hoped them to be. She shook her head and spoke to me as if I were a not-too-bright child—and a white one at that. “You don’t always get to control the screw-ups. Lots of times, they get you no matter what.”

“I want to help.”

“I know you do, Lee,” she said softly. “But sometimes you just can’t.”

I pushed myself out of the chair. “Any more of that fabulous chicken salad you made for lunch?”

Trina startled, as if she hadn’t expected me to give up so easily. “Ah, no,” she said quickly. “It’s all gone.”

“It’s okay. I’ll find something else.”

I was in the kitchen when I heard it. I inched to the cellar stairs and leaned toward the sound. The scrape of metal against metal, or manacle against stone. Of falling dirt. I saw the man from my nightmare as clearly as I had seen him in the eerie glow of the fieldstones. I clutched the door handle so hard it dug into my palm. The man was real. And he was back.

I forced myself to take a deep breath. It wasn’t the man. It was Beth or Michael or Gram. As I headed down the stairs, the shadows and the cobwebs and the musty, rank odor threw me back into the nightmare. The digging was closer, the sound more intense. I imagined I smelled sweat, and as I crossed the dirt floor to the door that led to the old cellar, I was filled with dread. Whatever lay on the other side was not going to be good. I wanted to turn and run, but I kept going. Nightmares weren’t real.

I stepped into the old cellar and the shadow of a figure holding a shovel fell before my feet. I gasped, and for a moment my dream and reality blurred into one another. My lungs ached with the air I was forgetting to breathe out. It was all true: the tunnel, the shovel, the dirt, the man. Then my vision cleared. I blinked, and the air rushed from my mouth.

I slumped against the rough-cut doorway in relief, watching my grandmother rhythmically fill the tunnel with dirt. Her back was to me, and she bent her knees as she lifted each shovel-load, just as Beth had instructed this morning. Sixty-nine and stubborn as hell. Gram had never planned to work with Trina. She had just been waiting until Beth and I weren't around to get her hands on that shovel. She was incorrigible—and she was going to give herself a heart attack.

Gram abruptly stopped digging and jerked the shovel toward her stomach. "What?" she said, her voice full of confusion. "What the hell . . . ?" Her breathing became rapid and labored, and she tugged on the shovel as if someone were trying to take it from her.

I was reminded of a mime I once saw fighting on the streets of New Orleans. He was alone on a corner, boxing with no one, throwing punches into the empty air, taking hits, but he was so good he made his invisible partner visible. In the same way, I could see the shape on the other side of Gram's shovel.

Gram's eyes widened, and the horrified awe that was squeezing my heart pinched her face, distorting her features into a startled white mask. Her hands tightened on the handle, and her entire body shook as, for a second, her eyes connected with mine. And in that endless moment, I knew and didn't want to know, understood and didn't want to understand, that I was watching the man from my nightmare.

I couldn't actually see him, yet he was there: strong and powerful, angry. Against all laws of physics, all laws of nature, an invisible being was trying to wrest a shovel from my grandmother's hands.

"Gram!" I shouted. "Let go! Let him have it. Just let it go!"

But she didn't hear me, or chose not to listen, for she stumbled backward, pulling the shovel with her. The shovel yanked in answer, dragging her forward again. Gram let out a long gasp and her knees gave way. She crumpled in on herself, collapsing as if she had no bones, no strength.

The shovel flew toward the tunnel as soon as Gram let go, then it too dropped, lifeless, to the dirt.

CHAPTER SEVEN

The Jews do a much better job with death than the Presbyterians.

When my father's mother died, the entire extended family arrived within what seemed like minutes. Grandma Ray was buried within twenty-four hours (Jewish law has a stricture against embalming which necessitates immediate burial; this has the unintended but fortuitous consequence of getting the funeral over with as soon as possible), then everyone stuck around for a week eating and talking and generally helping each other over the initial hump of grief. But the Presbyterians are too tough and too New England to do anything that emotionally supportive. The Presbyterians must go it alone.

Although I'd always felt a strong attachment to the liberal politics of my mother's family, when it came to emotion, I was pure Jew. None of that stiff upper lip crap for me: Gram was dead and I was aching and hollow with grief, wishing more than anything that everyone hadn't left me here alone. Gram died on Tuesday, was buried on Friday and now it was Saturday, time to pull that chin up and get back to the living. "Life goes on," my mother reminded me before she left last night. "Don't let it go on without you." But the house felt so horribly vacant and wrong. The fact that it was filled with Gram's papers and books and the faint smell of Chanel #5 made it all the emptier. I didn't bother to wipe the tears away, the truth was that I hardly noticed them. Over the last few days, crying had become as natural as breathing.

I was in the west parlor, sitting at the Congressman's desk and staring at the mounds of paper piled before me. There were condolence notes mixed with bills and the paperwork for the Park Service. There was an unfinished letter Gram had been writing to her brother Joe, and a note she had scribbled to herself about a hair cut next Wednesday. I supposed I'd have to call and cancel it. I looked at her calendar; it was sprinkled with notations of doctors' appointments and tennis matches and meetings with the Lexington Historical Society. I supposed I'd have to cancel all of those too. I was tired, exhausted actually, completely and totally wrung out. I didn't have the strength to do all I was "supposed" to do.

I flipped listlessly through the mail; some of it was for me, but most of it was addressed to Mrs. Clara Barrett or Mrs. Jonathan Barrett or Clara Harden Barrett. There were so many letters to write, people to contact, bureaucracies to inform. And I was so very tired. Beth had offered to go through Gram's personal things while I had opted for the desk. I didn't think I could bear the smell of her clothes. Her name showing through the little window of the electric bill was tough enough.

"Your grandmother had a good life," my mother had told me at the funeral, annoyed with my inability to control my grief with what she considered "the proper dignity." "Almost seventy years," she continued. "Gram went out the way she would have wanted: quick and painless, while she was still in good heath. You should be happy for her, instead of focusing on yourself."

I supposed my mother had a point, but Mom hadn't seen the horror on Gram's face as she wrestled over a shovel with no one. I hadn't told anyone about the scene in the cellar. It was all I could do to keep from constantly reliving those unlivable moments, from once again thinking those unthinkable thoughts. When I failed, I was overwhelmed by a dazed, frightened awe at what it might mean.

I stood and aimlessly wandered through the house. The air in the rooms seemed thinner, somehow less substantial, than it had been when Gram was alive. The dust lying on the furniture and bookshelves gave off an odor that evoked the relentless passage of time.

I paused in the east parlor before a Chippendale table; carved leaves and berries and other complicated foliage adorned its raised lip, and its slender cabriole legs supported an oval tabletop covered with family photographs: old ones dating back to the Colonel's time, pictures of Beth and me and our brothers as kids, a brand new photo of Adam and Mindy's baby daughter. There was an extended family shot taken in 1915 in which everyone, including the small children, looked stern. I scrutinized the sulky faces of the women, wondering which one was Dotty Aunt Hortense, both fearful and hopeful I might detect something in her eyes that would shed light on what had happened in the cellar. But my great-aunts and nameless cousins just stared morosely back, frozen in time, their secrets as remote to me as their lives.

I put down the family photo and picked up the sepiatone of Sarah Harden that Gram had shown me the other day. I was again touched by the compassion and sorrow in her expression. What had happened to this woman to make her so sad? Could Beth have been right about the painful, untimely death of her young husband? Or had it been something else, something quite different? There was so much we would never—could never—know, and this not knowing had its own bittersweet poignancy. I returned Sarah's picture to the table and headed back to the west parlor.

I had just settled in behind Gram's desk when I heard the kitchen door slam and the refrigerator door creak open. I jumped up. Gram was home.

"It's me!" Beth called. "You got any more Diet Coke?"

I dropped back into the chair. "In the cabinet to the right of the stove," I yelled back, surprised at the strength of my voice. "Bring me one, too."

Beth was as shook up as I, but she had Presbyterian stoicism on both sides of her family so her veneer was tougher and shinier than mine. Still, when she came through the door with two cans of warm Diet Coke, the eyes staring out from behind her impassive expression were dark and haunted. "No ice," she said, dropping one can on the desk and popping the other open. She took a sip. "Tastes like shit."

I opened mine and tried it. "At least it's warm shit."

"The only kind I'll drink." She sat down in the chair across from me, and we sipped our sodas in silence. There wasn't much to say. And there was so much to say. It had occurred to me that, as Gram hadn't finalized the deal with the Lexington Historical Society before she died, Beth would probably still inherit Harden House. I wondered what Beth and Russ would do with it, but I wasn't curious enough to ask, even though a faraway, detached part of me knew I needed to be concerned about the disposition of the house in which I was living.

"—call them on Monday?" Beth was saying.

"Huh? Who're you calling on Monday?"

"I asked what you think we should do about the Park Service inspection," Beth said, exasperated patience coating her words. "It's scheduled for this Tuesday, isn't it?"

I shrugged.

To my surprise, Beth burst into tears. "I can't do this

alone," she sobbed. "It's too scary and too hard, and I'm in no shape, no shape at all, not after everything that's happened, I'm in no shape to handle it. I can't, I just can't. I, I need you to come back and help me get through this."

Beth's tears seemed to reach me from a long way off, but they did reach me, and they reminded me of something. Of something someone had told me the other day. At the funeral. No, at the funeral lunch. I was standing in the east parlor and Michael was explaining something about the inspection. Uncle Joe was there. And Aunt Doris. "Trina," I said. "Trina."

Beth looked up, confusion mingling with the fear and sadness in her eyes. She grabbed a tissue from the desk. "What are you talking about?" she mumbled into the tissue, then wiped her cheeks and blew her nose. "What does Trina have to do with anything?"

"Trina called and postponed the inspection. Michael told her to. The Park Service people said they'll get in touch to reschedule."

Beth leaned back in her chair and closed her eyes. "Thank God that guy's got the hots for you," she said. There were dark crescents of sleeplessness under her eyes, but she was beginning to sound more like herself.

"He liked Gram a lot too," I reminded her.

She smirked at me.

I smiled, maybe for the first time since I had found Gram in the cellar. Perhaps my mother had a point after all: life did march along no matter how much you wished it was still last week. And who would have guessed a week ago that it would be Michael's mom who was still alive and Gram who was dead? I sighed. "Are you going to start going through the things in the bedroom?"

Beth looked down at her hands.

I noticed her nail polish was chipped—something she would never tolerate under normal circumstances—and the cuticle of her right thumb was all chewed up the way she used to do when she was a kid and was expecting a bad report card or had to tell her parents she'd cracked up the car. I was touched. "It really doesn't have to be done right away," I said. "Or," I hesitated, "or I could help you with it if you want."

Beth shook her head. "No," she said softly. "Let's stick to our original plan. I'll start in the bedroom and you try to get this mess under control." She pressed her hands to the desk and pushed herself to a stand. She stared down at her fingernails as if seeing them for the first time, then headed toward the front stairs. "But I'm not going to stay around all that long today," she called over her shoulder. "I've got to get a manicure."

I didn't know if it was Beth or the Diet Coke that got me going, and I didn't much care. It just felt good to be moving again, to be out of the fog. I opened all the mail and sorted it into piles: to be trashed, to be paid, to be sent to my mother, to be informed, to be dealt with in some other manner. Then I paid the bills and tried to bring some semblance of order to the Tubman Park materials. But it wasn't easy. Even with Trina's recent intervention, the papers were a mess.

Gram had been the center around which the project and all its players radiated: she delegated and kept track of who was doing what and what needed to be done next, but not in any organized manner I could discern. I was far from the world's most orderly person, and no one had ever accused me of being compulsive or even of keeping my desk too neat, but Gram's system—if you could call a lack of system a system—was out there. Or maybe it wasn't there at all.

She must have kept it all in her head. Impressive, but given the present situation, also exasperating. We all think we're going to live forever.

I felt bad that I hadn't gotten the chance to say good-bye, to tell Gram how much she meant to me, how much I loved and respected her. Perhaps seeing the Tubman Park project through to completion could be my parting gift to her. I lifted up a pile of unruly papers. "I'll get it done, Gram," I said out loud. "I promise."

"Talking to the walls?" Beth asked as she came through the door into the parlor. She had a funny look on her face.

"Find something?"

"It's not what I found—it's what I didn't find."

I could feel my energy draining away like air in a punctured balloon. "You know I hate riddles." I pressed my hands to my closed eyelids.

"And I don't like thieves."

I didn't move my hands. Beth was always on the look out for high drama—whether it was there or not—and I had had enough drama for one week. "Just tell me what you're talking about." I could hear a touch of irritation thinning my voice, and added, "Please."

"Gram's diamond-and-emerald bracelet is missing."

"No it's not."

"You have it?"

I slowly peeled my hands from my eyes. "No," I admitted, "but I'm sure it's there somewhere. I just saw it the other day."

"So did I," Beth said triumphantly. "And so did Trina."

"Are you suggesting Trina took Gram's bracelet?"

Beth crossed her arms over her chest. "She was staring at it the day we were up in Gram's room. The day you climbed into the tunnel."

I pinched the bridge of my nose to try to ward off the headache I could feel gathering. "If you stole every piece of jewelry you stared at, you'd be drowning in diamonds," I said, but Beth would have none of it, and I finally agreed to go upstairs with her and look for myself. As she had said, the bracelet didn't appear to be anywhere in the room.

"Maybe Aunt Doris or my mother has it," I suggested.

"You know we agreed to wait for the will."

I did know this was true. "Maybe one of them took it for safe keeping?"

"And not the ruby brooch?"

The ruby brooch was the most valuable piece of jewelry Gram owned. It had belonged to Charlotte Abbott Harden—the Colonel's wife, Sarah's mother—and was rumored to have once belonged to some minor Spanish princess. The brooch was in the jewelry box.

I sat down on the edge of the bed and squeezed my nose again. I wished I was sleeping—or at least swallowing some Tylenol. "When we go through Gram's clothes and things, I'm sure we'll find it in a pocket or a purse somewhere. She might have even taken it to the jeweler—she was always complaining that the clasp wouldn't stay closed. The slip might be in her wallet. Did you check there?"

Beth raised a single eyebrow and she looked so much like Gram I winced. But her words didn't remind me of Gram at all. "Think what you want," she said, "but when all the searching and checking's done, I'm betting we aren't finding that bracelet anywhere Gram put it."

CHAPTER EIGHT

November 15, 1858

The snows have come early this year and it seems darker and colder than it has ever been. I have just received a letter from Cousin Lizzie in Hartford and she is heart-broken that we shall not be together for Christmas as we have in the years past. She writes that Lewis Campbell has asked her to send his warmest regards and to tell me he is disappointed I won't be able to attend the Buffrum-Chase Christmas Ball. I am heart-broken also, but Papa is resolute in his decision to remain in Lexington, and neither my pleas nor those of Aunt Elizabeth can sway him.

Uncle Benjamin is in textiles, and he has no sympathy for the abolitionists as he needs Southern cotton for his factory. Papa and Uncle had a discussion of this last Christmas which ended with much raising of voices, and according to Lizzie, the breaking of two glasses and a plate. Uncle said that although slavery might be wrong in the eyes of the church, the founders of the Republic had consented to it, and it was his duty as a citizen to uphold the laws of the land.

It took Mama two days to calm Papa after this "discussion," and I fear that now that poor Mama is no longer with us, I shall never go to another Buffrum-Chase Ball, visit with my dear Cousin Lizzie nor see Lewis Campbell ever again.

November 18, 1858

Papa's edict that I may have no visitors was difficult enough when it was possible for me to walk to the homes of Nancy Southwick or Mrs. Childs for a cup of tea or go into the city for dinner parties. But now that the snow drifts sweep the landmarks clean, I am unable to move beyond the confines of Harden House.

Mrs. Harrington comes in each day to do the washing and cleaning and preserving, and as my studies were completed last year, I am mostly left with little occupation aside from my handwork. In the past, my correspondence was extensive, but now that Papa reads every letter I write to ensure I have not "divulged," I can take little pleasure in that. I attempted to make a new type of candle today with horse chestnuts and oil, but it failed to set correctly and had to be thrown away.

Papa, Caleb and Wendell are busy with their Vigilance Committee and their chores. Not even Wendell appears to notice whether I am about. It is only Silas who is willing to take a few moments to speak with me. If not for Silas, I think I should surely be mad by January.

November 19, 1858

Silas told me such a sad tale today. It happened in the Borderland, the long strip of forest between the Northern and Southern states through which most slaves must make their way to freedom. These woods are constantly patrolled by constables and bounty hunters looking to claim the rewards put up by the plantation owners. These rewards could be as little as a quarter-eagle or as grand as a fifty-dollar gold piece, but as Silas pointed out to me, it is not the dollar value which has meaning, it is the fact that an amount of money is equated to a human life that gives true expression to this horror called slavery.

The story Silas told was of a mother and her small son. The bounty hunters had set a bear trap to catch the pair of runaways—yes, a bear trap laid down with the intention that it close around the leg of a woman and child! On this day God must have turned his back for a moment, for the little boy became caught in the trap. His mother, of course, would not leave him, bleeding and surely dying, his arm crushed by the rusted teeth of a trap meant for an animal. He was but maybe five years of age. She was unable to free him from the grip of the trap, so they sat together in the woods, consoling each other as best they could as they awaited their fate.

They did not have to wait long, and when the bounty hunters found the pair, the men laughed with glee. The mother begged the men to release her boy, to staunch his bleeding, to get him to a doctor, but the men just laughed more loudly, and then one pulled out a rifle and shot the little boy between the eyes. He told the grief-stricken mother that he was just putting the boy out of his misery.

November 20, 1858

Today Silas told me he did not want to speak of himself, but to hear of me. I protested that I had lived a dull life, but he persisted, so I told him of Mama and my studies and of my favorite books. "I keep a diary," I confessed shyly, and then explained that although I tried to write every day, I was often too fatigued in the evening to carry out my good intentions.

"Might I read your diary some day?" he asked.

I'm sure I became quite red when I realized he was teasing me and told him I certainly thought not. He was a man of such experience—a married man, a widower!—and I a young girl of none.

He smiled at me, that warm, gentle smile, that told me that although I was right, I was young and inexperienced, that he did not hold that against me. "That would be its charm," he said.

November 21, 1858

Today when I visited Silas in the barn I brought along a book with my afghan. We did not speak much, yet it was one of the loveliest afternoons I have enjoyed in a long time. Silas went about his tasks as I read in the hayloft.

I am reading Pickwick Papers *by Charles Dickens, a novel which Nancy brought to me last month, and I have kept hidden as Papa would never allow me to read it. Papa says that the "indiscriminate reading of novels" by young women is a "most dangerous tendency." Silas laughed when I told him this. He said white men have many strange ideas. I told him this might be true, but Papa's ideas were stranger than most.*

I did not feel the least bit guilty saying such things about Papa, as Silas understands that I meant Papa no disrespect, that Papa is who he is: a man of great moral conviction, but a bit old-fashioned in his ways. The only person to whom I have spoken in such a way was Mama, and in many ways, Silas understands me as she did, listens as she did. Strangely, being with Silas makes me miss Mama all the more.

November 22, 1858

The anti-abolitionists are becoming bolder with each passing day, and Wendell has advised Papa that it is too dangerous for Silas to work in the daylight. He also suggested that all the dirt Silas excavates remain in the cellar. Wendell fears if Silas digs during the day a stranger might hear him, and if piles of dirt were to suddenly appear on Harden House property, suspicions might be raised.

So Silas now works on his tunnel only at night, oblivious to the discomfort of the cast on his leg or the dirt and dust that are his constant companions. I am very lonely and imagine Silas must be also. It is very dark and cold in the cellar after sundown, and although I know his heart is in the right place, I wonder if Wendell has done Silas a service.

It has begun to snow again.

November 23, 1858

The storm continues unabated, and I fear I shall lose my mind if I do not leave the house soon or at least have a decent conversa-

tion with a person of some interest and intelligence. Wendell has gone home to his family, and Papa and Caleb are busy with their whisperings on issues not deemed proper for a young lady. Mrs. Harrington is as grumpy as I at being trapped at Harden House by the snow, and her company is even more unpleasant than usual. Silas has spent the last three nights in the cellar digging behind the canning cupboard. He sleeps during the day.

Papa tells me to content myself with the Bible and Ladies' Repository, *but reading* Ladies' Repository *is like reading the parson's Sunday sermon, and although I do try, I find I cannot sustain interest in the Bible. I would much prefer* Graham's Magazine *or* Harper's Monthly*—both of which I have read at Nancy Southwick's—or the new novel by Jules Verne about traveling to the center of the earth or perhaps the latest by the writer George Elliot who Nancy declares she knows to be a woman! (I find this assertion very difficult to believe and, at times, Nancy has been known to stretch the truth.) But whether the author be man or woman, Papa will allow none of these books or magazines at Harden House. I have finished* Pickwick Papers, *hiding it in a back drawer of my chiffonier once again.*

The rooms grow smaller and tighter and closer with each passing day.

November 25, 1858

The skies have finally cleared, but the snow rises to the sill of the parlor windows and it is not yet December! No one remembers there ever being this much snow this early in the season, and there is much concern for animals and crops and floods in the spring.

Wendell rode his horse through the drifts to speak with Papa and Caleb, and, perhaps I flatter myself, with me. When he arrived at Harden House, he was so covered with snow, for a moment, we did not recognize that it was he! It was a great relief to be in the presence of someone besides Mrs. Harrington, and even Wendell seemed less dull than usual. He was only able to stay for a few moments, as some of his animals are sick and need his attention.

I pray for an early spring.

November 26, 1858

With no word of his brothers, and no hope of word soon, Silas has become very reclusive. He is no longer interested in telling me tales of either his life or of the horrors of slavery. He is only interested in digging. He has begun to sleep in the cellar as it is difficult to trek back and forth to the barn. Mrs. Harrington leaves his dinner at the top of the stairs. Often, I add pieces from my own plate to Silas', as Mrs. Harrington's servings are as meager as her heart.

I have not spoken with Silas in five days nor seen him in three, but I confess to you, dear diary, I have begun to dream of him. Last night, in my dream, he had no cast on his leg nor sadness in his smile. We walked together through the apple orchard. I blush to remember that we were holding hands.

Is this an evil vision for which I should repent? Dreaming of myself, a young unmarried girl, walking with a widowed, runaway slave? It was springtime and Silas and I were both so happy in the orchard. I cannot believe it is sinful to dream of peace and contentment.

November 27, 1858

The mails were finally able to get through, and in my little bundle I found a letter from Cousin Lizzie with the most distressing news. She has it on good source and in great confidence that Lewis Campbell is to be engaged! It is rumored that they are planning an announcement at the Buffrum-Chase Ball! He is marrying the second oldest of the Perkins' girls, a dull sort called

Hallie who is always wearing unattractive dresses with those horrid leg-of-mutton sleeves.

Although I did not wish to move all the way to Connecticut, I find myself most disappointed and extremely vexed. Why must it be my father who is so devoted to the cause? Why must it be my family who suffers for his righteousness? I am certain that if Lewis had believed I would be at the ball, he never would have betrothed himself to Hallie Perkins.

November 28, 1858

While Papa and Caleb were in the barn tending to the horses, I slipped into the cellar to visit Silas. I told him I was curious about his progress, but I confess to you, dear diary, I was lonely and wanted to see him. He appeared quite pleased that I had come and showed me the long tunnel he has dug. I cannot believe he has covered so much ground and think that surely he will be all the way to the well very soon! I only wish the post which brought me such distressing news of Lewis Campbell had also brought some news of his brothers to cheer him. But there was nothing.

After I inspected the tunnel, he showed me how he had devised a means to hide the tunnel opening by making Mama's canning cupboard appear solid and fixed in front of it. It is as clever as the safe room above! Dear Mama, for all I miss and admire her, was not particularly taken with either the eating or the preparing of foods, and this is why the canning cupboard is so modest. (Mrs. Harrington, for all I dismiss and dislike her, does make a wonderful strawberry preserve and can rinse and scrub salted beef in some special way that makes it actually taste good.) Papa used to complain that the cupboard was too small for a family such as ours, but now its size is coming in quite handy, for Silas has built a rack of shelves with a false back that fits right into the shallow cupboard. The shelves can be filled with cans and jars and strings of dried fruit—but the whole rack can also be lifted out to expose the tunnel behind it.

December 1, 1858

I had a dream last night in which Silas and I stood on the edge of a wintry forest. It was snowing and windy and I was horribly cold, shivering within my heavy wool cloak. Suddenly, Silas lifted a huge old oak tree right out of the ground as if it were a light as a sapling! He dropped the tree and held his hand out to ease my way over the hole where the tree had once stood, then climbed over himself. As soon as we passed beyond the spot where the oak had been, it became sunny and warm, and we were in a glorious field of sunflowers! I threw off my cloak and raced through the flowers. Silas laughed and followed me.

December 3, 1858

Papa, Caleb and Wendell have gone into Boston to meet with the Vigilance Committee. Papa left Mrs. Harrington in charge of the house and in charge of me, although I am surely old enough to look after myself. I avoid her whenever I am able. Papa and Caleb are staying at the home of Mr. William Lloyd Garrison and hope to get word of Silas' brothers while there. They have been gone for three days and shall probably be gone another two.

When Mrs. Harrington is busy with her chores and her grumbling, I slip into the cellar to talk with Silas.

December 4, 1858 (morning)

The snows have come again, and I fear Papa and Caleb may not be able to return from Boston for many more days. Early this morning, during a break in the storm, Mrs. Harrington left to check on her cows, but now the winds have picked up and beyond the windows we can only see white. I dare say she shall be unable to return either. How scandalized she must be at the thought of a white girl all alone with a Negro man. It amuses me to think of her, staring out her window at the unrelenting snow, horrifying herself with fantasies of sin and wickedness.

Silas has built a huge fire in the dining room hearth, and we are warm and safe and protected while nature and Mrs. Harrington rage on the other side.

December 4, 1858 (late afternoon)

The sun sets so early this time of year, and usually I am made melancholy by its disappearance, but as Silas and I sit together before the fire, reading and talking quietly, there is a gentleness to the approaching darkness that is comforting, beckoning. Like the softness of a black velvet gown.

December 5, 1858 (morning)

Silas has been telling me stories as we wait out the storm. Stories of the worst cruelties and the greatest kindnesses, of bravery and of cowardice. Of the power of the human desire for freedom and the equally human desire to keep others from being free.

I learned of a Negro man named Henry Brown who packed himself into a wooden crate and "mailed" himself to a Quaker meeting house outside of Philadelphia. I learned of a white woman named Nelly who sacrificed her own life to help a family of runaways escape across the Ohio River. And I learned of the practice of cathauling.

Cathauling is a form of punishment in which an angry tomcat is thrown onto the naked back of a slave and allowed to claw and maim the poor man until he faints dead away. When Silas told me this had been done to his youngest brother, Levi, who was tied down by leather thongs wrapped at his wrists and ankles, I was horrified. But when he told me the cathauling had been ordered and carried out by a Negro overseer named Luther,

I began to understand what true horror really is. Silas says Levi's screams still echo inside his head.

It broke my heart when Silas explained that after he took Levi's blood-soaked body back to his cabin, after he bathed his brother's wounds and tended to his fever, he did not go to the master to demand Luther be punished, even though the master had outlawed cathauling on his plantation. Instead, Silas went to the Negro conjurer and asked him to mix up a potion to be slipped into Luther's nightly brew that would bring the overseer the bad luck he deserved. The next morning Luther was dead.

Silas pulled the red-flannel Mojo from the inside of his shirt. He explained that his charm bag was made by the same conjurer who helped him with Luther, and that he wears it around his neck always to keep him safe. "There's no justice for the Negro in the white man's world," he said. "That's why we find ways to make our own."

"But how can you say that when you're more of a white man than a Negro?" I asked. "When three of your grandparents are white?"

Silas gazed at me with the weary, sad expression I have come to know so well. He touched my hand, but then pulled back and his expression hardened. "In this world, the smallest drop of Negro blood makes a man a Negro," he said. "The white man's world is only for the white man."

I could not hold his gaze and looked down at my hand, feeling the warmth and sweetness of his fingers upon mine as I felt how very dull and stupid I was: I have experienced nothing, seen nothing, understand nothing. I stand humble before this man.

December 5, 1858 (evening)

I write in the warm glow of the lamplight as I am unable to sleep. It must be well past midnight, and Silas sleeps before the fire. I am curled on the chesterfield, wrapped in Mama's afghan. I watch the gentle rise and fall of Silas' broad chest, the way his well-muscled arms glisten in the firelight, and wonder what it would be like to have that chest pressed to mine, to feel those arms around me. Despite the warmth of the room, a shiver of imagined pleasure ripples through me.

I have grown more in two days in the company of Silas than I have in the past two years in the company of Papa and Caleb and Wendell Parker. Silas stirs in his sleep, turns toward me and opens his eyes. I drop the afghan from my shoulders and kneel next to him. I reach out and touch his cheek. When he pulls me to him and cradles me within the warmth of his body, I learn what it feels like to have those arms around me. I learn what it feels like to be a woman.

It is all far more wonderful than I could ever have imagined.

CHAPTER NINE

I went into work Monday morning hoping that getting back into my routine would make the world feel right again. To my disappointment, but not to my surprise, it didn't work. On the drive over, I kept wondering how everyone could be doing their usual Monday thing when it wasn't a usual Monday at all, and when I got to SafeHaven, everything felt off, as if someone had come along and put things at a slight slant while I was away. The shoemaker's elves with diabolical intent.

Kiah's condolences and concerned expression seemed to be coming at me from the wrong end of a telescope, and I could have sworn I'd never met the two new residents washing the dining room floor—although Kiah assured me I had. My desk, crammed under the eaves of my tiny attic office, was larger than I remembered, and the ceiling dipped lower than it had last week. I sat down and scanned the room. The last time I had been here, I was finishing up the Health and Human Services report, pleased that the project was complete, but dreading my return to Gram's cellar. How prophetic that concern had been.

I knew Gram had lived a good life, and that her sudden and quick death was just what she would have chosen for herself. Still, I missed her with an ache that belied my logic, and although her last moments were indelibly etched into my consciousness, I couldn't quite believe it had happened. When my mother told me that an autopsy had been ordered, that it was standard practice when a sudden death occurred outside a hospital, I refused to discuss it, fearing the image it evoked of a cold room filled with sharp tools, a long metal table holding a naked blue-white body.

Gram wasn't dead. It was some kind of bad joke. She just couldn't be. I began to sort through the messages and mail that littered my desk, but even as I read the letters and made a list of calls to be returned, I found my mind wandering from the tasks before me to the place it had been gravitating since last Tuesday afternoon: to Gram's bizarre death scene in the cellar.

I still hadn't told anyone what I had seen, and although I knew Kiah would claim it wasn't good for my mental health, I wasn't planning on it. What would I say? That Gram had been fighting with an invisible being over a shovel? That the sight of it, or the power of it, or the fear of it, had killed her? I thought of the conversation I had had with Trina about an afterlife being no more improbable than life itself. I didn't think I believed in an afterlife. I never had before. But maybe a ghost would explain Dotty Aunt Hortense's behavior. Or maybe, just like she, I was losing my mind.

A sharp rap on the doorjamb startled me from my reverie. Kiah strode into the office and planted herself in front of my desk. Her eyes were worried, and there was a slight twitch at the left side of her mouth. I wondered if I had screwed up something in the report.

"Got a second?" she asked.

I pushed back in my chair and motioned her to sit on the corner of the desk. The room was too small to hold any furniture other than my desk and a narrow bookshelf. "What's up?"

She remained standing. "It's your friend Trina."

The way Kiah said, "your friend Trina," was not promising; it reminded me of the way my mother used to say, "your daughter Lee," to my father when I'd done something wrong.

"What'd she do?"

"It's not what she did, but how she's doing it." Kiah crossed her arms over her chest. "There're two uniforms downstairs."

Cops, I thought. Shit.

Kiah stared at me impassively. "It's that sweet-talking, pretty-boy Lionnel Matthias."

"So Trina's not in trouble herself?"

Kiah shrugged. "Your guess."

I massaged the back of my neck. "Are you going to tell me what's going on, or are you just going to keep giving me non-answers to my questions?"

Kiah had the grace to smile. She sighed and draped her lanky body over the end of the desk. "Lionnel's been busted for fencing hot goods, and the cops think Trina knows something about it."

An image of Gram's diamond-and-emerald bracelet flashed through my mind. "Did they recover anything?"

"Why?" Kiah jumped on my question immediately. "Why do you ask that?"

Although Kiah was only ten years my senior, she seemed much wiser and more worldly than I. She had grown up in the projects and done the old pull-yourself-up-by-the-bootstraps thing after a long bout with drugs and prostitution. She once told me that the aunt who had raised her—if you could call what the aunt had done "raising"—had instructed her to "be nice to men" when they were nice to her, and that it had been real clear to Kiah exactly what the aunt meant. Kiah was twelve. "I was too young to know any better," she had explained without the least bit of self-pity.

"I just wanted money so I could be stoned out of my mind for as many waking hours as possible." But Kiah had also wanted more. After putting herself through two years at Roxbury Community College, she got a scholarship from Harvard to finish up her BA. She founded SafeHaven when she was a senior. The woman could smell something fishy a thousand miles inland.

"Do you know something I don't?" she pressed me.

I moved a pile of papers from the right side of my desk to the left side. "No."

Kiah's narrowed eyes told me she guessed I wasn't telling the truth, but that she had bigger fish to fry. "Trina's copping a major attitude," she said. "You know, the too cool, kicked-back sulky bit. She won't give up anything except that some base head is probably setting Lionnel up."

"You think it's true?"

She shrugged again. "Sure."

I was touched Kiah trusted me enough to be honest. In my single year at SafeHaven, I had seen druggies setting up druggies, pimps setting up pimps, and cops setting up any poor hapless bastard they could find—especially if his or her skin was a few shades darker than white. There was a reason the people who lived here weren't long on trust.

"Trina told 'em Lionnel makes bank on blow, not fence. She said if they want anyone to believe their bullshit, they'll have to get their story straight." Kiah's voice contained a touch of respect.

"Compelling argument."

"Not to the man."

"They aren't talking arrest, are they?"

"Just trying to scare her, I think. But Trina doesn't scare easy, and she's holding her own."

"Do you think Trina has done something wrong?" I

asked because Kiah appeared more concerned than she usually would under these circumstances. Cops were always showing up at the door, wanting to question this one or arrest that one. SafeHaven was, after all, a drug treatment facility for poor, minority women, and these women lived in a world where suspicious police were as common as substandard schools.

"I don't think anything. It's like I was saying last week: I just don't like the signs."

I watched Kiah warily. The stubborn jut of her chin told me we were reaching that peculiar edge of our friendship where black was black and white was white, and no matter what else we shared, Kiah wasn't going to believe that anyone but her own could really understand.

"How do you mean?" I asked carefully.

A look of distressed patience passed over her features. "This kind of attitude and protection of the shit boyfriend is a freshman thing," she said, as if explaining the obvious to a child who should have known better. "Sophomore, tops. If Trina were anywhere near ready to go back out there and beat the street, she wouldn't be acting like this."

"Are you thinking of demoting her?"

"That's not the point," Kiah said.

I didn't say anything because I didn't want to ask what the point was. I waited for her to tell me.

Instead, she asked, "Why did you want to know if anything was recovered? Did Trina tell you anything the other day that I should know about?"

"No," I said quickly. This was a sticky issue at SafeHaven. While the staff was urged to offer friendship to the women, to gain their trust and develop mutual respect, if secrets were shared, we were supposed to turn around and tell all. I'd never been able to buy into this: if a friend told me something in confidence, it meant I didn't tell anyone else. As far as I was concerned, that was what confidence was. But, as I said, trust was in pretty short supply around there. And it looked as if Kiah's trust in me had just dried up.

"Lee," she said coolly, "this isn't about some promise you made to your little girlfriend when you were all playing in your suburban backyard. This is the real world—there's more at stake here than who peed in the sandbox."

It really annoyed me when the women at SafeHaven started talking down to me like that—and I'd heard it from both staff and residents. Why did they always have to believe we couldn't understand, that we were so different from them? A few months ago, a dispassionate discussion I was having with Trina about the possibility of a black person receiving justice in a white world—I said it was possible, although acknowledged it was difficult, and Trina insisted it was always impossible—blew up when I told her I didn't think I was a racist. Trina claimed every white person was racist, and that it was racist of me not to recognize my racism. If I was a racist, I had asked her, what was I doing there? Why would I bother? She had just shaken her head with the same look of distressed patience on her face that had been on Kiah's.

"I don't know any more than you do," I told Kiah. "I couldn't get Trina to tell me anything."

Kiah's smile was tight, a sad granting of the reply she had expected. "Just thought I'd check before I laid into them," she said. "Lionnel may be an asshole, and he's surely done lots of things way worse than fencing a few hot computers, but that doesn't mean they've got the right to hassle him like that—or Trina either." Then she turned and walked out the door.

I stared into the empty hallway for a long time after Kiah disappeared. Why did I have the impression she thought I disagreed with her? I was relieved when the phone rang. It was Michael.

"I'm at the house," he said, his voice terse. "I stopped by for a minute and found the police waiting in the driveway."

"Are they looking for Trina?"

"No," he said. "They're looking for you."

Trina watched the two uniforms leave, avoiding eye contact with Kiah. It was obvious Kiah was pissed off, but Trina wasn't exactly sure who Kiah was pissed at: Lionnel or the cops or her. Probably all of them. Trina glanced over real quick, and just as quick Kiah gave her the red eye. It was pretty clear Kiah thought she was fencing for Lionnel, or else that she was doing something else she shouldn't be doing. If Kiah believed Trina was turning, how could Trina expect the uniforms not to? Trina didn't look again. She just went back to the kitchen sink, which was where she had been when the cops had showed up.

One of the cops was a brother and the other a know-it-all white boy who didn't stop yapping the whole time he was sitting there. Yapping about how Trina knew what Lionnel was up to and how she was helping him dump all his shit all over town. Right. Here she was in drug rehab, for Christ's sake, locked in and watched every minute, on the edge of going to prison every day. How would she be getting rid of Lionnel's hot watches and boom boxes? When she told them so, they didn't believe her. They just thought she was giving lip.

The cops figured that because of Hendrika and the smack, Trina was lying. And Lionnel sure wasn't helping, sniffing around even though he wasn't supposed to, knowing it could land her in jail. "As long as you know me, don't you come near me," she had told him when he showed up at the kitchen window last week. But he kept coming. He didn't believe any more than anyone else that she really wanted to get her shit together.

Even Kiah, whose whole life was supposed to be dedicated to believing, didn't believe Trina could change from what she'd been. From where she'd been. Trina wanted to tell them all that a dead baby can change a lot of shit for a person. But, then again, maybe even a dead baby wasn't enough.

She pressed her finger to a spot above her upper lip to keep from crying and washed the rest of the dishes with one hand. What did the police know? What did Kiah and Lionnel know? They didn't know shit. Kiah had never even asked her if she was okay about Clara.

Trina felt real bad about Clara. It was like there was this huge hole where Clara had once been. One minute, she and Clara were shooting the breeze, and then the next thing Trina knew, Clara had passed. Trina hadn't wanted it to be like that, that wasn't how things were supposed to go, and even though she knew nothing hardly ever worked out the way you wanted it to, it still hurt to think about how it had come down.

Trina pushed harder on the spot, but a tear rolled down her cheek anyway. Maybe the cops and Kiah and Lionnel were right. Maybe they were just seeing what she didn't want to.

"Poison?"

"Only a possibility, ma'am." The cop swallowed and his Adam's apple bobbed. He appeared to be all of sixteen and quite uncomfortable. He had introduced himself as Detective Raymond Langley. His partner was Detective Lynn Blais.

"Are you telling me it's possible my grandmother was poisoned?" I looked at the policewoman who sat to the young cop's left. She obviously had seniority, but she didn't offer an answer to my question. I turned back to Langley. "Are you saying that someone gave Gram poison on purpose?" Although I knew this was impossible, a part of me recognized that if Gram had died from some kind of poison, she couldn't have been scared to death by a ghost.

Michael placed his hand over mine. We were in the east parlor. The two cops sat across from us in Gram's yellow bergere chairs. Michael and I were squeezed together on the old chesterfield. "I told you that no one would want to hurt Clara Barrett," he said. "It's not possible."

"And it's probably not," Blais said. "This is all very preliminary. We're making no assumptions at this point. Just checking into possibilities."

"Following through," Langley added. "Procedure. We'd like to know everything Mrs. Barrett ate or drank last Tuesday. What medications she took. Where she went, who she saw." He pulled a small notebook from his pocket. "Everything necessary to reconstruct her day."

"You think it could have been some kind of drug interaction?" I asked, latching onto the only thing he had said that made any sense. "I know she took blood pressure medication. And estrogen. Her doctor's name is Larry Starr. He's right here in town, and he's sure to have a record of everything she was taking." I jumped up and turned toward the front stairs. "Would you like me to get her pills for you?"

Blais waved me back into my seat. "You were the one who found Mrs. Barrett?"

I clutched the arm of the chesterfield. "Yes, yes I did. In

the cellar. I've always had the feeling that something bad was going to happen down there."

"You knew something bad was going to happen on that afternoon?"

"No, not then, anytime. I mean, it wasn't that I thought something bad was going to happen on that particular day, it's just that I always thought something bad was going to happen down there period—ever since I was a little girl and my older cousins used to tease me. You know how you are when you're a kid and there's this dark, creepy place?"

Blais didn't seem to know. "Was anyone else in the house at the time?"

"Trina. Trina Collins. She's a young woman who works—worked—for Gram. Helping her with paperwork and stuff."

"Do you have an address?"

While she was writing down the address, Langley asked, "Why was a woman from Roxbury doing paperwork for your grandmother?" When I explained about SafeHaven and SafeHaven furlough, he and Blais exchanged glances. "I see," he said.

But I knew he didn't. "This has nothing to do with Trina," I told him. "She may be a recovering drug addict, but she's doing really well, and she really liked Gram—they were good friends."

"Good friends," Langley repeated.

"They swapped books."

Another shared glance.

"Recovering drug addicts do read books," I said. "They do have friends."

"Was anyone else here with you, besides Mrs. Barrett and Ms. Collins?" Blais asked smoothly.

I sighed. "My cousin Beth—Beth Conyers, she lives in

Wellesley—was here in the morning. She had lunch with us, then left to bring her son to a baseball game."

"Who made lunch?" Langley asked.

"Trina did," I said before I realized the implications of my words. "But that doesn't mean anything—"

"Were you and Ms. Collins with Mrs. Barrett all day?" Blais interrupted.

I took a deep breath and tried to remain calm. "I went into work for a couple of hours after lunch, and Trina stayed here with Gram. I got home about three. It was right after that that I, that I," my voice shook, "that I found her . . ."

"And you're sure Ms. Collins was still here when you returned?"

"She was in the other room doing paperwork." I waved to the west parlor. "I talked to her."

"And exactly how long were you on the premises before you discovered that your grandmother was dead?"

Dead. My grandmother was dead. But Gram was still here. She was here in her arrangement of dried flowers on the mantle, in her afghan, in her collection of family pictures on the Chippendale table. I could still feel her. Maybe the idea of an afterlife wasn't as scary as I had thought.

Michael put his arm around me and patted my shoulder awkwardly. "Is this really necessary?" he asked. "Couldn't you wait to do this for a couple of days?"

I squeezed his hand.

Langley cleared his throat. "I know this is a difficult time," he said, "but it's important for us to get as much information as we can as quickly as possible. Memories are faulty, and it's a known fact that the more time that passes, the less chance there is for a satisfactory resolution." His Adam's apple bobbed wildly. "So, Ms. Collins was alone with Mrs. Barrett for a good portion of the afternoon?"

I stared at him. He sounded as if he were reciting lines of dialogue he had learned at the police academy in a class entitled, "How to Investigate a Murder."

"Now just a minute—" Michael began, but I stopped him by standing. This fishing expedition was over.

"I think we've answered enough questions for one day," I said, surprised by the strength of my voice and the smooth certainty of my words. "I can assure you that neither Trina nor my cousin Beth nor myself had anything to do with my grandmother's death. It's an absurd concept, and it just isn't true."

The detectives didn't argue; they stood and Langley snapped his notebook shut. "We'll probably need more information at some point," he said. "Most likely from all three of you."

I held out my hand to him. "We'll be sure to have lawyers."

"I doubt that'll be necessary," Blais said. "But we would like to take you up on that offer to see your grandmother's medications."

CHAPTER TEN

Beth raked her hands through her hair; it whirled wild and out of control around her face. "I can't believe it," she said for the third time in two minutes. "I can't believe I was just interrogated by the police. It was horrible. Just horrible."

I poured two glasses of wine and sat down at the kitchen table across from her.

Beth gulped the wine as if she had been starved for liquid for days. "Boy, that woman detective was a real bitch, wasn't she?" She refilled her glass. "And that outfit! I don't know what was worse, the polyester jacket or her pointy little teeth."

I had to smile. Beth's obsession with appearance was apparently undaunted by the horror of her interrogation. "I don't trust her either."

"She thinks Trina did it."

"They don't think anyone did anything—he said it was just procedure. To follow up."

"There is the missing bracelet."

"Sounds like you're the one who thinks Trina did it," I said, my sympathy quickly switching over to annoyance. "You've been reading too many of Russ' magazines. Just because Trina's black and lives in Roxbury, you figure she's got to be a thief and a murderer? Do you really think she'd hurt Gram?"

"There's a bit more to it than—"

"No there isn't. We don't even know that anything was stolen or that anyone was murdered. And even if we did, what sense would it make? Say Trina took the bracelet—which she didn't—why would she kill Gram? She'd just give it to some fence and pocket the cash." I stopped abruptly. Give it to some fence. I supposed I had to consider the possibility that Trina had taken the bracelet. In many ways she was still just a kid, struggling with a new sobriety, with new rules and a new life, trying to withstand the temptations that surrounded her. The bracelet had just been lying around, and there was the influence of "pretty boy" Lionnel to consider. I thought about Kiah's reservations. But even if Trina had taken the bracelet, I knew she hadn't hurt Gram. "Did you tell the cops about the bracelet?"

Beth shook her head and continued to stare into the depths of her wine glass; the mascara around one eye was smudged and her face was pasty. "At first they thought it was me."

"That's just their style. That's what they do: try to intimidate. I'm sure they never really believed you did it."

"They were grilling me, especially the bitch, about inheriting Harden House. About how much it was worth, about all the 'valuable antiques.' "

If they had "grilled" Beth—although given its source, "grill" was most likely a bit of an exaggeration—I wondered how the interview with Trina had gone. I was sure it hadn't been pretty.

Beth raised her head and her eyes were glazed, but they contained a gleam that hinted that the real Beth was still there. "Now you tell me," she demanded, "what could those two possibly know about antiques?"

"Did you tell them about the Lexington Historical Society?"

Beth slumped back into her chair. "Yeah, but that didn't impress them much. What impressed them was my alibi."

"Your alibi?" I felt like we were in a bad television drama. This was getting way, way out of hand.

"The young cop told me that if it was poison, then it was some kind of fast-acting stuff. He said whoever gave it to Gram had to have done it within an hour of when she died."

"How could they possibly know that?"

"He said the lab didn't know exactly which poison it was yet, but that their first guess was something called . . . Oh, I don't remember, it was some fancy chemical name, but it causes a real high fever, real fast, hallucinations and then respiratory arrest. 'Rapid onset,' he said."

"There was obviously a mistake at the lab," I insisted, although the similarities between the symptoms Beth described and the facts of Gram's death were impossible to ignore. "Lab errors happen all the time—apparently, a lot more than they let on. The cops also said it could've been some kind of interaction between the prescription drugs she was taking."

Beth shrugged. She looked horrible: disheveled and weary, almost old. I figured I probably looked similar, but it was a much greater divergence from normal for Beth, and I felt a rush of compassion for her. Despite the different ways we lived and dressed and viewed the world, we were family, and we were sharing a grief only family can share.

I reached out and pushed a piece of hair behind her ear. "There's something I didn't tell you about what happened the afternoon Gram died," I surprised myself by saying.

Beth jerked her head up.

"It's not really anything," I back-peddled. "I mean, nothing all that important. That's why I didn't tell you before."

Beth's blood-shot eyes were large and her hands trembled slightly.

I twirled my wine glass on the table. "Remember how I used to walk in my sleep when I was a kid?" Who but your family knew the peculiarities of your youth? Who but your family allowed you those peculiarities and let you move on?

"Dotty Aunt Hortense." Or didn't allow you to move on.

"No one knows for sure that Aunt Hortense walked in her sleep."

"Just that she talked to the walls." Beth took another drink of wine, and I checked the level in the bottle. Although Beth had never abused anything but diet pills—and that was only because of the obsession with thinness her mother had instilled in her during her chubby childhood—I saw the devastating effects of substance abuse on a daily basis.

I corked the bottle and put it in the refrigerator. When I sat down, I said, "Well, the other night I did it again—walked in my sleep, I mean. And after all these years it was really strange . . ." I paused and looked at Beth, who just stared back at me. "I woke up in the cellar."

"Lee . . ."

"I dreamed there was black man down there. A big man, really big, with a shovel and a scruffy looking cast on his leg. Light-skinned—and very handsome."

"Did you talk to him, Hortense, dear?" Beth flashed me her evil grin. "What did he have to say?"

"This isn't a joke, Beth. He was digging."

Beth sobered. "You mean like Gram?"

I nodded.

"But I don't understand . . ."

I sighed and told Beth about Gram's last moments, about her battle with no one, about her confusion and her fear, about my confusion and fear.

When I finished, Beth polished off her wine and went to

the refrigerator to get the bottle. She added a little to my glass and refilled hers, sat down and looked at me for a long time. She held onto her glass as if it were a stabilizer. "Are you suggesting Gram had the crazy gene after all? That she was perfectly sane for sixty-nine years and then went bonkers?"

"No."

"So then you're saying you think Harden House is haunted? That a ghost killed Gram?"

"Or that maybe she was scared to death by one."

"You realize what you're implying? If you believe Gram was scared to death by a ghost then that means you believe in life after death, in the eternal soul and God and heaven and hell and all that shit."

I shrugged.

"Angels and harps and pearly gates? God sitting up there checking in to see if you're naughty or nice?"

"That's Santa Claus."

"Does that make it more or less absurd?"

"It might sound absurd now, discussing it rationally, now, here, but at the time, when I was watching Gram, I mean, I don't know, Beth, it was so real. I couldn't actually see anyone trying to take her shovel away, but I could see that Gram was fighting with something, someone, who was real." I felt the stirring of the awe I had experienced that afternoon, of that odd astonished sense of terrified fascination.

"Or real to her."

"I guess."

"That Langely guy said that this poison could cause hallucinations."

"Gram wasn't poisoned."

Beth took another sip of wine, then leaned toward me.

"You know, I saw part of this show on PBS last week about this well-known hot-shot scientist who goes out to houses that are supposed to be haunted with all sorts of fancy equipment. He records ghosts."

"Did he find anything?"

"Well, there were a lot of fuzzy pictures with weird shadows and shit. Some very weird noises. But there really wasn't anything you could put your finger on and say, 'now there's a ghost.' But, of course, that's not what he said. According to him, he had proved the house was actually haunted."

"But you didn't think so?"

"I don't know," Beth said. "Maybe. Maybe not."

"I got the impression that the man in my dream came from a long time ago. Maybe from around the time of the Civil War."

"You mean like he was a runaway slave? From the Underground Railroad days?"

I smiled wanly.

We sat in silence for a long time, then I said, "But it doesn't make any sense. If Harden House is haunted, then how come we didn't know it before? If the ghost's been around since before the Civil War, where's he been for the last 150 years?" I knew I was contradicting myself, but this topic compelled contradiction.

Now it was Beth's turn to flip-flop. "You knew he was here. You've always been afraid of the cellar."

"I was afraid of a woman with iron teeth, not a ghost."

Beth shrugged. "Well, if it wasn't the ghost who killed Gram, maybe it was Trina."

I was suddenly very tired. "No one killed Gram," I said, resting my forehead in my hands. "She just died, that's all. People do."

* * * * *

After Beth left, I wandered around the house, lost in a haze of unanswerable questions. Nothing made sense, and the slight tilt of the wide pine floorboards didn't do anything for my sense of balance. It was late and I had had one hell of a day. I only hoped I'd be able to sleep.

As I turned off the kitchen lights, I wondered again what Beth planned to do with Harden House. I couldn't imagine her living here—there was no master bath, no garbage disposal and no central air, none of the amenities that Beth considered necessities—and it would be a pricey second home, especially when it was only a fifteen minute drive from her first home. I knew nothing about inheritance taxes and wondered for a moment if the taxes would be too steep for Beth and Russ, if they would have to sell the house. But it didn't seem likely; even with all the economic ups and downs lately, I was pretty sure Russ did extremely well. Between his dental practice and apparently bulging stock portfolio—if the time he spent in front of his computer bore any relationship to his returns—they would surely be able to come up with the cash. But I supposed either way, it was possible I'd be looking for a new place to live.

I paused in the long dining room and stared at the old molding that ran along the edge of the ceiling. It was chipped in places, missing for a two-foot stretch over the fireplace, but mostly intact, amazing after all those years. The house had stood before the Civil War and would presumably stand many years more. The things we built lasted so much longer than we did.

Or did they? Could the soul of a man survive 150 years? I walked into the entrance hall and climbed to the first landing. I unhinged the hidden door to the safe room and peered in; it was dark and smelled of dampness and lumber and something that had once been alive, but now was dead. It smelled like the cellar, but more so. I closed the latch and sat on a stair. If the soul of one runaway slave still existed, then did all souls live beyond the death of the body? But if the souls did survive, then where were they all living? Where were they now?

I headed up to my bedroom. This was nuts. Ghosts were no more plausible than angels and harps and pearly gates. Perhaps even less.

I was standing in the dining room, looking at the molding that ran around the edge of the ceiling. It had been recently painted and glowed in the light from the fire, which roared from within a huge open hearth, much larger than the fireplace I knew. I was alone, and the silence of the house was thick with waiting; it enfolded me like an unwanted, oversized shroud. I didn't like it.

Shadows flung themselves from the fire, licking at the edge of the rug, brushing the wall. They wavered and slithered and mutated themselves. Changelings. Elusive and cunning. I didn't like them either.

But I knew the silence and the shadows were not what I feared. There was something else. Something lurking, huddling, burrowing, hiding. A secret. A horrible, horrible secret. Here. Waiting for me.

Despite my overwhelming desire to stay where I was, to allow the unknown to remain unknown, I was pulled out of the dining room and through the west parlor. It was as if I was being propelled by a force outside my body, for I didn't move my legs, yet I walked. I walked into the entrance hall and up the stairs to the first landing.

I didn't want to open the door to the safe room. I didn't want to see what was in there. I wouldn't. I wouldn't. Yet I did. My fingers, of their own volition, tweaked the hinges and the door fell toward me. The smell of death and decay rose like a living phantom, wrapping its fingers around my face. I turned away. I wouldn't look. I wouldn't. Yet I did.

I peered through the small opening and gasped: there was no safe room. The door opened into nothing, and all I could see was the earthen floor of the cellar far below. Then I heard a moan and saw a flicker of movement. It was the man. The man from my dream, illuminated as he had been before by an eerie green glow from the fieldstone. He lay on the ground, and his blood darkened the dirt around him. He had a huge wound in his chest, gaping and gleaming and raw. A shovel lay at his side, turned up, open and beseeching, clumps of earth still clinging to its mouth.

Another moan.

I cried out in alarm and he turned his head slowly toward me.

"Sarah," he called, his voice a hoarse whisper. "Please help my brothers."

I was terrified and wanted to run from the house, to tear screaming into town, to the police station, to somewhere filled with people, light and commotion, somewhere that was safe. But the man was alive. He was real and he needed me.

I went back through the dark parlor and dining room; my hands trembled as I opened the cellar door. He was hurt, possibly dying. I had to help him. I had to get him out of there. Sharp needles of sweat sped up and down the back of my neck, and I could hear the pounding of my feet on the stairs through the pounding of blood in my ears. I was pulled across the new cellar and into the old.

But when I reached the spot where his bloodied body had been, the same spot where Gram had lay, there was no blood and no man. There was only me, once again, alone and barefoot, shivering on the cold earthen floor.

CHAPTER ELEVEN

December 8, 1858

Papa, Caleb and Wendell returned to Harden House late this morning as the snows have finally abated and the sun is strong and bright. Wendell stayed to dinner at Papa's insistence, and although he was seated to my left, he only spoke of Mr. Garrison and his uncle and the Vigilance Committee. The men are so full of themselves that they do not see I am changed. As remarkable as it seems, they perceive me to be as I was last week. But the girl Papa left behind is no more: she has been transformed into a woman.

The news from the city is not good, and Papa is much troubled by what he has learned while in the home of William Lloyd Garrison. He brought with him a placard he and Mr. Garrison had written which is now being posted about the city by the Vigilance Committee. It reads:

Caution to Colored People of the Commonwealth of Massachusetts.
Avoid conversing with the Police Officers of Boston!
The Mayor has empowered them to act as
Kidnappers and Slave Catchers.
Have a Top Eye Open!

As I read the placard, I am filled with fear for Silas, whose only crime was to be born of a mother with dark skin. How is the mayor able to ignore the words of the Constitution of these United States? "All men are created equal," the Bill of Rights clearly states, specifying nothing about the color of that man's skin. It is the same contradiction Mr. Garrison commented upon when he was jailed for his writings in The Liberator. *It seems to me that this country is not as free as we wish to believe.*

Papa, Caleb and Wendell spent the last two days of the storm patrolling the city for slave catchers. Papa has caught himself a very bad cold for his efforts, but he says it is a small price to pay for his convictions, that if he must, he will cough and sneeze every day until slavery has been abolished and all men are truly free.

Still, I went to the chemist to procure a small quantity of Peruvian bark for him to chew upon. At first he refused to take it from me, but then I insisted, explaining that his irritated throat was going to do nothing to further the abolition of slavery. Finally he acquiesced. Often, men are much like small children.

December 9, 1858

Papa went into the cellar to speak with Silas this morning. He did not bring good tidings. It is a harsh winter all down the entire eastern seaboard and well into the south. Snow is said to lay deep on the Maysville Road—which is in Kentucky—and Pittsburgh and Philadelphia have suffered the same blizzards as we. Steamers are unable to move on the Ohio River. Needless to say, there has been no word of Silas' brothers.

Papa told Silas the Vigilance Committee shall remain watchful for news of the boys, but that it may be late spring before the brothers are able to reach Boston. Quilts are being hung and messages are being sent for each of them to come to Lexington, so it appears that Silas will have to wait here until they arrive. It would not trouble me if Silas should have to remain even longer than springtime.

December 11, 1858

After dinner, Papa and Caleb went to Lexington Common to visit the dram shop for an apple brandy and the news of the day. Mrs. Harrington returned to her farm, and Silas and I were able to be together for the first time since Papa's return from Boston. Silas is much troubled by the thought of his brothers on the road in bad weather and frets that not only will their travel be made more difficult, but that food will be harder to procure. As we sat before the warm fire, he worried that they were cold. He was concerned especially for the youngest, Levi, who he said has not been well since the cathauling.

Silas has such a kind and tender soul, wrapped in a powerful intellect and body. If only he were not so bruised and angry. If only he had lived the life he deserves. But I know neither his bruises nor his anger will disappear until all men are free. He and Papa are much alike in that way. But when I told him this, Silas disagreed. "No white man can be like a Negro, and no Negro like a white man," he said. "Although it may look the same from the outside, the Negro and the white man live in two completely different worlds."

"What about me?" I asked him.

He smiled and gently cupped my cheek in the palm of his large hand. "You, my dear Sarah, are a woman."

Papa and Caleb arrived home at early candle-light and found me sewing in the east parlor while Silas dug his tunnel under the ground. Papa commented on how pretty I looked, and I knew that I did. For I cannot restrain my happiness, and indeed, I shall not restrain it. I feel not at all condemned.

December 12, 1858

As Christmas draws nigh, I can barely remember my earlier distress over not partaking in our annual trip to Hartford. Al-

though I miss Mama dearly, and will indeed miss my visit with Cousin Lizzie, I feel that it was a child who pined for Lewis Campbell and the Buffrum-Chase Christmas Ball. I am no longer that child. I am, as Silas said, a woman. A woman grown and fulfilled by the love of a remarkable man.

December 13, 1858

Wendell has asked Papa if I may spend Christmas Eve in the home of his parents and join them in their pew at the First Parish Meeting House for the midnight service. Although Papa does not believe in celebrating Christmas while men are in bondage, he gave his permission. I wish he had not, that he had insisted that his strictures applied to me as well as to him, but I shall take the path of least resistance for the present.

December 14, 1858

Papa had Silas come up and take dinner with us today. Although she made it abundantly clear that she disapproved, Mrs. Harrington cooked roast beef with potatoes and turnips and her famous rice pudding. She would not sit at the table with us, and instead pretended she had too many chores to take the time to eat. She fooled no one.

Caleb engaged Silas in a lively discussion of the Bible and the work of Harriet Beecher Stowe. It was apparent that Caleb was most impressed with both Silas' knowledge and his intellectual acuity as he sparred with Papa over whether Mrs. Stowe held that a man must reject Christianity if he accepted slavery, and the other side of that argument, that a man who had lived under the injustice of slavery would never be able to believe in the mercy of the God of those who held him hostage.

I could not contain my pride and could barely contain myself from shouting our secret to Papa and Caleb. Silas has forbidden me to speak of it, claiming that Papa would not understand, that at best, Papa would order him to leave Harden House, and at worst, that Papa would kill him.

But I believe Silas underestimates Papa. I shall show him that all white men are not evil, that some of us are of a different sort. Silas will not hear me say it, and silences me every time I try, but it is my promise to you, dear diary, that Silas shall know this someday.

December 20, 1858

What is sin? I do not know, but I know it cannot be the consequence of love.

December 24, 1858

Wendell Parker has asked me to be his wife. I was not surprised, and had actually anticipated the possibility, but still, I do not know what I shall do. I thanked him for his kind offer and told him I should need to think about it until the new year. Then I allowed him to kiss me. He seemed quite pleased, and I'm sure he is certain I shall say yes.

December 25, 1858

It is the birthday of our savior, but Papa has mandated that we shall not celebrate His birth until human freedom and human dignity are given to all men equally. When I told Silas of Papa's decision in an effort to convince him to allow me to tell Papa we are keeping company, he just laughed bitterly. He said if I believed Papa would be willing to have his daughter courted by a Negro just because he was willing to give up Christmas, I was even more naive than he had thought.

Sometimes I fear that Silas has seen so much evil in his life that he will never be able to see anything else. It makes me very sad, but I love him all the more for his pain.

January 2, 1859

A new year has come and with it a new fear. I dare not write of it here, and only hope I am mistaken.

January 3, 1859

I have managed to postpone giving Wendell an answer to his question as I have been feeling very fatigued and quite ill these past few days. I miss my dear Mama so much and with a great aching pain. I long for her to wrap me in her arms and bring me tea and toast as she did when I was feeling poorly as a small girl. I smell her toilet water in my dreams.

But I am a child no longer, and must be the woman I am.

January 8, 1859

Silas and I have been unable to be together for almost a week as there has been too much activity about Harden House for any privacy. I ache for his arms, for his whisper, for the beat of his heart against mine. I feel his presence beneath my feet as I do my chores, and it is both a comfort and a torment to know he is so close.

January 9, 1859

Although it is Silas with whom I wish to speak, this is not possible at the moment, so this afternoon I went out to the barn to speak with Caleb of my fears, but my courage failed me, and I sat quietly for a long time as he shoveled hay. Finally, I asked him if he really believed that all men were equal, that Negroes were exactly the same as whites.

He looked at me oddly, but didn't answer for a long while. "Yes," he finally said, "I do believe that. But it isn't as simple as you make it out to be."

"Why not?" I asked. "Doesn't Papa believe that it is?"

Caleb smiled at me the same way Silas had when I asked if I wasn't different from the whites he believed to be so alien from him. And, just as Silas had done, Caleb did not answer my question.

January 10, 1859

Wendell came to call this afternoon, and I had Mrs. Harrington tell him I was still ill. She admonishes me that if I lie abed too long, another young lady shall set her bonnet for him. I think she says this in the fear that I might miss my opportunity to move from Harden House and out from under her feet. Often I feel her eyes upon me and wonder what she knows.

It occurs to me that Wendell might offer an answer to my dilemma, but I refuse to imagine that this could be my only means of salvation.

CHAPTER TWELVE

On the west side of Lexington Common, not far from Harden House, an old burying ground was tucked behind the First Parish Meeting House. Only a few timeworn letters chiseled into a boulder at the corner of the property mark the cemetery's presence and date of origin: 1690. One has to know to follow the crumbling asphalt drive at the left of the church to find the graves. Hardens have been laid to rest in this place since before the Revolutionary War.

The cemetery was on a small rise, its only gate a granite threshold, now sunk deep and unevenly into the earth. I stepped carefully between the tilting gravestones in the oldest area of the burying ground, unpolished chips of weathered bluestone, so close together it didn't seem possible that each could be the resting place of a full-sized human being. And many of them were not: the birth and death dates engraved on the stones were often within a few years of each other, sometimes days.

As I walked toward the Harden family plot, I could see the mound that rose over Gram, the dirt raw and exposed among the old stones. It was a beautiful May day, and the huge maples and oaks overhanging the graves sprouted clusters of chartreuse leaves shiny with new spring. The azaleas and early rhododendrons were in full bloom. It felt both incongruous and fitting that the cemetery smelled of hope and life. Gram loved azaleas. I knelt and pressed my hand to the damp earth. I missed her, but I knew she would be happy here. It was pretty and peaceful and she was surrounded by her family.

I rocked back on my heels and surveyed Gram's closest neighbors. "Loving Mother," Sarah Harden's lichen-mottled marker read to Gram's left, "1842–1900, AEt 58." Sarah Harden, dead for one hundred years and suddenly everywhere. "Sarah," the hoarse voice of the dying man had whispered in my dream last night. "Please help my brothers." Why was a runaway slave calling for help from Sarah Harden? Had he thought I was she?

No, I reminded myself, "he" hadn't confused anyone with Sarah Harden. There was no "he." There was only my subconscious mind, my nightmare, my extravagant imagination. Last week, Gram had been talking about Sarah, and since then, I had been looking at her picture, wondering about her lost husband, the unhappiness in her eyes. The workings of the human brain were truly wondrous—and truly bizarre.

Sarah's mother and father were buried under a single marker to their daughter's left: Colonel Stanton Harden and Charlotte Abbott Harden, the original owner of the ruby brooch. The parents' memorial was taller and wider and much more regal than Sarah's, topped by an intricate carving of a wide-eyed skull with wings at the back of its neck. The Colonel was born twenty years earlier than Charlotte, in 1800; she was dead eight years earlier than he, in 1857, AEt 37. Sarah had been fifteen when her mother died, twenty-three when she lost her father, and from Gram's tale, about the same age when she became a widow.

To Charlotte's right were two small stones with no names and but a single date each. "January 21, 1838," read one. "March 3, 1839," read the other. Along the top of each tiny marker, the same two words were hewn: our baby. There was no sign of Sarah's husband or of the younger brother Gram had mentioned—Caleb, I thought she had said was his name—but Sarah's son, Ulysses Harden, born in 1859, was here, as was Ulysses' wife, Alice Dillaway Harden, and two of their children, Elijah and Zane, AEt 9.

So much could be read from these names and dates, and yet so little revealed. Poor Charlotte had most likely married before she was seventeen, lost two babies before she was nineteen, and died before her two surviving children were grown. Sarah must have left her childhood even earlier than her mother had done, for Ulysses had been born when she was only seventeen, and her husband, the distant Harden cousin, must have died soon after that.

I walked along the crooked rows, searching for a man whose name and dates might match those of Sarah's husband. I found many Hardens, one born in 1650 and another in 1672. I found a single, tragic marker for the six children of Emily and Thaddeus Harden, who had all died between August 17 and September 6, 1778—probably a smallpox or typhoid epidemic—and I found an odd little verse engraved on Alice Dillaway Harden's headstone: "Death like an overflowing flood; doth sweep us all away; the young, the old the middle-aged; to death becomes a prey." But I didn't find anyone who fit the description of Sarah's husband. He must have been buried in Ohio.

I sat down next to Gram. All these dead Hardens added weight to my argument against ghosts: If all the spirits of just this one family were still in existence, where were they all right now? I glanced at the hundreds of graves that surrounded me. There just wasn't room for all those disembodied souls. They'd be hitting up against us, nudging us, smothering us, suffocating us. We'd be constantly fighting each other for the scarce space. I flashed on the image of

Gram's final battle with no one, then pushed the image quickly away.

I sat there for a long while, studying the names and the dates, and the startling number of children who had died before the age of five. I thought about Hendrika, about all those tiny dead souls and heart-broken mothers. So much had changed—and so little. We married later now and had fewer children, who lived much longer and healthier lives, but we also yearned for love and made families just as Sarah and Charlotte had done. And we still grieved for our lost babies.

I swiped at the tears that were running down my face, knowing I wasn't just crying for Gram. I was crying for Sarah and Charlotte and Trina and all the lost mothers and babies and husbands, crying for the spirit of the black man with the shotgun wound calling to Sarah for help. I was crying for all who had come before and weren't anymore. For all I longed to learn, but never would.

I looked at the floral arrangements withering at the edge of Gram's grave and remembered Gram telling me that she had given a large batch of Harden family papers to her friend Nancy Winsten at the Lexington library. Letters and ledgers and receipt books, she had said. Maybe I could learn more than I thought.

I stood, brushed off my jeans, and headed across the Lexington Common to the library. The common was a wide swatch of newly greened grass, bordered by steepled churches and white clapboard houses with plaques commemorating their construction dates—usually late seventeenth century—and their role in the revolution. This was the site of the first conflict of the Revolutionary War, the Battle of Lexington, the shot heard ' 'round the world,' a fact in which Lexington residents take great pride. Guides in Colonial dress mingled with the small crowd, answering questions, pointing to markers and taverns and the spot where the first Redcoat was killed.

I crossed the grass to the Minuteman statue—rumored to be a likeness of Jonas Parker, whose mother had been a Harden and who was also buried in the cemetery behind the Meeting House—and stood among the gawking, camera-toting tourists. I read the inscription and thought about the historic events that had occurred at this very place over two hundred years ago. I looked at the old houses, and even older trees, ringing the common; they had stood here long before those long-ago events. To my right two boys played a raucous game of Frisbee, and behind them a young couple leaned against a gnarled oak and nuzzled each other's necks. A car alarm screamed, a baby wailed, and the Minuteman stood his silent vigil, musket resting on his knee, gazing eastward at nothing.

Once, when I was a little girl, we had visited Gram over Patriot's Day, the anniversary of the Battle of Lexington. The town throws a huge celebration each year, highlighted by a reenactment of the famous battle. At the crack of dawn, the skirmish is recreated by men in full period dress, wielding antique muskets filled with blanks, and watched by tens of thousands. My father had to perch me on his shoulders so I could see over the crowd, and I remember staring in open-mouthed amazement as the British "Lobsterbacks" tried to intimidate the Minutemen with their superior weaponry and fancy uniforms.

When the first Minuteman fell to his death, I burst into tears, so persuaded was I of the authenticity of the fight. "No one's really getting hurt, honey," my father assured me. "It's only make believe—the real men were killed two hundred years ago. They've been gone a long, long time now."

"But how can you be sure they're not still here?" I had wailed at him. "How can you be sure it doesn't still hurt?"

My father had laughed and taken me to drown my fears in a big plate of pancakes, but he brought me back to the common when the reenactment was over. He showed me there was no blood and no dead soldiers, and tried to get me to speak with a Redcoat who was having breakfast with his family. But I refused to talk to the Redcoat and refused to believe my father's unlikely tale. I was certain that my father was protecting me from something he didn't think I was old enough to understand.

Now, as I looked up at the sightless Minuteman, at Jonas Parker, dead over 225 years, I wished I could be as certain of anything as I had been that day.

Cary Memorial Library stood cattycorner to the Minuteman, behind a tall garden maintained by the Horticultural Society. I walked up the wide stone steps and entered the domed atrium, a remnant of the original library. I breathed in that unique library smell of paper and paste and slightly sweaty children, and felt immediately comforted. Libraries have always had that effect on me: the summer after my junior year in college, I back-packed alone through Europe, and whenever I felt lonely, I'd find the local library and spend a few hours curled in a chair with a book. It never failed to make me feel better.

A dozen blinking monitors were lined up along the top of the card catalogue; the rows of ornately carved drawers and tarnished brass handles looked anachronous and forlorn, downcast over their demotion to a stand for the new technology. I went up to an empty keyboard, pressed the search button and typed in "Harden."

Leo F. Harden had written a book about quantum mechanics; Leslie Harden had written a children's book about ducks; Harden and Hayden was a book about two composers. The list contained 17 items and filled three screens, but when I had scrolled through all the entries, it was clear none related to my family. No Harden Papers, no listing for The Letters of Colonel Stanton Harden or The Diary of Sarah Harden. I knew it had been a long shot, but still I felt disappointed as I resigned myself to going to SafeHaven, where last week's work was piled high on my desk.

On my way out, I stopped at the reference desk and asked for Nancy Winsten. She wasn't in, so I asked the librarian if she knew anything about historical papers that had been donated by a Lexington family named Harden. The plaque on her desk identified her as Ms. Tosatti, which seemed a good librarian name, but she looked more like a model for a teen magazine with her platform shoes and short black skirt. She hit the search key and typed "Harden."

"I already did that," I told her.

Ms. Tosatti didn't appear to hear me. "Doesn't look to be anything like that here," she muttered as her fingers flew over the keys. She made noises like a doctor examining a very sick patient. "Hmm," she said, her eyes glued to the screen. "Tsk." She typed and scrolled and scowled. Finally, she looked up at me. "Do you have a few minutes?"

I shrugged. "I guess." The piles on my desk had waited a week; they could wait a while longer.

"Come back in fifteen minutes," she said, ducking back toward the monitor. "I'll be able to tell you something then."

I returned to my computer and hit the search key again. This time I typed the word "ghost." One hundred seven items, everything from *Haunted New England: Classic Tales of the Strange and Supernatural* to Edgar Allen Poe to *Successful Ghost Writing: Ten Easy Steps*. I read through the summaries and scribbled down a few call numbers. Then I went downstairs into the stacks. The pickings were much slimmer than the computer had led me to believe, and although *Haunted New England* was nowhere to be found, I did manage to come up with a collection of Victorian ghost stories, an odd little primer written by "professional demonologists" and a volume titled *Yankee Ghosts: Spine-Tingling Encounters with the Phantoms of New York and New England*. I took the three books upstairs.

Ms. Tosatti nodded as I passed by her desk and held up a finger to indicate it would be another moment. I sat down at a large reference table behind her and flipped through the books. The one about the demonologists was actually quite funny; a husband-and-wife team who investigated "bone-chilling phone calls from beyond the grave" claimed to have spoken with John F. Kennedy and Mrs. Douglas MacArthur. They described graveyards similar to the one in which I had just spent a peaceful hour as "eerie and violent places whose dark influence wreaks havoc on those unlucky enough to live near them." I put the book aside and opened *Yankee Ghosts*.

In his introduction, Hans Holzer, a "world-renowned" spectral investigator and parapsychologist, stated that ghosts were real people, or parts of real people, who were misunderstood by the living for the same reason psychotics were misunderstood: they weren't in touch with reality as the rest of us knew it. Mr. Holzer went on to explain that all ghosts required was a little acceptance and sympathy, that they were "caught in the web of their own unresolved emotions at the time of their physical death." He pleaded with the reader to empathize with any ghost he or she encountered because the ghost "needs your full understanding and, where possible, your help to move on into the wider world of the spirit." As I read his words, I wondered who was—and wasn't—in touch with reality here.

I was relieved when Ms. Tosatti waved me over to her desk. "It does appear that something was logged in almost a year ago under the heading of 'Harden Papers,' " she told me. "Do you think that's what you're looking for?"

"Yes," I said eagerly. "That must be it."

"Unfortunately, that's all there is."

"What do you mean? The papers aren't here?"

She turned her palms upward, and I saw that she had a ring on every finger. "Oh, they're probably here. It's just that we got a new computer system recently, and things often aren't where you'd expect them to be."

"But you would be able to find the papers, given some time?"

"Maybe . . ." She didn't look happy.

"Would it be possible for you to check into it for me? To see if you can find them?" I smiled encouragingly. "It really would mean a lot. The Hardens are my ancestors."

Ms. Tosatti hesitated, then returned my smile. "Okay, sure," she said. "I'll see what I can do. Leave me your name and phone number, and I'll get back to you sometime within the next couple of weeks."

"That long?"

"Maybe I'll find them sooner, but I wouldn't count on it."

I thanked her, and even though I felt a bit foolish, I retrieved the books I had left on the reference table and checked them out. What the hell? I thought as I walked down the library steps. What the hell?

That night I walked in my sleep again. I dreamt I was in

a department store with Gram, searching for a dress for her to wear to her great-niece Karen's wedding. It was extremely important that we find one immediately, for the ceremony was in an hour, and the fact that I knew the dress Gram had bought for the wedding was hanging in her closet didn't faze me in the least.

I sped through the aisles, pulling dresses off racks, throwing them frantically over my shoulders.

"Hurry," Gram kept saying in a most un-Gram like manner. "Hurry."

I was sweating as I staggered to the dressing room door, bowed down by the weight of my load. But when I stepped into the tiny room, I saw that hundreds of dresses were already in there: dangling from hooks, piled on the floor, hovering near the ceiling. I dropped the clothes I was holding as a single dress floated down and hung motionless before me.

"Hurry," Gram repeated. "Hurry."

I struggled to remove the dress from its hanger, but it refused to unhook. No matter how hard I tried, I couldn't get my fingers around the buttons or get the zipper to unzip. Then the dress raised an empty arm and reached for my hand, as if to invite me to waltz. I yanked my hand back, but the dress wouldn't take no for an answer. It came at me again, with both arms open wide, grabbed me and swung me around in a wide circle. I yelled and woke myself up.

I found that I was indeed in a tiny room surrounded by dresses. But I wasn't in a department store. I was standing barefoot in Gram's closet, the sleeves of the black dress she had planned to wear to Karen's wedding grasped in my hands.

I was sitting at my desk when Trina walked by; it was

obvious from the way she slipped across the open doorway that she didn't want me to see her, but we needed to talk. I wanted to apologize for getting her involved in the mess around Gram's death, and, although I assumed she knew it already, to tell her there was no way I thought she was involved. Trina and I hadn't spoken since Gram's funeral, and hadn't really spoken then. "Hey," I called. "Trina."

I heard the sound of reluctant footfalls in the hallway. Trina leaned against the doorjamb and stared at a spot over my left shoulder.

"How're you doing?" I asked. "I heard you got stuck with kitchen duty. How bad is it?"

"Sucks." Her voice had no affect, and it was clear that although she was willing to go through the motions of this conversation, motions were all I was going to get.

"Give me a break, Trina. Come in and sit down."

Her eyes moved from the wall behind my head to scan the small room for a place to sit.

"On the desk," I said. "Please?"

She walked into the office and rested the side of her hip against the desk's edge.

"I'm really sorry about all this stuff with Gram and the cops."

Trina reconnected with the spot behind my head.

"It's stupid," I said. "Like anyone would want to kill Gram."

Trina didn't say anything, and I remembered what Kiah had said about freshman attitude.

"They were at my house on Monday," I tried again. "Then they went over to Beth's too. Beth said they really grilled her. That they were talking as if they thought all three of us were suspects."

"Like they really believe you or Mrs. Lily-White

Wellesley committed murder."

"I know they're always jumping to the conclusion that the black person did it, but that doesn't mean it's going to go anywhere."

Her eyes connected with mine, and for a fleeting moment I caught a flicker of hope.

"And anyway," I continued, "I told them it was ridiculous to consider you a suspect—just as ridiculous as considering me or Beth. Just as ridiculous as thinking Gram was murdered at all."

"Lee," she said so softly I almost missed the words. "You just don't get it."

"Try me," I said. "Maybe I can."

"The cops can take it anywhere they want. It doesn't need to be real."

Of course I knew she was right—you'd have to be completely deluded to believe that the American legal system was colorblind—and I didn't know how to respond in a way that would be both truthful and encouraging. But before I could say anything, I saw Kiah standing in the doorway.

"Those Lexington detectives are downstairs again," she informed us.

Trina threw me a rueful look, then she pushed off from the desk, squared her shoulders and faced Kiah.

"No," Kiah said. "It's not about you. They're looking for Lee." She turned to me. "They're waiting in my office."

Now it was I who stood, and although I wasn't anxious to speak with the police, I was relieved it was me and not Trina for whom they were looking. If Trina saw she was wrong about this, maybe she'd consider the possibility that she was wrong about other things too.

I gave Trina's shoulder a squeeze as I slid by.

CHAPTER THIRTEEN

January 28, 1859

I know now for certain, and I am filled with fear. I have not spoken of it to anyone and cannot imagine what I shall do. If only Mama were still alive, my own sweet Mama to help me and guide me in my hour of need. But even as I long for my mother, I know I no longer have the luxury of these girlish yearnings. From this day forward, my position and my concerns are forever changed. I am no longer just a daughter, no longer a child, and I must turn my attention to what shall become of my child.

Mrs. Harrington squints her beady eyes at the waistband of my skirt, and although she believes she knows what ails me, she cannot even imagine the truth. When I told her to send Wendell away again today, she was most surprised. Her confusion provided the only light moment in my dark day.

I pray to God for guidance, but all I hear is silence. I think He is telling me that I am on my own, that I am the only one who can set my destiny—or perhaps He is saying I already have.

January 30, 1859

I received a letter from Cousin Lizzie today, full of the news of her festive Christmas and her latest beau, Mr. William Sinklar Whaley, Junior. William, or "Junior," as Lizzie calls him, was born on a plantation in South Carolina and moved to Hartford just this past summer. Lizzie says that his father, William Sr., is a business associate of her father's and, of late, has become a close family friend. I shall not contemplate what views William Sr. and Uncle Benjamin might share.

Lizzie writes that the holidays were not nearly as gay without me to accompany her to the many teas and parties, and that she prays next Christmas the whole family will dance together at the Buffrum-Chase Ball. She very delicately told me of Lewis Campbell's engagement to Hallie Perkins, which was indeed announced at midnight during the Ball. It does not seem possible that I once had such strong feelings about this event, as it now seems as distant and unimportant as what time the sun sets in South Carolina.

I am unable to venture where I might be next Christmas or what form my life will have taken a year hence. I press my hand to the flat of my stomach and wonder what Lizzie should think of my news. I dare say I know all too well what Uncle Benjamin will think.

January 31, 1859

I reread Lizzie's letter and feel so apart, so separate, from this world I so recently inhabited, and I am filled with sadness and longing. I cannot put Wendell off for much longer, and I wonder if I should.

February 1, 1859

Papa asked today if something was troubling me. He said I appeared wan and pale. My eyes filled with tears at the expression on his dear face as he resettled his spectacles on his nose: so concerned, so sad, and loath as I am to write it, so very old.

How shall I answer him? Shall I tell him I am carrying a child without benefit of wedlock? Shall I tell him that although the blood which flows within the child's veins is seven-eights white, my child is, nonetheless, the sire of a Negro? An octoroon, subject in all Southern states to the strictures of slavery.

Although I know Papa is the most fair-minded of men, I tell him I am just missing Mama, which is not a lie. I must speak with Silas.

February 2, 1859

This afternoon there was no one about the house, and I slipped into the cellar to speak with Silas. He stopped digging and leaned against his shovel as I came toward him. His broken leg was still in its splint, and he looked very tired, worn down by work and worry. I did not have to utter a word for him to know that I had something important to tell. At first, I could not speak, and Silas waited patiently, silently, until I pulled my thoughts together.

I think he feared I had brought bad tidings of his brothers, and when I was finally able to blurt out my news, his grip on the shovel loosened and his shoulders relaxed. For a long moment, he said nothing, then he put his arms about me and held me to him. I could feel his heart beating against mine. He gently, sadly, pressed his lips to my forehead.

"This doesn't make you happy?" I asked.

He held me even more tightly. "It fills me with fear."

February 3, 1859

I waited until Papa was in the west parlor with Dr. Ward, and Mrs. Harrington left to go to the chemist, then I slid into the cellar, making my way as silently as was possible down the rickety stairs.

As soon as Silas saw me, he dropped his shovel and took me in his arms. "I've been thinking and have decided that you must marry Wendell Parker," he whispered into my hair. "As soon as possible."

"I can't do that," I cried, as if I had not had the same thought myself. "I don't love Wendell, I love you."

Silas held me closer. "This isn't about love. This is about saving your life and the life of your—our—child."

"But you have just lost a child," I wailed, burying my head in his neck. "I won't let it happen to you again, and I cannot

bear to even contemplate a life without you."

"Sarah," he said softly. "Look at me."

I did as he asked and saw that he was not to be deterred.

"A life without me is the life you were meant to live. Wife of a wealthy white man, home, children, tea with Nancy Southwick. And it's the life you shall have. It's better for everyone if you do this, I promise you."

"It won't be better for you," I said defiantly.

His voice was as soft and gentle as it had been before. "If I know you and the baby are safe, it's better for me."

"You don't want me?"

"Not like this. If things were—" Silas stopped speaking as we heard the scraping of chairs overhead. Papa and Dr. Ward. "Go," he urged. "Now."

I was too stunned to argue, so I went.

February 4, 1859

Mrs. Arabella Parker, Wendell's mother, came to call today. She brought with her a note from Wendell. He wrote, "Herein, I do solicit the honor of your hand in marriage. If you should so graciously allow it, I shall call on you on the eighth of February at two o'clock in the afternoon. I hope with all my heart that my question will be answered in the affirmative and that we may set the date of our marriage vows at that time."

I poured Mrs. Parker's tea and we chatted of my mother and Aunt Elizabeth and Nancy Southwick's sister Emily's new baby. As Mrs. Parker was taking her leave, she held my hand a moment longer than is customary and called me dear.

Mrs. Harrington came up behind me just as I had closed the front door. "One would be wise to keep the bird in the hand," she hissed in my ear.

I pretended I did not know of what she spoke, but it scares me to think that perhaps the old crone is right.

February 5, 1859

It is the darkest and coldest hour of the darkest and coldest of nights. I have just had the most terrible nightmare and am afraid to return to sleep for fear the dream shall also return. I sit with the lamp lit and a heavy shawl about my shoulders, but neither can dispel the gloom that has taken hold of my heart. All I can feel are the icy cold tentacles of trepidation. All I can see is the endless blackness of dread.

I dreamt I lost my child. His cradle lay empty, and, lo, though I looked and looked everywhere, I could not find him. I searched the house and looped through the rooms again and again, then I searched a whole city—I think it was Boston—but he was in none of these places. I tried to cry out, but no words came from my mouth. When I awoke, I knew with the certainty of the dreamer that he was gone from me forever.

I believe dreams augur the future, and my fingers tremble around my pen to imagine what this nightmare might portend. Yet I also believe dreams may be messengers sent to aid the dreamer in averting the events revealed. I shall not allow my wild imaginings to get the better of me, I shall not. I shall search the forms of this dream until I discover what I am meant to learn to make it not come to pass.

I shiver in the void of darkness and fear; emptiness and silence surround me. I press my hand to my belly and remind myself that I am not alone. There is someone with me, someone who I wish to keep with me always. What is best for my baby? What is best for us all? I worry that the baby may be born with skin too dark to pass for Wendell's child. I worry that the baby may be born with skin so light that he easily passes for Wendell's child and never knows who he really is.

No matter what I choose, the baby shall know me to be his mother and shall suckle at my breast until he is able to stand on his own. But although Silas is his true father, it is upon me to decide if he grows to manhood knowing this or believing he is the sire of Wendell Parker. If I choose Silas, Papa, my home and my family shall be lost to me, and I will set my poor babe on a perilous and unpredictable journey. But if I choose Wendell, Silas shall be lost—to both myself and the baby.

February 6, 1859

As this child grows within me, so too does my resolve to discover a way for Silas, the baby and me to all live together in safety and happiness. Thus far, I have been unable to discover this way, but I shall continue to search even as the avenues appear to be closing around me. What is best? What is best?

Week's end is fast approaching and Wendell shall arrive soon for his answer. Silas will not hear of my doing anything other than accepting Wendell, and although, of course, we have not spoken of it, I know this would be the course preferred by Papa and Caleb. I am just as certain that Nancy and Cousin Lizzie would counsel the same. Mama also. And yet, I find myself unable to imagine speaking the words that would link my life, and that of my child, to Wendell Parker.

February 7, 1859 (morning)

I have found it! My scheme is so simple and so perfect, I cannot believe I did not think of it sooner. Silas and I shall marry and leave for a place where it will be safe for us to make a life. With the aid of the Vigilance Committee, we shall use the Underground Railroad to go to a free Western state! Instead of heading north to Canada, Silas' brothers shall meet us there also, and their nephew shall be born in a place where he can grow to manhood unfettered by hatred and laws which are a sin against God.

I know this to be a difficult course, but it is one I can embark on with vigor, for it embodies not only a solution to my problem, but all that I believe is moral and good. I'm just as certain that Silas will feel the same way and am most anxious to speak of it with him.

I shall tell Wendell I cannot marry him.

February 7, 1859 (afternoon)

Although I did not tell him why I wished to know, I asked Papa how the abolitionists were faring in the west. He explained about the forthcoming vote for statehood in Kansas Territory which will determine if it is to be a free or slave state. He also told me that Joshua and Sally Kensington left for Kansas in September, and that the entire Locke family—Job and Mae and their six sons—plan to follow in the spring. The Vigilance Committee has raised money for their journey as it is imperative to have a majority of voting men on our side.

Kansas Territory is where Silas and I shall go! It is fitting that Papa's kindness to those he does not know should provide for the survival of one of his own.

February 8, 1859 (afternoon)

Wendell came for tea today promptly at two o'clock, as he had promised. I told him I was in love with someone else and could not marry him. He was a gentleman in every way, so much so that, for a short moment, I wondered if I wasn't making a horrible error. Then I remembered Silas working beneath our feet, and I knew I had made the correct choice.

February 8, 1859 (late afternoon)

Silas was most displeased with me when I told him what I had done. "That was very foolish, Sarah," he said, his eyes hard with anger. "You must write Wendell Parker a note this afternoon and tell him you have made a mistake."

"No," I said, then burst into tears. I reached toward Silas,

but he stepped away from me. "I shall not marry Wendell. I shall only marry you."

"Sarah," Silas said, holding his arms open to me. "My sweet, foolish Sarah. Don't you know this is just an impossible dream?"

I rushed to him, pressing myself as close as I could. "No it's not," I managed to say between sobs. "I have a plan."

Silas traced the line of my jaw with his finger. He did not ask about my plan.

"We can go to Kansas Territory," I cried. "Together. There are many abolitionists already there. It's to be a free state. We'll be safe. We'll be together, a family."

He shook his head. "There'll never be a state where a white woman and a Negro man can be safe."

"Then you can pass as white! You're light-skinned enough. You speak as well as any white man, better than most. If you're traveling with me, we'll be able to fool everyone. We'll go wherever we want."

He cupped my chin in one of his large palms and wiped my tears with the flat of the other. "Look at my lips, Sarah. Look at my nose. My features will fool no one."

"It can work!" I pressed. "I know it can. Papa will know what to do. So will the Vigilance Committee. We'll tell Papa and he'll help us. He'll find a safe route. I'm certain he will."

"It is a brave idea, my darling," Silas finally said, "but it's far too dangerous and risky for a woman in your condition, and I cannot allow it. But even if we did decide to go, I would have to insist that your father not be told."

Although I was crushed by his words, I held out hope that within this last comment lay the seeds of my future.

February 10, 1859

Silas has stood his ground for two days, but he is weakening as he listens to the stories I spin of our life together in the free west with our child, unhindered by the strictures of slavery and old ideas. Although Silas still insists that we cannot tell Papa of our plans, I can see that the idea of Kansas Territory has taken hold of his imagination.

Oh, dear diary, I am so happy. I know I shall be able to convince Silas that Papa can be trusted to stand behind me, my husband and his grandchild, that Papa is a good man whose beliefs go far beyond rhetoric. Then, after we receive Papa's blessings and aid, we shall be married and go off to forge a new life in a new land in which all are free!

February 14, 1859

Yesterday Silas told me of a plantation custom in which Negroes are married by a ceremony called "jumping the broom," a ritual he says seals vows as certainly as any minister. I decided that this is what we should do, and today Silas and I were wed. Although we may not be married in the eyes of the church, or in the eyes of the Commonwealth of Massachusetts, we are truly married, for we are married in God's and our own eyes, the only eyes of import.

Now, dear diary, I am certain that this is the course I was meant to follow, that this is why I have always felt a bit apart from Mama and Cousin Lizzie and Nancy Southwick. I shall follow my destiny into a new life, take me where it may. I write the truth when I tell you jumping the broom felt more proper to me than if I had stood at the front of the First Parish Meeting House, Papa and Caleb at my side. For now I have become one with Silas, one of his own.

We placed a broom on the earthen floor of the cellar, directly in front of Silas' tunnel so his brothers could be our spiritual witnesses, and then, hand-in-hand, we leapt backward over the broom handle. "This is your husband," Silas said to me, solemnly pointing to his chest. "This is your wife," I said to him, just as solemnly pointing to my own.

Then we laughed and kissed, and Silas finally agreed to allow me to tell Papa of our plans. He said he was still uncertain, but that if it meant that much to me, his dearest wife, and if I was so confident that Papa would stand with us, then he would not bar my way.

February 15, 1859

I shall speak with Papa tomorrow morning.

CHAPTER FOURTEEN

Kiah's office was two small parlors separated by a sliding pocket door that didn't exist anymore, its rich Victorian detail barely discernible beneath the years of neglect and bad paint jobs. The original owner of the turn-of-the-century house, an elderly Italian woman who had never lived anywhere else, had sold it to Kiah for a dollar to avoid taxes; ten years later it wasn't clear which one of them had gotten the better of the deal.

I dropped into the worn brown-and-orange couch in the bay window and stared at Detective Blais. "I what?"

Kiah had followed me in and stood at the end of the couch. She placed a hand on my shoulder.

"That can't be right," I said, both horrified and thrilled by the policewoman's claim. "It doesn't make sense."

"That's what the lawyer told us."

"What lawyer?" Kiah asked.

"Jan Rosenthal," Blais said calmly. "Her grandmother's lawyer."

"But no one's even seen the will yet." I glanced up at Kiah, then over at Raymond Langley. "How could you know who's inherited what?"

"We got a subpoena," Langley said helpfully, leaning forward in his chair. Blais shot him a look, and he sat back and pressed his lips together.

I pushed my palms into the nubby fabric of the couch. It was ugly and scratchy and had obviously been someone's yard-sale cast off, but in the world of urban drug rehab, a couch is a couch. I continued to push into the cushion until I could feel the nubs branding my hands. Could Gram have really left Harden House to me?

"But Gram was planning to give the house to the Lexington Historical Society," I said. "She just told us last week."

Detective Blais flashed her pointy teeth. "Apparently, your grandmother died before she had time to change her will."

"But then it would've gone to my cousin Beth. The eldest child of the eldest child always inherits Harden House." I looked at Kiah, as if for confirmation. "Aunt Rhoda, her mother, is dead."

"Michael Ennen is the contractor renovating your grandmother's house?" Blais asked. "He told us that was why he was there Monday afternoon."

"Michael Ennen?" This was getting more confusing by the moment. "What does he have to do with this?"

"There were a number of smaller bequests."

"Still pretty generous," Langley offered, and Blais silenced him with another glance. He cleared his throat and his Adam's apple bobbed.

"Bequests?" I repeated. "Gram left money to Michael?"

Kiah leaned over and whispered in my ear, "To Trina too."

"Although the largest bequest, the house, was to you, Ms. Seymour," Blais said.

"Just what do you want here, officers?" Kiah asked, drawing out the word "officers," knowing full well they were detectives. "Exactly what are you implying?"

"Oh, we're not implying anything, Ma'am," Blais said, stressing the "ma'am" in a way that made it as insulting as Kiah's "officers." "We just stopped by to establish exactly where everyone was on that day."

Again, I felt as if everything was off-kilter: unexpected inheritances, alibis, murder. This was someone else's life, not mine. "Are you saying that you think I could have possibly—"

Kiah squeezed my shoulder to silence me. "Ms. Seymour will not be saying any more without her lawyer present."

"My lawyer?"

"Oh," Blais said breezily, continuing her conversation with Kiah as if I hadn't spoken, "I doubt that will prove necessary. This is all standard operating procedure. We just need to verify the exact hours Ms. Seymour was here on the afternoon of the fourth, as well as the comings and goings of Trina Collins."

I couldn't help but notice that Blais referred to me as Ms. and to Trina by her first name.

Kiah must have noticed it too, for she said stiffly, "Ms. Collins already told you she was at Clara Barrett's house all day. I'd think that would be all the verification you'd need."

Blais' smile was warm and pleasant. "Detective Langley has already talked with your secretary, who unfortunately could not verify either Ms. Collins' or Ms. Seymour's departure times that day, but I spoke with a Ruth Thompson—I understand she's one of your department heads?" She paused and waited for Kiah's confirmation, as if that would also confirm the veracity of her suspicions.

"Ms. Thompson," Kiah corrected.

"Ms. Thompson told me she's almost positive Ms. Seymour left at 2:00 on the afternoon of the fourth. She said Ms. Seymour was walking out the door just as her 1:00 group was letting out—a group which she remembers did not include Trina Collins, as Trina was on a SafeHaven furlough assignment in Lexington."

"Ms. Collins."

Blais stood and said to Kiah, "Now, if we may, we'd like to take a look at Ms. Collins' records and Ms. Seymour's computer files."

"You absolutely may not," Kiah retorted. "Not without a warrant."

The detective nodded, as if Kiah's response was exactly what she had expected. "We'll stop at the courthouse on our way back to Lexington," she said, "and drop by again in a couple of days." Langley stood too, and the two detectives sauntered out the door.

Kiah crossed her arms as the door slammed behind them. "Shit," she said.

"Shit," I agreed.

Trina couldn't believe it. Ten thousand dollars. Shit. Clara had said she was going to leave her "a little something" in her will, but Trina had never expected that much. One thousand maybe, two. But ten thousand dollars. Shit. She never figured she'd see that much money all at one time. Ten thousand dollars. Of course, the cop made sure to tell her that you couldn't inherit money from someone you were convicted of murdering. But Trina already knew that.

Kiah came up to Lee's office and said that the cops were there to talk to Lee, but in the end Trina knew they'd want to talk to her too. No big surprise there. The surprise was the money. All that money. Cash money. Ten thousand smackers. Clams. Greenbacks. Whatever, there were ten thousand of them. She could finish up her time here and jet out. Get a new life going some place different. On her own. Really make it work.

But Trina knew the same money that was her ticket out also gave the man a suspect with black skin and a motive. She had told Lee that the man could take his suspicions anywhere he wanted, that nothing had to be real for him to decide to make it real. And now, he had more real than he needed to hang this around Trina's neck.

A sister with old tracks in her arm is a sister with old tracks in her arm, and the world wasn't gonna see anything else. So they'd just prowl around, watching her every move, waiting for her to screw up.

And Trina knew you didn't need to screw up to get screwed.

When I got home from SafeHaven, I went straight to Gram's Rolodex and called Jan Rosenthal, who for some unknown reason was Gram's lawyer although she practiced in Connecticut. Jan had already left for the day, but her secretary assured me she'd return the call first thing in the morning. I dialed my mother in New York without much hope that she'd have any information for me, but she turned out to be more knowledgeable on the subject than I had expected.

"Well," Mom said slowly, "yes, I did actually know your grandmother had decided not to stick with family convention."

"Why didn't you tell me?"

"How did you find out? The will hasn't been probated yet."

"I thought her break with family convention was leaving the house to the Lexington Historical Society."

"Well," Mom said again, even more slowly, "that was your grandmother's other plan."

So it was true. Harden House was mine. I looked around

the west parlor, the room in which Gram had chosen to spend most of her time. It was a beautiful place, well-proportioned, with hand-carved, built-in bookcases surrounding the fireplace and multi-paned windows on two walls. The house was on a slight rise, and the west windows caught the full evening sun. I leaned back in Gram's chair and put my feet on the desk. My desk. But even as I basked in the glow of new-found home ownership, I felt the clutch of anxiety. Beth was going to be really upset. "Gram underestimates—underestimated—Beth," I said.

"Perhaps," Mom agreed vaguely, and I knew from the thin tone of her voice that she didn't want to talk about Beth. Mom preferred to pretend everything was as she wanted it to be. "I'm sure Beth will understand."

Right. Beth was going to understand real well. "So no one knows about this but you?" I asked.

Mom's sigh was long and deep. "Your grandmother really loved that old house. I guess she thought you'd take better care of it than Beth would. That you'd make sure Tubman Park happened."

It hurt to think how much having Harden House a part of the Park had meant to Gram, that she would never see it happen, that she had entrusted it to me. "Do you think she knew she was going to die?"

"We all know we're going to die, Lee."

Right. Another deep insight from my mother. "Do you know anything about Sarah Harden?" I asked.

"Who?"

"Sarah Harden. She must have been your great-great-great grandmother, maybe great-great. Something like that. The Colonel's daughter."

"Where did this sudden interest come from?"

"It's not so sudden," I argued. "I've always been interested in the family history." My mother had a way of putting me on the defensive about the most absurd things. "Since I was a little girl."

"Well, this is news to me," she said curtly.

I swallowed my annoyance. "Oh, you know, with the whole Underground Railroad thing, I've just been thinking about the house and the family . . ."

"Well, I'm sure you know far more than I do about it all."

I tried one more time, although I didn't know why I was bothering. "How about anyone ever being killed here? Did you ever hear about anything like that? A runaway slave maybe? In the cellar?"

"Now, Lee Anne," Mom admonished in the same tone of voice she had used when I was a small child, "please don't start this again. Aren't you getting a bit old for this foolishness about the cellar? I thought we put all this nonsense behind us years ago along with your nightmares and sleepwalking."

"Like they put away Dotty Aunt Hortense."

"What? What are you talking about?"

"Forget it," I grumbled, in the same tone I had used when I was a small child. "Forget I mentioned it." I told her I was running late for a date, which was clearly the first thing I had said that pleased her, and hung up the phone. As I had no date, I wandered into the kitchen to see if there was any food in the fridge.

There was a half-eaten pan of lasagna and an untouched mystery casserole, along with a bunch of cakes and gooey desserts people had brought over after the funeral. There were also three cartons of milk turning bad now that Gram wasn't around to drink them. I poured the sour milk down the drain and sat down at the table with a fork and half a chocolate mousse cake. I could hear Gram telling me to drink milk, how women needed lots of calcium, how chocolate cake just cries out for a tall cold glass of milk. I hoped wherever Gram was, she was able to get her daily milk quota.

As I was flaking bite-size pieces off the side of the cake, I noticed the boxes that still sat on the floor in front of the old couch. Could it only have been a week ago that Michael had brought them up from the cellar, that Gram and Beth and I had sat around talking about Sarah Harden? I licked the frosting off the fork and knelt next to the boxes. Gram had said it was a disappointing haul, but she had never had time to go through it. Maybe there was something in one of the cartons that would give me some insight into Sarah's life—or into the life of the black man who had called out to her from the cellar floor.

I hadn't gotten far into the moldy baby clothes and water-stained photos when there was a knock at the back door. I looked up as Michael walked in. I jumped up, awkwardly balancing one of the cartons in my right hand, and smiled. Michael had been very sweet yesterday with Blais and Langley. I hadn't had a chance to thank him.

"Hey," I said.

"Hey yourself." He smiled back at me, and his dimples flashed.

I made a rather large production out of putting the carton back on the floor, remembering the warmth of his arm across my shoulders when Blais began pushing a little too hard. I gave the carton a shove with my toe. "Those detectives came back again today."

"What'd they want?"

"It was at SafeHaven. They were checking out alibis, but it's still supposedly just procedure. They'll probably be calling you soon."

"Me?"

I dropped into the couch. "Did Gram ever say anything about leaving money to you in her will?"

"I thought she was joking."

"You better hope Blais and Langley believe you."

Michael's face paled, and he leaned into the wall. "Clara really left me some money?"

"Trina too."

"Shit," he said. "That was really nice of her."

"I don't know how much."

He shrugged. "You got any beer?"

"Just wine."

"I've got some out in the truck. Want one?" When I told him no, he left and returned with a six-pack under his arm. He turned a kitchen chair around and draped his lanky body over it, then he removed a bottle from the pack and took a long drink. "You think the police are going to think I killed Clara because she left me some money?"

"I suppose it'll depend on how much it is."

He frowned.

"I wouldn't worry about it too much—they're looking to hang it on Trina."

"Predictable," Michael said. "Is she doing okay?"

"As okay as any innocent person suspected of murder might be."

"Where is this coming from? There's no evidence. They don't even know for sure how Clara died."

"Trina says evidence doesn't matter: if the cops want to make it real, they can make it real."

He grunted, then glanced at the cartons at my feet. "Those the boxes I brought up from the cellar last week?"

Instead of answering, I surprised myself by asking, "Do you believe in ghosts?"

Michael seemed more amused than surprised. "Nope."

"Do you believe in dreams?"

"Yes."

His ease with my odd questions was disarming. Too disarming. "How's your mom?"

"Better, they think. Still in the ICU though."

"Want to talk about it?"

"I'd rather talk about ghosts."

"You just said you didn't believe in them."

"Just because I don't believe in something doesn't mean I'm not willing to talk about it. You're having dreams about ghosts?"

"No," I said, then changed it to yes. "I mean, I'm having dreams, but they're about real people. Or at least I think they're about real people . . ." I paused, feeling foolish. "I guess," I continued, "if I believed in ghosts, I'd say I was dreaming about people who had once lived in this house, but since I don't, it must just be my overactive imagination . . ."

"This is really bothering you, huh?"

"I guess I've always thought of Harden House as such a proud place, with such a moral history—you know, the Colonel, the abolitionists, the Congressman, all those liberal women who worked for the vote. But these dreams—nightmares really—are always about hatred and violence. Awful things. About people hurting each other, about slaves being killed, not saved . . ."

"And you think these dreams are telling you that the house isn't what you believed all these years?" Michael asked. "That maybe your family isn't either?"

I was unnerved by his perceptiveness. "I don't know. Maybe."

"Dreaming it doesn't mean it's true—it just means you're worried about it."

I told him about the black man with the shovel and the cast on his leg digging behind the root closet. Then I told him about the same man with a mortal wound to the chest, lying on the cellar floor, bleeding and calling for Sarah. "Sarah's buried right next to Gram. I saw her grave yesterday. Her picture's in the east parlor."

Michael reached out and touched my arm lightly. "Your dreams sound a lot like what's been happening around you: digging and death and thinking about the Underground Railroad and the people who've lived in the house."

"I suppose . . ." I could feel the warmth of his fingers even after he removed them. "I have been thinking about Sarah Harden quite a bit this past week."

Michael nodded toward the library books on the kitchen table. *Yankee Ghosts* was on the top of the pile. "And ghosts?"

"That was afterward."

"Anything in the books?"

"Only if you're looking for instructions on how to help a ghost 'move on into the wider world of spirit.' Something I'm sure you've just got to know how to do."

His eyes were amused, and I wondered, not for the first time, what it would be like to kiss him. "And why would I want to know this?"

"Beats me, but this guy, Holzer, seems to think it's a good thing. He says you do it through empathy. That first you've got to understand the ghost, and then explain to him what his misconceptions are—apparently, they don't usually know they're dead—and once he understands what you understand, then he's freed to go on to wherever it is he's supposed to go on to."

"Sounds like resurrection and the Eucharist and all that other Catholic bullshit my father's sisters are always spouting on about."

"I think this is a lot weirder than your aunts could ever be."

"Take it from someone who knows: nothing's weirder than my aunts." His smile was slow and sensuous, and I felt a warmth spreading through me that was so powerful, so familiar, that it scared me.

"Good," I said abruptly, stupidly. I broke eye contact and reached into the box at my feet. I pulled out an old doll with one leg and a ripped dress. "Why would anyone save this?"

"Nothing like the historical restoration business to show you that people will save anything." Michael leaned back easily in his chair; he looked like a man who was willing to take his time.

The idea of Michael taking his time nearly made me blush, and I quickly handed him an old photo album in which there were no photos. "Like this?"

"I've seen entire attics filled with newspapers from fifty years back that're impossible to read." He put the album aside and reached into one of the other boxes. "There's got to be something interesting here—there almost always is." He pulled out a stack of pictures that were stuck together from years of being stored in the damp cellar. When he tried to pry them apart, they fractured between his fingers. He put the photographs carefully back into the box. He had nice hands, large and callused and hard working, but gentle, deliberate, somehow intelligent.

I raised my eyes from his hands and burrowed further into my box. I took out a long piece of tattered rawhide; at the end of it hung a cloth sack about the size of a man's fist. The sack appeared to have been made from red flannel, but was so old and worn it was difficult to know for certain. There was a small hole at the bottom; it looked as if it had been scorched in a fire.

"Any idea what this could be?" I asked.

Michael took the sack from me and turned it over in his hands. He whistled in appreciation.

"What?" I asked. "What is it?"

"It's an old charm bag," he said slowly. He carefully pried open the top of the sack and looked inside. "I think they also called it a Mojo."

I leaned toward him, watching intently.

"There's something in here." He shook the bag over his open palm. A small object fell out.

I jumped back. It looked like the deformed stick Hansel and Gretal had pushed through the bars in lieu of a finger to convince the witch they were too thin to eat. "What is that?"

Michael cautiously lifted it between his thumb and forefinger, holding it up to the light, turning it in all directions. "I think it's a frog's leg," he said, his voice full of awe. "Or at least the bone from one."

I wrinkled my nose. "Gross."

He looked over at me with an expression of mild disappointment. "Not really," he said. "It was probably a good luck charm. Slaves wore these bags for protection from evil." He pointed to the knot at the end of the rawhide. "You tied it around your neck and let it hang over your heart. It had a talisman inside—to bring luck, or ward off illness, or whatever. A rabbit's foot, horse hair, sometimes a piece of snakeskin. I never heard of anyone using a frog's leg, but it seems to fit."

"How do you know so much about this?"

"Doing historical preservation is a good excuse to waste a lot of time reading things you're interested in, but will never have any use for."

I forced myself to touch the bone. It was smoother and stronger than I expected. "You think this could be from the Underground Railroad days? That it could've belonged to a slave who was hidden in the house?"

"Hard to know for sure," he said, "but the historians at the Park Service should be able to date it pretty accurately." He ran his finger along the burnt edge and turned the bag over. One side was quite a bit darker than the other. "Definitely hand-sewn, well-worn, full of stains—could be sweat, blood, who knows? Could easily be nineteenth century." He paused and continued his examination. "Can't tell if these burns are from fire or a bullet." He pressed the cloth to his nose, then shook his head. "Smells like the cellar. No carbon. But then, that's what you'd expect after all these years."

I stared at the charm bag and once again saw the black man, prostrate and bleeding, beseeching me—beseeching Sarah—to help his brothers. Had he been wearing a charm bag next to his heart? Could it have been this very one? "Are you saying that this bag was once worn around the neck of a real slave?" I asked, my heart pounding. "That it could have blood and gun residue on it?"

"Whoa," Michael said, holding up his hands. "It's quite a leap from this bag to the man in your dream."

"So you don't think it's possible?"

"No," he said with a certainty I envied. "No, I don't."

I didn't realize what I was going to do until I did it: I leaned over and kissed him.

CHAPTER FIFTEEN

September 17, 1859

It has been seven long months since last I wrote to you, dear diary, for I have been too filled with despair to take pen in hand. All that used to give me pleasure, whether a walk in the woods, a quiet hour with a book or a whisper with Nancy Southwick, now requires far too much effort. For what purpose? I find myself wondering. For what purpose?

It seems I am always tired.

I remain broken-hearted, even more broken-hearted now than before, but after what happened today, I feel I should chronicle the horror of all that has transpired between February last and the present, though I know it will be most painful to me.

Yet now that I have found the courage to take up my pen, I do not know where to begin. Shall I begin at the end, with the emptiness and defeat, or begin where I left off, when I still had hope and faith, when I still believed in human goodness and a merciful God? I suppose it is always best to begin at the beginning, but find, as with most things, I don't really care.

I never had difficulty with the making of decisions before, nay, Mama always claimed I was far too headstrong for my own good. But now, even the simplest of judgments, such as whether to arise or remain abed, requires more strength than I possess.

Perhaps I shall try to do this some other day.

September 18, 1859

Silas is gone, and so too is my child. Now it is time for me to leave also. I am to be sent to Columbus Ohio, where I shall live with Cousin Hattie and help tend to her four children. It is thought that my repentance shall be more complete if I am far from the place of my sins. I find I care little if I go or if I stay.

September 20, 1859

I am to leave for Ohio in three days, and feel that I must take pen in hand once again. I shall begin at the beginning and go to the end. If I tire, I shall rest and begin again when I rise.

On the day after Silas and I became man and wife, I was determined to take action. First, I would speak with Papa about my situation and then explain to Wendell why we could never marry. When these discussions were past, and the truth was finally known, I would seek advice from the Vigilance Committee as to the best route to Kansas Territory. Then Silas and I, and our unborn child, would be on our way to our new life.

Silas warned against this plan, arguing that we should leave for the west without telling anyone, for my husband was convinced that Papa would be furious, Wendell horrified, and the Vigilance Committee of no help to us at all. Silas tried to explain that I could not understand the response of white men as he did, but I told him I was a white woman and could understand my own father and his friends quite well. Silas didn't contradict me, he just touched his charm bag.

I convinced him to remain in the cellar, to continue digging his tunnel, while I went into the west parlor to speak with Papa. Silas was not happy, but he loved me and did as I asked.

I entered the parlor with both excitement and fear, although, the truth be told, I was quite apprehensive and my hands trembled as I approached Papa's desk. He was entering numbers into his account book and barely acknowledged my presence.

"Papa," I said loudly, trying to speak over the pounding in my ears. "I have news."

He looked up, surprised, and resettled his spectacles on the bridge of his nose. Then he said, not unkindly, "Please be quick about it, child. I have much to do."

Before I could lose my nerve, I told him I was in love.

"Well, my dear," he said with a chuckle. "This is indeed news. I hope it doesn't mean I am going to lose you too soon?"

I took a shuddering breath. "We want to be married as soon as possible," I said, not so foolish as to presume Papa would consider jumping the broom a suitable marriage ceremony. "Then we shall leave for Kansas Territory."

A frown creased his brow. "Kansas Territory?"

"To help insure it is a free state when it enters the union. Just as you told me so many others of us are doing," I reminded him.

"Harumph," he grumbled. "And just who is this young man who wishes to take my daughter from all she knows and loves so she may join him on a dangerous journey into the wilderness? I dare say, I didn't suspect Wendell Parker would have the gumption."

"It isn't Wendell Parker." I raised my chin and met his eye.

"Not Wendell Parker? Who then?"

"It is Silas."

"Silas?" he repeated, and it was clear he had no idea of whom I spoke.

"Silas Person."

His eyes opened wide. "The slave?" he whispered. "You wish to marry a slave?"

"He's not a slave," I corrected my father, perhaps for the first time in my life. "He is a man—a man whose ancestors were taken from their homeland and made into slaves—and although it is of no matter to me, only one of his grandparents was a slave. The other three were free—and white."

"It's impossible," Papa said. "I shall not allow it. Ever."

"But Papa—"

"Never!" he roared. "Now leave me and speak of it no more."

But I stood my ground. "I cannot and I shall not."

"You shall do as I say!"

"I love him, and he loves me."

"Silence!"

"I am with child," I told him softly.

Papa stared at me blankly, obviously unable to comprehend my words. I said nothing, but could feel the heat of embarrassment rising up my cheeks as understanding finally dawned in his eyes. He bolted from his chair with the bellow of an enraged bull, knocking the account book over in his agitation. I tried to stand tall before his fury, but my knees betrayed me, and I sank to the carpet.

I hesitate here, as the pain of relating what happened next is so great. At the time, I believed the events of that afternoon were the worst I would ever experience. Of course, now I know they were just the beginning.

As I lay huddled on floor of the west parlor, Papa's shadow towering over me, his anger surrounding me, I hid my face in my hands. But I hid from no one. Papa grasped me by the shoulders and yanked me erect. He held me more roughly than he had ever done before, and my legs dangled uselessly above the floor. He shook me and said horrible things, but nothing as horrible as when I told him it was indeed Silas who was the father of my child. His face became red and mottled, as if he were suffering from apoplexy. He could barely speak. He sputtered and coughed and shook me even harder. "You are carrying a Negro child?" he hissed. I tried to explain that my baby was seven-eighths white, but he would hear none of it. "A Harden the progeny of a colored man?" he cried. "May God have mercy on your soul!"

I thought for a moment he might strangle me, but then he let go of my shoulders, and I fell back into a heap on the carpet.

Papa turned to the fireplace and tore his rifle from where it hung over the mantle. I watched in horror as he ripped open a paper packet of gunpowder with his teeth and began to load the musket.

"Don't!" I howled, throwing my arms around his legs. "Don't!"

Papa ignored me, pushing the bullet home with his thumb and drawing the ramrod. For a moment, I lay stunned, dumbfounded and unable to move. But I had to move, I had to warn Silas. As Papa pulled back the hammer and marched toward the cellar, I hauled myself up and stumbled after him. I tripped on the edge of the carpet, fell again.

I was just entering the dining room when a single rifle shot shook the house. It seemed as though I felt the blast before I heard it, and I grasped onto the chair rail. "No!" I screamed. Maybe Papa was just trying to scare Silas, I prayed as I raced down the stairs. Maybe he had missed.

When I reached the bottom of the stairs, I saw my worst fears had been realized. Silas lay on the ground, his blood darkening the dirt around him. Silas had a huge hole in his chest, and his shirt was blown to shreds. I could see he was gravely wounded. I knelt down and took his hand. It was icy cold.

"Sarah," Silas said, his voice a hoarse whisper. "Sarah, please help my brothers."

CHAPTER SIXTEEN

I think I was more surprised by my impulse than Michael, but we seemed to be enjoying the kiss equally. I hadn't kissed a man in two years, and it was better than I remembered. As the kiss deepened, the warm sensation in my center swelled into a wanting as ancient as life itself. I told Michael it was a dangerous thing to be the one to release two years of pent-up desire, but he didn't seem too concerned. He laughed and kissed me again.

I felt giddy and carefree; all the concerns that had been crowding me for the past week drifted away, became elusive, formless, unimportant. I was only aware of this man, of his arms and his lips and the way the palm of his hand was pressed against the small of my back. I only cared about the desire that overwhelmed me, about the desire I could feel overwhelming him. I arched my body closer to his and imagined leading him upstairs to my bedroom, undressing him, letting him undress me . . . I pulled away.

Michael looked at me with a puzzled expression.

"Need more time," I managed to gasp. "Can we take this a little bit slower?"

He ran his finger along the line between my ear and my chin, leaving a trail of tiny shocks in its wake. "As long as we take it somewhere."

I tried to still my ragged breathing and surprised myself by saying, "How about dinner tomorrow?" That wasn't very slow.

"You cooking?"

I shook my head. "Cooking's not my thing, but I'll treat." I stood before I could change my mind, and he reluctantly followed my lead. We walked together to the door, but I leaned away from him when we reached it.

"I've got a bunch of books on slavery at home," Michael said calmly, as if no kiss and no images of lust and nakedness had passed between us. He nodded in the direction of the small sack on the couch. "I'll see if I can come up with anything else on charm bags before tomorrow night."

Charm bags, I thought stupidly. Tomorrow night. "Sure," I finally said, when it became clear he was waiting for an answer. "Sure," I said again.

Michael kissed me lightly on the end of my nose and told me he'd see me about six. Then he slipped out the door.

I watched from the window as his truck pulled out of the driveway. When the red taillights disappeared from sight, I dropped into the couch. "So, how do you like that, Gram?" I asked out loud. If Gram were here now, she'd pour us each a big glass of milk, and we'd polish off the remains of that chocolate cake, debating how slowly I really wanted to go. "Just because Michael's good-looking and it didn't work out with Richie, that doesn't mean it won't work out with him," Gram would say. "Life's short. Take a chance." Maybe I'd even drink some of the milk, just to make her happy.

I picked up the charm bag laying on the couch next to me. It was too bad Gram wasn't here to see this. She'd have been thrilled by the notion that it had belonged to a slave who had been "riding" the Underground Railroad, perhaps one who had been sheltered under the eaves of Harden House.

Gram had told me that no one knew for certain why the network of safe houses was called the Underground Railroad, but one story was that in the early 1830's, the owner of an escaped slave was overheard to say, "Those damn abolitionists must have a railroad by which they run off the coloreds." Whatever the truth, the railroad analogy had stuck, with "conductors" as those who helped the slaves "ride" from one "station" to another. Harden House had been a link of this chain, the Colonel, one of the "damn abolitionists." It was a family history to be proud of, and it bothered me to think that a tragedy might have taken place here. Could an anti-abolitionist band have raided Harden House and discovered a slave hiding in the cellar? Could one of them have shot the runaway, who then bled to death on the dirt floor, calling out to Sarah Harden with his last breath?

I pressed the charm bag between my hands. What must it have been like to be a slave? To never be able to call your life your own? To believe only the plantation sorcerer and a small sack could protect you from the evil that surrounded you? Michael had been so understanding when I told him about my dreams and my irrational fear of ghosts and what might have transpired at Harden House one hundred fifty years ago. *"Dreaming it doesn't mean it's true,"* he had said, *"it just means you're worried about it."* But why should I be worried? What would make me think a slave had been killed in the cellar? The only answer was that I had already known. Gram must have told me the story when I was a young girl, and I had forgotten—or my conscious mind had forgotten, but my subconscious had not.

Sitting quietly on the couch, pressing the charm bag between my hands, with only the creaking of the old house for company, my thoughts finally began to slow. My breathing followed, then my eyelids closed.

I dreamed I was sitting on the couch, pressing the charm

bag between my hands. I was alone, but not afraid. It was peaceful, comforting, to sit there, lost in a web of conjecture, contemplating the impossible. Gram drifted in and told me what a nice boy Michael was and reminded me I had forgotten to pick up my navy suit from the cleaners. Then Linda Lubin, a childhood friend I hadn't seen since she moved to California after high school, walked into the kitchen. She was wearing the maroon prom dress with the slit up the leg that we had thought was so daring. "You've always been a risk taker," she said, and I couldn't tell if she thought this was a good or bad thing.

I opened my hands and the charm bag rested in my right palm. I cupped it protectively, and it began to stir in my fingers. At first I was only marginally interested as the sack twitched slightly and lay still. But then the bag leapt from my grasp, jumping up and out as if snatched by an invisible hand. I shouted as the red sack flew across the kitchen and through the dining room doorway. Then I froze. He was back. The man with the shovel. The man with the hole blasted through his chest. He was dead. He was back.

Sweat rolled down my neck, and I wasn't sure if I was asleep or awake. I jumped up and went to the refrigerator, grasped the metal door handle in my hands, pressed my cheek to its smooth coldness. I was awake. I was standing in the kitchen. A dead slave had returned to the living. He wanted to reclaim what was his. He wanted his charm bag. The ghost of my dreams. He was real and he was here.

I streaked through the house and yanked open the front door, thrusting myself into the night, out and away from all that scared me, all that I couldn't understand. I ran right into the arms of Raymond Langley. Behind him was Detective Blais.

"Whoa!" Langley said, catching me as I tripped over his shoe. "Whoa."

Blais raised an eyebrow. "Is everything all right?" she asked. "Are you feeling unwell?"

But I didn't care what she asked or even that she had used the pretentious word "unwell." I was just happy to see them. To see anyone. To be with people. Living people. Even if one was Detective Blais. I took a shuddering breath and leaned heavily against Langley's arm, as much for the physical support as for the brush with reality the contact offered. "Fine," I finally managed to answer. "I'm just fine."

Langley looked dubious, but Blais said, "We'd like to talk with you."

"Sure," I agreed readily. Talking was fine. Anything was fine as long as they didn't leave. Nothing could be worse than being alone in the house. If I had been alone in the house.

"How about we go inside?" Blais suggested.

"It's such a nice night," I said quickly, not ready to go back, even with two detectives by my side. "Why don't we just sit out here?" I looked around the yard. It was dark and getting chilly, and there was nowhere to sit except for the front stoop, which was a single slab of slate, about three feet wide and two feet deep, barely large enough to hold one person. Never three.

Langley glanced at the stoop and then back at me. "I think we might be more comfortable in the house," he said reasonably.

The shadow of the house fell over me as the moon rose behind it. The two-story facade seemed taller than usual, longer and flatter and somehow more ominous. "There are no lights," I said, as if this made it all make sense. I had fallen asleep on the couch while it was still dusk, and night had come while I dreamed. "It's dark in there."

"We could turn the lights on," Blais suggested in the soft tones one uses with slow and skittish children.

Langley cleared his throat, and his Adam's apple bobbed. "Is, ah, is there some reason you don't want us to go into your house, Ms. Seymour?"

"You can call me Lee," I offered, although I had extended this privilege when we first met, and he had obviously chosen to decline it.

"Is there some reason you don't want us to go into your house, Lee?" Blais asked.

"No," I said quickly. "No, of course not. It's, it's just that I lost something—a charm bag. It's a sack, actually." I held my forefingers about three inches apart. "A small sack that slaves wore around their necks for protection against evil." I knew I wasn't making any sense, but I didn't know what else to say. I couldn't tell them why I didn't want to go back into the house—I couldn't tell them I was afraid of a ghost who had snatched his charm bag from my hand—but I had to tell them something. "I was looking for the bag when you got here. I can't find it anywhere."

Langley took a small step backward. "You don't want us to go inside because you lost your charm bag?"

It was clear I had no choice. I consoled myself with the fact that I wasn't going to have to go back into the house alone, that I was accompanied by two armed police officers. "Shall we?" I asked with a false heartiness that fooled no one. "I'll just turn some lights on."

"You do that," Blais said as she pushed the front door open.

When we got into the house, I was even jumpier than I had been when we were outside. I walked through the downstairs rooms, turning on all the lights and jabbering about safe houses and slaves and the Underground Railroad. I kept throwing furtive glances into the corners and under the furniture. Langley and Blais trailed behind me, not saying much but watching me closely. When we reached the kitchen, I offered them coffee or tea or soda or water or anything else that they might like to drink or even eat.

"I still have all these leftovers from the funeral—casseroles and lasagna and such—lots of cookies. People bring way too much food to these things. Some kind of offering to the dead, I guess. I don't know exactly who they think will eat it all. Please," I begged, not at all sure why, "can't I please give you something?" I looked over at the couch, at the cartons. No charm bag.

"We're fine," Langley said. "We just want to ask you a couple of things."

"Sure," I said. "Sure. I'll be happy to talk. Just sit down here." I pointed to the couch in the kitchen. When Langley started to sit, I changed my mind. "No," I said. "Not there. It's too cramped. All these cartons and things. Not enough space for us to sit comfortably. How about the east parlor? Or the west—that was Gram's favorite room."

"Are you sure you're okay?" Blais asked again.

"Fine," I said as I led them into the west parlor. "Fine," I repeated as I waved them into the wing chairs in front of Gram's desk. As fine as anyone could be who had just had an object snatched from their hands by a ghost.

Langley waited until I was seated, then cleared his throat and explained what it was they wanted to know. They had come to ascertain if I had a computer in the house (I didn't), if I had access to cocaine (I didn't), if Trina had access to cocaine (I didn't know), if I had ever seen Trina with cocaine (I hadn't), and if Trina had ever offered me cocaine (she hadn't). I didn't understand their interest in cocaine, but knew it didn't bode well for Trina.

"Would you mind if we took a look in the cellar?" Langley asked before I could get any information on the cocaine.

"The cellar?" I remembered Kiah's protective stance at SafeHaven, Trina's assertion that the police didn't need evidence to make an accusation real. Could someone have really killed Gram? Did they think it was Trina? Or me? Maybe I should do as Kiah had suggested and call her friend, Mike Dannow, supposedly the best defense attorney in the state.

"Ms. Seymour?" Blais asked. "It may be a crime scene."

"No. No, I don't think so," I said, then thought better of what might be construed as unwillingness to cooperate with the police or perhaps even obstruction of justice. "That is, unless you have a search warrant?"

"Unfortunately we don't," Blais said. "We'd hoped you'd be more cooperative. But there won't be any problem arranging it. It usually takes a day or two, but we got one quicker for your computer at work. We'll have someone at your office first thing tomorrow to make a copy of the hard disk. We'll probably be able to get someone here with a warrant to check the cellar the next day."

"Warrant," I said stupidly. "Check the cellar." Somehow a search warrant for the house seemed much more ominous than one for SafeHaven. Mike Dannow would know how concerned I should be. "Why all the questions before about cocaine?"

"The preliminary lab report indicates that there might have been cocaine in your grandmother's body."

"That's ridiculous. Gram wouldn't have done cocaine."

"We assumed that," Blais said, a bit smugly. "We're guessing someone gave it to her without her knowledge."

"Someone like Trina Collins?" I asked.

"The lab is running more sensitive tests to be certain," Blais continued smoothly, ignoring my sarcasm. "But we also talked with your grandmother's doctor, Larry Starr, and he said she was taking Inderal, a beta blocker for her heart."

"So?"

"It turns out that an overdose of that is another possibility. Or there's always the chance of a false positive."

"What about natural causes?"

"A possibility too."

"How could Gram take an overdose of heart medication she'd been taking for years?"

"It happens," Langley said. "Older people sometimes forget that they've already taken their pills."

"Gram wouldn't have done that. She wasn't old."

Langley nodded sympathetically. "According to the lab the symptoms of an overdose of Inderal and cocaine are quite similar."

Blais flipped through the pages of her notebook. "An overdose of either drug can cause hallucinations, disorientation, convulsions, coma, delirium and death."

I thought about Gram's final battle with no one. Hallucinations? Convulsions? Delirium? It had certainly ended in death. I thought about the charm bag flying from my hand, and it occurred to me that "scared to death" might be more than just a metaphor.

CHAPTER SEVENTEEN

September 21, 1859

It has taken me a full day to regain the strength I need to continue my story.

As I knelt by my dying husband, Papa stood with his rifle resting on his knee, silent and still as a statue, staring at nothing. He did not try to stop me from speaking to Silas. He did not try to do anything.

"Of course I'll help your brothers," I promised Silas. "I'll do all I can, but you'll help them too. Dr. Miller will come and mend you and make you well. We'll help them together, and then we'll all go to Kansas Territory. We'll raise our family there, and grow old together. You and I . . ." I began to choke on my tears, for it was all too apparent how short our future was to be. "You and I will . . ." But before I could tell him of all we would surely do, before I could tell him how we would raise our son to be strong and proud in a free land, he squeezed my hand once, then his eyelids dropped closed.

I knew Silas was gone because I felt his spirit, his essence, separate from his body. I could almost see him, feel him, as he wrapped himself around me. "I won't leave you," the spirit of Silas seemed to whisper in my ear. "I'll stay with you forever."

The charm bag Silas had been given by the plantation conjurer hung around his neck. I gently removed it and pressed it to my heart. The "Hand" Silas had said it was sometimes called. I would keep the hand of Silas close. Papa jerked me up toward him.

"Go to the barn and get Caleb," Papa ordered as I slipped

the small sack into the pocket of my dress. "Then go to your room and wait for me to come to you."

"How could you—"

"I have done nothing," he said. "You have seen nothing, and you will not speak of it to anyone. Ever."

"But—"

"But nothing!" he roared. "Go get your brother."

My pen quivers and shakes and falls from my hand. I can write no more this night.

September 22, 1859 (morning)

Papa and Caleb buried Silas at the far end of his tunnel, then they filled it with dirt and placed the canning rack Silas had built in front of the hole. It is as if neither the tunnel nor Silas had ever been. Papa informed the Vigilance Committee that Silas had left for Canada and that his brothers should be sent straight on to Montreal. The Committee said they would attempt to get the messages through, and as no brother of Silas' has arrived at Harden House, I can only hope word reached them rather than the alternative.

As for me, on the following Sunday, Papa announced in church that I was suffering from a severe case of tuberculosis. Dr. Miller was the only one we took into our confidence, and he preserved the charade of my illness throughout the long, hot summer.

I was alone all those months, save visits from Caleb and Dr. Miller. I did not see Papa in all that time, nor did I wish to. I lay in my bed, overwhelmed with guilt. Why had I been so stupid, so trusting? Why hadn't I listened to Silas' warning? If I had we'd have been on our way to Kansas. I was extremely contagious, and even Mrs. Harrington did not dare to come near.

I do not remember much of that time, but I do remember Caleb telling me of John Brown's raid at Harper's Ferry, of the thwarted slave rebellion, of John Brown, dead. Just like Silas. Just like me, though I still breathed.

I mostly slept during those scorching months, dwelling in a hazy dream world of cold winter nights with Silas alive beside me. When I woke, hot and covered with sweat, I would turn over and dream again so that the spirit of Silas could come to me. He whispered the same words in my dreams as he had on the day he died. "I won't leave you," the spirit of Silas promised over and over again. "I'll stay with you forever."

September 22, 1859 (afternoon)

On September 1, our son was born. He was a beautiful baby, and although his skin was as white as any child born into the Harden family, I could see his father in his wise, thoughtful eyes. Just looking at him caused me to ache with love and anguish, to long for what was not anymore, and to give thanks for what was. I named him Levi, for Silas' youngest brother, the one Silas worried about so.

They allowed me to keep Levi one week. One marvelous, wonderful week in which we were never separated, in which my sweet babe slept in the crook of my arm. He was a wonderful baby, hardly ever crying, easily satisfied, happy to be near me. He had the calm of an angel. He was my angel, and I loved him with all my heart. I still do. I always will.

But on the morning of the eighth day, Levi was not in my arms when I awoke. He had been taken from me in the night! I raced down the stairs and discovered Papa reading in the west parlor. I demanded to know what he had done with my baby.

"You have no baby," he said calmly.

"I do and you stole him from me!" I cried.

He pushed his spectacles up on the bridge of his nose. "I dare say, child, you are still delirious from your illness. Please go rest yourself before you take sick again."

"I shall not rest until you return Levi to me!"

"Please don't upset yourself so, dear," he said, then called for Mrs. Harrington. He told her to take me upstairs and returned to his book.

September 22, 1859 (evening)

I refused to eat for five days in the hope that Papa would relent. But he is a stubborn man, and would say nothing. I was determined to starve myself until he capitulated. If I died along the way, so be it.

Three more days passed before Caleb took pity on me and confided that Papa had instructed him to bring Levi to a Negro foundling home on Boylston Street in Boston. I began to eat. I would need my health to reclaim my child.

With each passing day, I grew stronger and more resolute. I had hope for the first time in seven months. I had a plan.

My plan was to tell Papa I must go into the city to purchase clothing for my journey to Ohio. He would insist that Mrs. Harrington accompany me, and I would acquiesce. Once in Boston, I could easily become separated from Mrs. Harrington and "lose" my way. From there I would go directly to Boylston Street. I would find Levi and I would take him with me to Ohio.

The thought of the long train ride with my baby cradled in my arms filled me with joy. I could see the mountains and the rivers and smell his sweet baby smell. Because of Levi's light skin, I knew I would be able to devise a credible story of his parentage and raise him as my own along with Cousin Hattie's children. We would be together, happy, and I would never return to my father's house.

September 22, 1859 (very late evening)

Five days ago, Mrs. Harrington and I traveled to the city. All went according to my plan, and I arrived at the foundling home without mishap. But then my dreams fell apart.

The rooms were run-down and small, but clean, and I eagerly approached the first woman I saw. She was a Negro, as was everyone there, and she looked at me with a world-weary sadness as I explained my quest. She told me to wait and spoke with another woman. They spoke with two more, and then the four took me on a tour of the home. The women stood silent and somber as I walked through the warren of rooms, looking into every tiny cradle—every one—then looking again. I retraced my steps and looked one more time, but as the silent women knew before I began, my sweet boy was nowhere to be found. There were many children, large and small, with skin of light chocolate or shiny rich ebony, many children running or playing or sitting quietly, many children, but none of them Levi.

Levi was not there. Not there!

No one knew where he was. No one knew of him at all.

When Caleb had no answers for me either, I fell into the deepest despair, caring little if I lived or died. Five days later, I am still completely crushed, without hope, overcome by the impossibility of finding answers to the only questions about which I still care: Where is my precious baby? Where is my husband? Where is the father I thought I knew?

At dawn tomorrow, I go to Ohio. For what purpose? I find myself wondering, then realize I do not care.

CHAPTER EIGHTEEN

The computer technician the Lexington police sent to SafeHaven wasn't what I expected. Joe was at least seventy-five, bald, paunchy and quite a talker. He was wearing suspenders and looked more like the guy who worked in the corner hardware store than a techie cop. But, of course, he wasn't a cop. He told me he was a "retread," that he had quickly bored of retirement after selling his business making Venetian blinds and gone back to school to learn about computers. Now he worked free-lance for a number of small police departments in the Boston area, making enough to nicely augment his Social Security—thank you very much—and keeping him busy.

Joe acted as if he were installing new Venetian blinds in my office rather than copying computer files for a murder investigation, and soon I began to forget why he was there. He told me about his grandson, Josh, and his wife—now dead eight years, God rest her soul, she had never even gotten to see her first grandchild—and asked me if I was married and where my parents lived and if I didn't think it was about time to settle down and have a family. His daughter was a "career girl" too, but he didn't think it was enough, not nearly enough, and he was sure she was going to be sorry if she didn't start acting more agreeable toward some of those nice boys she dated—very sorry indeed. I nodded and smiled and answered when it was necessary, but mostly I just listened.

The binding of *Yankee Ghosts*—which I had impulsively

grabbed from the kitchen table and tucked under my arm on my way to work—was visible through the open zipper of my briefcase. Although Harden House had been peaceful and calm this morning, the dust motes dancing innocently in the sunlight, I wanted to see if Hans Holzer had written anything about ghosts who stole things in the night—and it seemed safer to read up on the subject at SafeHaven. I had searched the house for the charm bag before I left for work, but it hadn't been anywhere I looked.

"All righty, then." Joe stood up and flipped a computer disk the size of a cassette tape into its plastic case with one hand. "My work is done here," he said as he wrapped the cord around the small machine he had used to copy my files. He held the tape up for me to see. "This is exactly what you should do to back-up your system. At least once a month. Bet you don't do it, do you?"

I shook my head.

"Nobody does," he told me. "Mistake. Big mistake. With all the viruses and bugs around, these babies break down more than people think." He patted my computer affectionately. "And once your data's gone, it may be gone forever. Do yourself a favor, Lee, do a back-up every month."

"I'll take that under advisement."

He touched a hand to his heart and added, "And find yourself a nice guy." Then he waved and slipped out the door.

I wondered if I had already found myself a nice guy and where I should take Michael for dinner tonight. Tonight. A jolt of both fear and excitement blazed through me. My track record with men wasn't the greatest, and I wasn't at all sure I wanted to run that race again. Sometimes it was better to sit on the sidelines. The only problem was that I didn't know if this was one of those times.

"Hey." Trina was standing in the doorway. "Heard the man was giving you some shit."

I was pleased to see Trina so cheerful—even if it was because she was bonding with me over the shared experience of being a murder suspect. "Yeah," I said, "they came to the house yesterday, but I wouldn't let them into the cellar, so they're coming back with a search warrant. Probably tomorrow."

"Watch out for the bitchy one."

"I called a lawyer this morning—I'll talk to him about you too, if you want." I didn't want her to know she was the primary reason I had called Mike Dannow, that I, too, believed she had reason to be seriously concerned over the police jumping to convenient conclusions.

She perched herself on the edge of my desk. "Dannow?" she asked, and when I said yes, she nodded in appreciation of my choice. "He's good. Lionnel uses him. But don't worry about me. I'm cool." Trina leaned closer and said conspiratorially, "Heard about the blow." Blow is one of the many street names for cocaine.

"They asked you about that too?"

She barked a laugh. "Wanted to know if I 'had access.' Told 'em I was in drug rehab, for Christ sake. No drugs allowed in drug rehab. No suh, no ma'am. No drugs a'tal." She pressed her lips into an impressive pout and put her hands peevishly on her hips. "And they thought I was lying. Can you evah believe such a thang?" she twanged in imitation of a Southern belle.

I looked at her warily. The worst infraction a client could commit was possession of drugs or alcohol while in treatment, but this didn't make it an unknown occurrence. A freshman had been caught with some crack and kicked out just a few weeks ago; apparently her boyfriend had slipped it to her through the first floor bathroom window. Another time, an ounce of pot had been smuggled in inside a baby's diaper on visiting day. Had pretty boy Lionnel slipped Trina some cocaine? I leaned closer to see if her pupils were dilated. She was awfully cheerful. And jittery. But her eyes appeared normal. "Did Kiah tell you about this afternoon?" I asked, feeling her eyes on me long after I had looked away.

Trina frowned and moved toward the door. "Fine with me," she said stiffly. "If that's what you want." She knew exactly what I had been thinking.

"Of course it's what I want," I said, pretending to misunderstand. "It's what I need. You're the only one who has any clue about Gram's system—or lack thereof—and we've got less than a week to get it all together." The Park Service had called that morning to tell me they had rescheduled their inspection for next Wednesday. I had asked Kiah if I could bring Trina to Harden House this afternoon to help with the paperwork. I had also called Michael, but only reached his machine.

She shrugged. "I guess."

"Great," I said. "We'll leave about two. I'll meet you downstairs."

Trina looked disappointed. She clearly wanted to leave earlier—probably to miss lunch duty in the kitchen.

"I've got to hang around here for another few hours," I explained, "but I'll tell Kiah I need you for a full day tomorrow, so you'll have to catch the bus before breakfast in the morning."

"Thanks," she mumbled and clomped out of my office.

As I listened to Trina's footfalls descend into the stairwell, I wondered what the hell was wrong with me. Who was this woman who believed her dreams were a reflection of some past event? Who believed her house was haunted and that a friend was lying? I stared glumly at my overflowing in-box. I looked into my briefcase at *Yankee Ghosts*.

I pulled out the book and began to flip through the pages, searching for something that might convince me I had indeed just misplaced the charm bag, that there was no ghost in my house. Instead, I read of ghosts who were very connected to "things," how they often "tenaciously cling to earthly possessions," especially a possession that had great meaning in their lives. Such as a charm bag created by a sorcerer to bring the owner good luck?

Then I read that ghosts were unhappy creatures, caught between two states, often unaware of which realm they existed in at any given moment, unable to adjust to either one. Holzer said a ghost was "the emotional memory of a person who had died under tragic circumstances," one who was frequently seeking revenge for his untimely death. Such as a slave who had been killed by anti-abolitionists in one of the few places he believed himself to be safe?

I read on. According to Holzer, in the ghost's confusion, he was unable to differentiate between one time and another, thinking now was then, then was now. When a living person appeared, the ghost perceived that person to be in whatever time the ghost believed himself to inhabit. So, if the ghost at Harden House was the slave who had owned the charm bag, and he believed he was still living in 1859, he would also believe the anti-abolitionists were still around. And if a person from the present—Gram perhaps—stepped into his world, he might think she was the anti-abolitionist who had killed him, or another, just as dangerous.

I dropped the book back into my briefcase, but not before my eye caught the paragraph pleading with the reader to appreciate and understand the ghost's predicament, to help the ghost comprehend his situation so he would be released from his netherworld and freed to move on in peace. If I tried to talk to the poor man—the poor soul?—to explain to him what had happened and where he was now, would he then go away? Would he and I then find some peace?

Trina and I were sitting cross-legged on the floor of the west parlor, sorting through piles of papers. We had been at it for a couple of hours, and were making some headway, albeit slowly. Trina had perked up as soon as we left SafeHaven, apparently forgiving me for scrutinizing her eyes, and as we worked, we chatted about music and government stupidity and the dangers of being involved with a handsome man. "You want him, you got to tolerate his alley cat ways," Trina was saying, although she insisted Michael was the exception that proved her rule. I was inclined to agree with her.

As Gram often noted, Trina was great at getting to the heart of an issue, at seeing things as they really were, at assessing priorities. These skills were fortunate for more than my love life. We didn't have much time before the inspection, and the Park Service was more than sustaining the federal government's reputation as the master of superfluous paperwork. Strong organizational skills were going to be a necessity, and I, unfortunately, took after Gram in that department.

The kitchen door slammed open. At first I thought it was Michael—who had called to say he was on his way over to develop a game plan for the inspection—and my heart jumped, but then I saw it was Beth.

I hadn't spoken with her since Gram's will became family knowledge, and I had no idea how she was going to react to losing the house. I watched her progress across the kitchen and dining room with apprehension. I could tell by the shuffle of her heels on the hardwood floor that she was bummed out, and I scanned her face for signs that she was mad at me. There were none. She just looked devastated.

Beth's eyes grazed over Trina and the paperwork. "Do you have a minute, Lee?" Her voice was dull with pain.

I nodded and pushed myself up from the floor. "You got this under control?" I asked Trina.

"Sure," Trina said without acknowledging Beth's presence, a mask of willful blankness covering her face. Trina didn't like Beth, and given some of the careless things Beth said, I wouldn't have expected her to. It took some time to understand Beth, to learn to appreciate her; she had a good heart—and now she was hurting.

I met Beth's gaze and smiled as warmly as I could. "Want some tea?" I asked her, then looked over at Trina. Trina pulled a piece of gum out of her backpack and shook her head.

Beth didn't answer, but she followed me into the kitchen. She dropped sluggishly into the couch and sat silently as I put on the water. Her eyes were large and dark against her pale face, and she was staring at the hands in her lap as if they didn't belong to her. It was disconcerting to see her so still. I busied myself with the tea-making, trying to figure out what I should say.

"I feel so bad that she didn't trust me," Beth finally whispered, a tear running down her left cheek. "My own grandmother . . ."

I put down the teacups. "Oh, honey," I said, sitting next to her and putting my arms around her. "Gram was always too hard on you. I told her that lots of times."

"Guess it didn't do too much good."

I pushed back a wisp of hair that had fallen to her forehead. "You know Gram wasn't big on taking advice. Mom always says that once Gram makes up her mind, nothing is ever going to get her to change it, so it's a waste of good time and energy to even bother."

"My mom used to say the same thing," Beth allowed with the glimmer of a smile.

"She was a stubborn ol' coot, our grandmother," I said, hoping to nudge a laugh out of her.

Instead, Beth burst into tears. "I wish she wasn't dead."

I rested my head on Beth's shoulder. "Me too," I said. "Me too."

We stayed like that for a while, sharing our sadness, our connection, letting the tears run until they were ready to dry up. Beth's tears dried first. "My one consolation is that Gram didn't completely lose faith in me," she said. "She didn't completely cut me out of her will."

I swiped my eyes with the sleeve of my shirt.

Beth reached into one of the cartons that was still sitting open on the floor. She pulled out a child's pink dress, used it to wipe her face, then handed it to me. "I talked to Jan Rosenthal—Gram's lawyer—she told me about Michael and Trina. I guess you must already know."

I glanced up to see if Beth was going to use the inheritance against Trina, but, at the moment, she was too distracted by her own misery.

"A bunch of other people too," she continued. "The Lexington Historical Society, some blind woman she used to read to, the library."

"What about you?"

Beth sighed. "Jan said the will stipulates that I get first

pick of the furniture, and if you're 'unable or unwilling' to take Harden House, then it reverts back to the way it's always been." Beth tried to smile, but didn't quite make it. "I guess if she really didn't trust me, she wouldn't have taken the chance that you might not want the house."

I turned the little dress around in my hands. Was this Beth's way of asking if I was willing to give up Harden House? Did she think I didn't want it? I worked the dress until the sound of ripping cloth startled me. I had torn a seam in the skirt. "Beth, I don't know what to say. I really—" I began.

"No," Beth interrupted. "That's not what I mean. I don't want you to change anything. I don't want this old house—this old flea trap—I've got a perfectly nice house of my own that's air conditioned and has instant hot . . . It's just that I, that I just . . . I just feel so bad." She started to cry all over again.

I wrapped her in my arms and rubbed her back, smiling at her reference to air conditioning and the instant hot water dispenser she had at her kitchen sink. Beth was a character, there was no doubt about that, but I felt bad too.

Michael found us like that when he walked in a few minutes later. He stood at the door, shifting his weight from one foot to the other. "Hey," he said uncertainly. "Hope I'm not interrupting."

I wanted to run to him and let him hold me while I wailed out all the unfair and unbelievable things that had happened since I had last seen him. But I didn't, I just gave him a small smile over the back of Beth's head.

It was Beth who took control of the situation. "We're done," she said, standing and throwing Michael a forced smile—which was a pretty good imitation of the real thing considering the circumstances. "We've had our crying and our girl bonding and now we're all done. Come on in and sit down."

Michael looked at me.

"There's only so much bonding two women who have known each other their whole lives have left to do," I assured him.

Beth patted my shoulder and then turned to Michael. "We were having tea," she said. "Want some?"

Michael said he did, and we poured four cups of tea—despite Trina's earlier turn down—and went into the west parlor to discuss the inspection. Trina drank the tea once she had it in her hands, and the four of us spent over an hour working out a plan that would have everything ready in less than a week. It was going to be tight, but Trina said she could come out over the weekend, and Michael thought he could get his piece together if one of us was willing to complete filling the tunnel by Sunday morning, when the cement contractor was scheduled to arrive.

I participated in the conversation—even made suggestions and volunteered to do tasks—but I felt as if I weren't really there. How could I care about the inspection when Gram was dead and the cops thought Trina killed her and Beth was so unhappy and the charm bag had disappeared and Michael was so concerned and sweet? How could I not care about my grandmother's final dream?

The four of us tromped downstairs to assess that situation. "Jud's doing us a huge favor by coming in on a Sunday," Michael said when we reached the old cellar. "And if we don't have it ready for him, I'll be screwed with Lexington Cement and Gravel for years—not to mention the time and a half you're paying for him and two of his guys."

It was slowly dawning on me that I was the only one who

didn't have a hard and fast excuse to avoid the task. Michael's mother was having surgery in the morning—the doctors had finally decided a bypass was necessary—and Michael's crew was committed to another job through the end of the month. Beth was working all day at Zach's school, had a "no-excuses-accepted" business gala to attend that evening with Russ and claimed that on Saturday she was completely booked with back-to-back baseball games and a fund-raiser. Trina's time was more than absorbed by the paperwork. That left me and the promise I had made to my dead grandmother that I would see her project through.

"There's no one you can get to help out?" I asked Michael. When he said no, I turned to Beth. "How about your endless list of helpful servants?"

"I could try," she said dubiously. "But everyone seems awfully busy this spring."

"High school students?"

"None I can think of."

"All right, all right," I said reluctantly. "I've got to go into work in the morning, but I guess I can get back here by noon and start in on it." Michael gave my shoulder a grateful squeeze and promised he'd be over as soon as he could get away from the hospital. We tromped back upstairs.

Trina went back into the west parlor and Beth lingered in the cellar for a few minutes, which gave me the chance to tell Michael I just wasn't up for our dinner date tonight. "I know it was my suggestion," I said, "but can we do it some other time? There's just too much going on, and I'm completely wasted. I'd be lousy company."

Michael looked at me closely. "Anything you want to talk about?"

I didn't answer right away. "Not now," I finally said, although I did want to. "Maybe tomorrow."

He ran his finger along my jaw line with the same gesture he had used yesterday, and I felt the same shiver of excitement. "Leave a message on my machine if you change your mind," he said. "But, either way, I'll see you here tomorrow night—afternoon, if I can."

Beth came up the stairs just as Michael was leaning over to kiss me. We leapt apart, and Beth looked both pleased and guilty at her intrusion.

"Don't mind me," she said breezily and headed for the west parlor. "As you were," she called over her shoulder.

I heard her say something to Trina, then the slam of the front door. We listened to her car pull out of the driveway, then Michael touched my cheek and he left too.

Trina knew there was some weird shit coming down in that old house. Real weird. The cops knew something was up too, but they thought it was her. It never occurred to them it might be something much weirder and more sinister than a sister with a lot of baggage.

Lee was starting to wonder too, but Lee was wondering about a lot of shit these days. Trina had caught her checking out her pupils, and although it had made her mad at the time, when she thought about it, she couldn't hardly blame Lee, not with Kiah and the cops filling her with their negative thoughts.

The cops didn't appear to be at all concerned with the low-life cousin, but they did have part of an eye out for Lee, who wasn't half bad, even if she wasn't tuned into a lot of shit you would've thought everyone would be tuned into. Trina knew the man had a whole eye out for her, and that her main gig now was to make sure she got off his scope because suddenly it was like her ticket was being dropped from heaven. Things had changed, and she might not have to wait out an inheritance everyone seemed motivated to keep from her. Maybe there was a God.

Trina felt bad about how it was gonna look for Lee when she showed up gone after Lee had been going to bat for her with Kiah and the cops, even offering to get her hooked up with fat-cat Dannow.

But she also felt bad about Hendrika and Clara and a shitload of other stuff. And Trina knew feeling bad about something didn't make it any different than it was.

I didn't move from my desk all morning, furiously attacking all the work I had ignored for the last week, trying to catch up on enough of it so I wouldn't feel guilty about leaving to go home and dig. Oh goody. Digging in the cellar. My favorite thing.

I sorted through the mess in my in-box—filing a few papers, throwing away a few more, restoring most to where they had been—and returned the most pressing calls, but I kept an ear open for the intercom announcing that Mike Dannow, who hadn't returned my call from yesterday, was on the line. Kiah had promised to talk to him this morning to make sure he called today, although she was cool to the idea of Dannow representing Trina. "The guy's pro bono slate is full into the twenty-second century," she said. "Who's going to pay him? Pretty-boy Lionnel? You?"

When the intercom finally buzzed, it was Trina, not Dannow. "You got to get your ass home right now, girl." Trina was usually careful not to use street language when she talked to me, and I knew this wasn't a good sign.

"What's going on?" I demanded. "What's wrong?"

"The man," she said.

"The man?" I repeated to stall for time, although I knew exactly who she was talking about.

"The cops," she answered with exaggerated patience. "That little lady with the sparklin' personality and the—"

"Blais and Langley."

"Yeah. Them. They were here."

"But they aren't anymore?"

"He went with her in the ambulance, but there's another one—"

"The ambulance?"

"She got herself hurt. They were going into the cellar when one of the stairs came loose and she fell."

Those steep, narrow steps, no railing . . . "Is she okay? She's not? She isn't?"

"Nah, that kind always pulls through. Her leg was bent all around, and she was making a shitload of noise. Pissed as all hell. Said someone did it on purpose."

"Did what?"

"Screwed with the stairs. The uniform said it looked like someone pulled out the nails so the next person who came down would get themselves hurt—maybe even killed."

Someone pulled out the nails? I thought about angry creatures caught in a netherworld, neither here nor there, frustrated and enraged, fighting to keep what they believed to be theirs.

"Did they accuse you of doing it?"

"Not directly," Trina said. "But I got the distinct impression they're leaning that way. Said whoever did it was covering up the evidence against her."

"They had a search warrant?" I was surprised I was asking such logical and reasonable questions when my mind was racing with such illogical and unreasonable ones.

"You don't think I'd let them in without one, do you?"

Trina demanded indignantly. "You told me they were coming with one, so when they showed it to me, I told 'em it was cool. But now that they know I knew, they're busy digging my grave."

Digging.

CHAPTER NINETEEN

As I dodged the traffic crowding Dudley Square, I couldn't quite quell the uneasy sensation that I was somehow responsible for Blais' broken leg. I knew it had been an accident, an unfortunate accident, and that while it was true I had never wished the detective well, I had also never wished her ill. Her fall had nothing to do with me or Trina or Harden House or a ghost who inhabited the cellar. It had just happened. Things do just happen.

A few blocks beyond the square, I saw a lone little girl wearing a cloth coat at least three sizes too large for her slight frame. She crossed the battered asphalt, clutching a plastic lunch box and dragging the hem of her coat through the dirt. Sadness emanated from her like a bad aura. She was headed toward Garrison Elementary and was at least four hours late. Watching the tiny, dispirited form, it was clear her problems were far greater than mine. And far more real. There was no ghost, no one had killed Gram, and the police were mistaken about the broken step. In a structure as old as Harden House, hands—incorporeal or human—weren't necessary to cause a stair to fall apart. The stair was quite capable of falling apart all by itself.

But as I watched the little girl being swallowed by the oversized door of the school, I once again heard the voice from my dream. *"Sarah,"* the man had called out. *"Please help my brothers."* And although I knew he was just an errant flicker of my subconscious mind, I couldn't help but wonder if Sarah had been able to do as he had asked: if his last dying wish had ever been realized.

May 14, 1868

Papa is dead, and I have returned to Harden House. I feel little sadness at his passing and little joy at my homecoming. While I was gone, Papa became a great Colonel in the War Between the States, with many battles to his credit, but he lost his final battle to a flesh wound that never healed. Ironic that he too died of a gunshot. Ironic and fitting.

It has been more than eight years since I was sent from Harden House in disgrace, and more than eight years since I last spoke with you, dear diary. I found you just where I had left you, hidden beneath the brim of Mama's pink-and-white hat, nestled in the bottom of a box at the back of her closet. Silas' charm bag was there too. I placed the charm bag around my neck and shall wear it to my grave.

Much has changed since I left this place—a wrenching war has been fought in our great nation, with many lives lost and many freedoms won—but also, little has changed. Silas is still gone from me, now just bones huddling beneath the house, and only the merciful Lord knows where my poor Levi may be.

I now know the Lord is far less merciful than I once believed. A merciful Lord would never have taken my child from me nor allowed a man such as Silas to die before knowing Emancipation.

May 20, 1868

I am now twenty-seven years old, a spinster with much less ahead than behind. My brother, Caleb, too, has grown old, odd in his ways, and is without a wife. I presume he shall remain as such to the end of his days, as shall I. Perhaps the neighborhood children will grow frightened of us over the years, telling each other tales of the eccentric Mr. and Miss Harden, who busy themselves plotting ways to capture and torture small children. I smile sadly as I write these words, both because they are so fantastic and because they may become true.

Harden House is uncommonly still after Cousin Hattie's boisterous household, which was always full of children and servants and much comings and goings. I think I prefer it thus in my middle years, although I do miss the children, most especially Roderick, who reminds me of my own sweet Levi.

My time in Ohio, where I was "Auntie Sarie," as Baby Emma took to calling me from my first afternoon, is already far distant—eight full, long years, yet now fleeting and dreamlike. From the first, Cousin Hattie was kind and strove to include me in her busy life, but I was so dull at calling and dinner parties that, after a season, she finally yielded and allowed me to remain at home with the children, which is as it would have been either way, as the War ended social living as we knew it.

Cousin Hattie was never told the true reason for my extended visit, and although she may have guessed at a portion of my secret, it is certain she could never have imagined the horrible depth of the truth. It would have been a great relief to be able to reveal the bleakness that dwelled within me to such a kind soul as Hattie, but, of course, this was not possible.

Caleb is now the only one still alive who knows all that occurred in this house, but he has not spoken of it since my return, and I dare say he never will, for he is distant, ill at ease in my presence. He will not meet my eyes as we sit at dinner and does not wish to discuss great books as he did before I left.

For good and ill, I am alone with my memories, with the irrepressible burden of hidden truths, and I often wonder if these truths shall be my undoing. I like to think they were Papa's, and that the truth remains alive as a warning to those who would be driven by the hate in their hearts.

May 21, 1868

The War has brought many changes to these great United States and also to my small town of Lexington. Many of the faces with whom I was familiar are no longer here. Wendell Parker was killed at Gettysburg, Franklin Fiske at Second Manassas and Jedidiah Bridge at Antietam. It is said that dysentery took Quincy Clarke at Malvern Hill and no one is certain what felled the Esterbrook twins. Yet, as I had always longed for it to be, the Negro is now free, and I believe it was worth the price. If only Silas had been allowed to live to see it. If only I had listened to my dear husband. If only Papa had been the man I believed him to be.

Almost all of Mama's friends have passed on, and many of my own acquaintances have married and are busy with their lives and families in a manner I cannot be. Nancy Wallace, nee Southwick, now lives in Sudbury, almost a full day's ride, and she is the only one upon whom I might wish to call. I have let it be known that I am not well after my long journey home, and that I shall be unable to receive visitors or pay calls for at least three more weeks.

I sit alone in my room most of the day. My return to Harden House seems to be waking memories I had hoped would remain buried along with my poor Silas. The pain and horror of it all rises up to haunt my days and my nights, as fresh and as powerful as when it first happened. Perhaps I shall be allowed deliverance in madness.

"See?" Langley knelt down and pointed to the splintered wood along the edge of the stair.

I saw. The stair was torn apart, completely gone in the middle, obviously where Blais' foot had broken through. It looked raw, angry, menacing. "But she's okay?" I asked again, even though he had just told me Blais would be fine. "It was just her leg?"

"It was just her leg." Langley waved to three nails sticking meanly out of the left side of what remained of the tread. "It's possible these nails were purposely loosened."

I looked down at the nails and then over at Trina. She stood behind the detective, freshman attitude all over her face. She hadn't said a word since I walked in the door because Langley had come in right behind me. "This is an old house," I told him. "Things come loose all the time."

He nodded, as if he were seriously considering my words. "Yes. That's entirely possible too. The evidence techs will be here within the hour to take their samples. When all the lab work's done, we'll know what's what." He glanced up at Trina, who turned and stomped back to the west parlor. "Quite a chip that one's carrying around."

I didn't bother to explain about the abusive foster father, the drugs, the dead baby. It's not that Langley wouldn't have cared about the details of Trina's life, it is just that it wouldn't have made any difference. "She didn't do this."

"Did you?"

I looked him straight in the eye, the way innocent people and practiced criminals do on television. "No."

"Then who did?"

"No one," I said. "No one did anything here—it all just happened." But I couldn't stop myself from casting a nervous glance toward the old cellar and wondering if that was really what I believed.

"Look, Ms. Seymour—Lee," he corrected himself, holding my gaze, "your grandmother's dead and my partner's got a busted leg, so if you know something you're not telling, I think it's time to come clean."

So much for appearing innocent. I turned away and stared silently through the shadows to the uneven, earthen floor below. What I wasn't telling, he didn't want to know—and I didn't either. In the murky darkness beneath us, the dirt seemed jagged and unwelcoming, but certainly more welcoming than the detective's probing eyes. I leaned over, looking more closely into a place I didn't want to see. Then I jerked myself erect. There was something down there. Something caught on the edge of the lowest stair.

"You see something?"

I started slowly down the stairs, pressing my left palm to the fieldstone wall, feeling, as well as stepping, my way. The damp stones sent a chill through my hand, turning the bones inside my fingers icy cold. But it wasn't the dampness that numbed me, it was the feeling of dazed recognition seeping through me that congealed time and space, freezing me between here and there, between before and after.

Langley was right behind me. "What is it?" he demanded. "What's wrong?"

I kept moving stiffly downward, even though I knew what was there and knew I didn't want to find it or acknowledge the meaning of its presence. When my feet hit the cellar floor, I stopped and stared. In front of me was a small, red-flannel sack, old and stained by sweat, burned along the bottom.

"Ms. Seymour? Lee?"

I nudged the charm bag with the toe of my sneaker. Jesus.

"That the bag you were looking for the other night?" Langley asked.

I slowly reached down and picked up the tattered sack, pressing it tightly between my hands. Did this mean the impossible was possible?

May 23, 1868

The memories have not abated. If anything, they have grown more powerful, swirling around me like a maelstrom of pain, drowning my present in the horror of my past. I miss my dear Silas and my dear, dear Levi beyond all reason. I long for the love and the camaraderie Silas and I shared, the quiet hours reading by firelight, the stories told through the cold winter nights. I long for the weight of Levi in my arms, for his sweet baby smell, for the whisper of his breath on my neck. I long for my child, for my husband, for the life we should have had. I am full of anger as I press the charm bag to my breast, but mostly I am very, very sad.

I know it bodes ill for my sanity, but to soothe myself, I sometimes speak with Silas in my mind. I tell him of the smallest events of my day and of the deepest longings of my heart. I touch his charm bag through the fabric of my dress and tell him I love him and will keep him with me always.

Sometimes I imagine he hears me, answers me, that he is indeed still with me. I know this cannot be true, and instead of deluding myself with the pleasures of this falsehood, I turn my thoughts to a prayer that wherever Silas may be, he is finally a free man.

May 26, 1868

On Monday, I felt the touch of Silas' hand on my arm, on Tuesday, it was the brush of his lips along the back of my neck, and today, I heard his whisper in my ear. These imaginings are a great comfort to me, and although I may live within them more often than is wise, I find I am unable to stop the wash of belief that rises within me at these moments. I miss my dear husband so, and his companionship is such solace.

May 27, 1868

I went for a walk through the apple orchard today. The trees were in wild bloom and the fragrance was heady. I imagined the infant apples, tiny and determined, pushing from within to become round and rich and full of sweet juice. Soon I was crying, thinking of my precious Levi, wondering where he might be, how he might be growing. Then, with a certainty I cannot explain, I knew Silas was beside me. He took my hand and we walked to the edge of the orchard. "Do not cry," he whispered inside my head. "I am with you."

When I closed my eyes I could almost believe it was true.

May 28, 1868

I imagined Silas came to me as I worked on my needlepoint in the east parlor today. Again, it was while I was weeping, and again Silas told me not to cry, that he would never leave me. I know these visions are just the fantasies of my muddled brain, and yet he seemed so real, his words so clear.

I remind myself that Silas is not here. I was with him when he died, and I know where he lies.

CHAPTER TWENTY

The evidence techs were in the cellar for over an hour, and when they finally left, Langley did too. He took Trina with him, ostensibly to give her a ride back to SafeHaven because he "was going that way," but my guess was that he was looking for a chance to catch her with her guard down. Knowing how street-smart Trina was and how she felt about cops, I figured his chances were pretty much nil. Langley had been nice enough while he was at the house, polite and respectful to us both, but it was obvious he had a lot of suspicions, and, as good a suspect as I might make with my motive and opportunity, Trina's dark skin and drug use made her a far better one in his eyes. Even a nice cop can't help but think like a cop.

I punched the "play" button on the answering machine, and the blinking light disappeared as the tape rewound itself. I looked at the small red sack lying on Gram's blotter next to the telephone. Where had it gone when I lost it, and why had it been returned? I put the tattered bag under a pile of papers in the bottom desk drawer and closed the drawer with my foot.

The voice on the machine was Mike Dannow's. He apologized for not getting back to me sooner and said he would be in his office all afternoon. I was relieved to get his message, but instead of calling him, I looked up the number for the Lexington library. When the phone was answered, I asked for Ms. Tosatti, the librarian who had promised to try to find the Harden papers. At first she didn't remember who I was.

"Oh yes," she said after a long stretch of dead air. "Your name isn't Harden. You're the one whose grandmother gave some boxes to Nancy Winsten."

"It's really very important," I said, hoping she wouldn't ask why. I had no lie prepared, and the facts were too preposterous to state out loud. If I opted for truth, I would have to say, "You see, Ms. Tosatti, there's a ghost in my house, and I need to find out what's bothering him so I can get him to stop hurting people." Instead, I explained that I needed the papers right away, and that I'd be forever grateful for any help she could give me.

"I'm sorry I haven't called you back, but I don't have much to tell—nothing really. Nothing about your boxes anyway."

"But you found something?"

"Not me. One of the reference librarians came across it and—"

"Someone found something of my grandmother's?"

"Not of your grandmother's, I don't think, but it may have something to do with one of your other ancestors."

I felt like a dentist with pliers around a tough molar and remembered that Ms. Tosatti hadn't been easy to wrestle information from when we stood face-to-face. "What have you got?"

"It's very odd. No one seems to know exactly where the letter came from. Things got moved around a lot during the computerization—a lot more than necessary, if you ask me. Anyway, maybe this came from your boxes and maybe from somewhere completely different—a lot of people give old papers to the library, most of them not all that useful, and things do tend to get lost around here. Especially recently. Anyway, Mr. Sweeter, he's one of the volunteers to the archivist, happened to come across this letter and thought it was interesting so he showed it to Mrs. Schaye—that's the librarian I was telling you about. When I mentioned to her that you had been in asking about the Harden papers, she showed it to me."

"You've got a letter from one of my ancestors?"

"*To* one of your ancestors."

There must be hundreds of letters still in existence that had been written to any number of my ancestors, and I didn't hold out much hope this one would shed any light on the man in the cellar. "Who's it to?" I asked anyway.

"It's addressed to a Miss Sarah Harden, dated June 1860."

"Sarah Harden?" I repeated, not believing my luck. "Who's it from?"

"It isn't signed, but it appears to be from a Negro foundling home in Boston, responding to an inquiry from Maysville, Ohio."

The date and the Ohio address matched what Gram had told me about Sarah. I held my breath.

"It's very short," Ms. Tosatti continued. "Just says there's no record of a child named Levi placed with the home the previous summer."

I exhaled loudly. Very few blacks were able to read or write in 1860—in the South, it was actually against the law to teach slaves to read—and Sarah must have been writing in some poor woman's stead. This cryptic letter had most likely brought great sorrow to the grieving mother—and it wasn't making me too happy either. "That's all?"

"I'm afraid so," Ms. Tosatti said crisply.

I didn't want to appear ungrateful, so I swallowed my disappointment and asked, "Can I come down and take a look at it?"

The librarian sounded mollified by my request and assured me I could read the letter any time, although she reminded me it was the property of the library. Then she promised to "scout around" for the cartons, took down my number and said good-bye.

I slumped into the chair and tried to resign myself to the fact that I was not going to find the answers I sought. Although the charm bag was hidden in the closed drawer at my left ankle, not seeing it didn't stop me from feeling its presence, from knowing it was there, from wondering who else might be also.

I knew I couldn't go down that road, so I pulled myself up and dialed Dannow's number. When he picked up his phone, he sounded pleased to hear from me, but rushed and preoccupied. "Right," he said in a clipped, no-nonsense voice. "You're Kiah's friend. Talked to her this morning. Sounds like a mess. Want to tell me about it?"

I was surprised he wanted to jump right in. "To be perfectly honest, I don't think I really need a lawyer—this was Kiah's idea. If anyone needs a lawyer it's my friend Trina, Trina Collins, and I thought maybe you might be willing to help her. But, as I don't think there really was a crime, I don't think it's going to be necessary for you to help either of us."

"Let's hear the story before we decide who needs my help."

I recounted the events of the past eleven days as succinctly as I could. Dannow interrupted me a few times with questions, but mostly he just listened.

When I finished, he asked, "You ever say anything to the detectives about the missing bracelet?"

"It didn't seem important."

"So you didn't say anything?"

"No."

"So even without the bracelet, you're sure they're more focused on your friend Trina? Sure they like her for it better than you?"

"Reading a detective's mind isn't my area of expertise, Mr. Dannow, but Trina's a young, black, ex-drug addict with a manslaughter conviction who's currently living in a residential drug treatment facility. What do you think?"

"I think what's bad for her is good for you."

It seemed unnecessary to comment on such an insensitive statement—even if it was true—and I didn't know what to say anyway. I had no more experience with defense attorneys than I did with police detectives. "Does that mean you're not interested in helping her?"

"Here's what we do. I call my friend Steve Corr who's the lieutenant detective over there in Lexington. You and Trina go about your business."

"About our business?" I echoed.

"Corr's a good friend," he continued. "Skiing buddy. I'll be in touch after I've talked to him."

"But—"

"No point in going any farther 'til we know what the police've got. No point in wasting my time or your money. You're right. It'll most likely turn out neither of you'll need me."

"You really think so?"

"Doesn't matter what I think, Ms. Seymour. Matter's what the police think—and what they've got."

"Lee."

"Go to your office, Lee. See a movie with your husband. Work on that Underground Railroad project Kiah was telling me about. Look normal. Be normal. Assume everything is normal."

"But—"

"You going to be at this number all weekend?"

"Mostly."

"I'll call after I talk to Corr."

"Thanks," I said, but Dannow had already hung up.

I called SafeHaven to thank Kiah for hooking me up with Dannow and to make arrangements for Trina to come out to the house tomorrow. Without Trina, there was no way I'd be able to sort through Gram's system of no system. There was a ton of work to do before the inspection, and working hard seemed a good way to start trying to be normal. But my conversation with Kiah didn't go nearly as well as my conversation with Dannow. Trina had just been caught trying to pass Lionnel something through the kitchen window, and Kiah had put her on house restriction.

Trina wasn't going anywhere for the next two weeks.

Trina couldn't believe she hadn't known better. But of course she had, she knew what was happening, what was going to happen, she just hadn't wanted to admit it. Even to herself. Especially to herself.

All that whole time, while she was playing the game, mouthin' the words, actin' the act, pretendin' it could all be real, she had known in her gut that there was no chance. Still, she went on makin' believe like she was living in some little kids' fairy tale. And that's just what it turned out to be. The joke was on her.

So now she'd decided she wasn't gonna throw down for it any more. She finally had a way to get herself off the man's scope, and Lionnel was gonna help her get there. Even though Lionnel was no angel, he was smart, and she would be jetting out of here as soon as he got the sidewalks cleared.

First the cops said she killed Hendrika, then they liked her for Clara, and now with the bitch cop falling down the stairs and all the accusations flying, Trina was sure if she stuck around for long she'd be behind bars, that there was no way a sister could win at this game.

When they had come and told Kiah what they suspected, Kiah didn't even bother to say their thinking was screwed. Kiah believed she was smarter than everyone else, that she knew everything, just like Shirleen said about Trina, but with Kiah it was true. Ms. Oreo Kiah Wilkinson, always strutting around, showin' off, when all the time all she was doing was helping the white folks figure out how to lock up more black folks without the black folks getting riled about it.

Right before the cops showed, Kiah had caught Trina talking with Lionnel at the window. So she was already pissed off and had her mind all made up against Trina before it even got started.

"Girl, you have not changed," Kiah said to Trina in the kitchen after the man was gone. "And not changing is gonna get you right back where you were or put you in jail—or it's gonna get you dead."

Well, what did Kiah expect? Nobody changes. Nothing changes. It was what Trina knew all along.

"Go to your office," Mike Dannow had said. *"Work on that Underground Railroad project . . . Look normal. Be normal. Assume everything is normal."*

In the movies, the character who ignores her lawyer's advice always ends up in big trouble, and with Trina on house restriction, it was obvious which piece of Dannow's advice I needed to tackle first—but I didn't like it. I reminded myself this wasn't the movies, then sifted through the piles of papers on Gram's desk until I found a file labeled "cellar construction" in Trina's tiny handwriting. Gram didn't believe in files.

The largest single piece of Park Service paperwork that remained still undone was completing the forms that described the status of Michael's repair work to the cellar. I opened the file and scanned the packet of blank questionnaires, then I closed it and put it back on the desk. The movie character who ignores her gut feelings always ends up in big trouble, too.

I drummed my fingers on the manila cover, knowing I was going to have to fill out the forms sometime, and guessing if I waited too long, allowed myself to obsess too much, the task might never get done—and neither would the tunnel that had to be filled before Lexington Cement and Gravel showed up Sunday morning. Michael could be tied up with his mother for days, Trina was out of commission, and Beth was pretty much useless. I owed it to Gram to see her pet project through, but I didn't want to go into the cellar alone.

I reminded myself that there really was nothing to be afraid of. What did I have to worry about? A few dreams? A charm bag that had gone missing for a few days? I stood and tucked the file under my arm. If I was going to get into big trouble either way, I might as well err on the side of execution. I marched resolutely through the dining room, but when I reached the kitchen, I turned around and went back into the west parlor. I opened the bottom drawer of Gram's desk and scooped out the charm bag. I put it in my pocket. Whether for luck or protection, I wasn't certain.

As I stepped carefully around the missing stair tread, I

thought about Blais with her leg in a cast and wondered how it had happened, why it had happened. Maybe there were some things we weren't supposed to know. I touched the charm bag in my pocket, then flicked on the lights.

The illumination consisted of two bare bulbs: one in the new cellar, one in the old. Michael planned to install more light fixtures, but the electrician had shown up for two hours one morning and then never returned. Coils of wire were piled in the corner near the new sump pump, and a mass of thick cables hung from a metal box on the wall, but nothing was connected and puddles of standing water pooled on the floor. The light was feeble, just barely bright enough to read by, so I sat down on an empty spool to bring me closer to the bulb and squinted into the file.

I glanced at the gaping mouth of the tunnel to my right—a tunnel that may have once led the way to a man's freedom, a tunnel which that man might believe still did. Gram had tried to fill in the tunnel, and Gram had died in the attempt. Had the man been afraid she would block his way, stop him from reaching Canada, confine him to a life of slavery? Did he think he still needed to help his brothers? Would he continue to maim and kill until he succeeded? I forced my eyes back to the questionnaires.

It took almost an hour to fill out the forms, stipulating to the exact condition of each of Michael's repairs—although I did fudge on the status of the puddles and the tunnel, figuring that by the time the papers were submitted to the Park Service, the sump pump would be installed, the hole filled and the fieldstone wall reinforced with concrete. There were seven separate documents, three over five pages long, almost all the questions redundant, bureaucratic bullshit. Our tax dollars at work. I stood and stretched, annoyed by the task, but proud of having completed it—and of my ability to survive an hour alone in the cellar. There had been no sounds of digging, no ghostly sightings, no stairs ripped apart by incorporeal hands. Perhaps things were more normal than I had thought.

I glanced at my watch and saw that it was leaning toward dinnertime; I had forgotten to eat lunch, and my stomach rumbled now that I remembered. A shovel rested against the wall at my left, and two large piles of dirt lay in front of me. The tunnel opening yawned behind me; I could feel it, empty and waiting to be filled. I sighed and put the completed forms carefully down on the ground. I would dig for an hour, then take a dinner break and hope that Michael showed up; if he couldn't leave the hospital, I'd just have to finish the job myself. I took the charm bag from my pocket, pressed it between my palms, then put it back again.

The shovel was heavy in my hand. I bent my knees as Beth had instructed and reminded myself that nothing untoward had happened in the hour I had been in the cellar, and therefore nothing would now. I began to move dirt from the pile at my feet to the hole in the wall. It was easier than I had imagined, and I got into an almost pleasant rhythm: bend, push, scoop, raise, turn, dump, turn; bend, push, scoop, raise, turn, dump, turn. It was soothing, in a sweaty, dusty kind of way, flowing and repetitious, satisfying.

I was half-hypnotized within the cadence of my motions, feeling good, strong, capable, when I began to have the vague impression I wasn't actually accomplishing anything, that the tunnel wasn't getting filled. I double-checked and saw that the pile from which I was taking the dirt was growing smaller, and that the depth and width of the tunnel were too, so I went back to work. Bend, push, scoop, raise, turn, dump, turn.

Then I felt it again, this time as a certainty: the dirt wasn't staying where I was putting it. I was getting sloppy, or tired or hungry or all three, so I moderated the speed of my movements and promised myself I'd only work for a few minutes more. But even as I went more slowly, was more careful to put the dirt deep within the tunnel, when I turned back to the hole, my shovel brimming with dirt, the last shovel-load seemed to be at my feet.

I stared into the tunnel, at the soil on my shovel, at the growing pile of dirt on the earthen floor in front of the tunnel's mouth, and I deliberately placed the shovel into the hole. I patted down the dirt and this time did not turn away; I stood my ground and watched, still partially anesthetized by my rhythm, not knowing what I expected to see, not sure I was expecting anything. And that was what I got: nothing.

I picked up another shovel-load of dirt and started again. But on my third cycle, after I had swiveled and thrown the dirt into the tunnel, the dirt flew right back out at me, pummeling me with its power, stunning me with its force. I stood immobile, unbelieving, staring into the hole as small rocks and pieces of earth pelted my chest. Someone did not want the tunnel to be filled.

The dirt shot out with a fury, a viciousness—a hatred.

The base of the shovel quivered, then the whole thing jerked in my hands. It was as if someone were reaching out from inside the tunnel—from inside the grave—to seize it from me. To stop me. I flashed on Gram struggling against her invisible opponent, yelling at no one. Just as it was then, I now saw nothing, no one, only the penetrating blackness of the hole.

Then it came again: a powerful force on the other end of my shovel, pulling it, jerking it, trying to take it and stop me from filling the tunnel. My hands tightened on the handle, then when I realized what I was doing, what Gram had been doing, what was happening, I let go. The shovel hung in the air in a few seconds, defying gravity, then clattered to the ground. I turned and ran.

CHAPTER TWENTY-ONE

Lexington rush hour swirled around me: weary commuters, blank-faced behind tightly sealed automatic windows, listening to cerebral discussions on NPR or songs of their youth on classic rock; high school girls flirting with gangly boys smoking cigarettes; streams of young mothers dragging children to the bank or CVS, anxious to be done with their errands and home for dinner. It was amazing to me that the mundane world of the everyday could continue on so smoothly when my world had been rocked apart.

I was standing in front of the phone booth on Mass Ave, frantically searching my pockets for change. I needed thirty-five cents and didn't have my purse. I hadn't been thinking about purses and telephone calls when I raced out of the cellar—all I had been thinking about was getting as far as I could from whatever was down there.

An over-excited toddler bumped into my leg. His mother threw me a quick glance, grabbed the boy by the hand and led him hurriedly away. A black woman sitting at the bus stop looked at me suspiciously, turning as our eyes met. I didn't blame either of them; I would do the same had I been in their position. I was dirty and disheveled and obviously distraught. I probably looked deranged—and perhaps I was. Dotty Aunt Hortense.

I finally found two quarters in the back pocket of my jeans. I dropped them into the coin slot and punched Beth's number. Beth's son Zach answered and regaled me with the details of his baseball game. I waited as patiently as I could without screaming through the description of his three RBIs and his best friend's game-winning catch, then asked for his mother. When Beth came to the phone, I said, "I need you to pick me up right away."

"Where are you?"

"In Lexington Center. At the bus stop in front of Depot Square."

"I'll be there in ten minutes."

I sank gratefully into the bench at the bus stop. The woman who had been watching me moved to the far end, presumably to put more distance between us, but I didn't care. Beth was coming to get me. She hadn't asked any questions, and she hadn't hesitated; she had just said she would be here. If home was where they had to take you in, family was who came to get you without asking why. When Beth's Range Rover pulled up in front of me, I jumped in before she could come to a full stop.

"Well, aren't we all gussied up," Beth said, running a critical eye over my dirt-streaked clothes. "There's something on your left cheek."

"The least of my worries," I said, but swiped at my cheek with the back of my hand.

Beth drove me home without saying a word. She parked in the driveway behind my car and turned off the key. "Want to tell me what this is all about?"

I stared through the windshield at Harden House. It looked so inviting, so warm and cozy; even the paint flaking on the front door was appealing. "I read an article in the *Globe* about a bunch of theologians and physicists who got together at MIT last week to see if they could find any common ground in their work."

"And that's why you had me leave my dinner and pick you up in Lexington Center?"

"One guy was talking about how he saw the glory of God in the workings of the universe, in the goodness of the human soul."

"Lee . . ."

"And then this scientist gets up and says that the soul is nothing more than a series of electrical impulses. A collection of memories."

"Is this about your ghost?"

"I got a book from the Lexington library that says that a ghost is the emotional memory of a person who died under tragic circumstances."

"And you believe everything that you read?"

I looked down at my hands; dirt underlined my fingernails and clumped between my fingers. "I felt him," I whispered.

"You mean his spirit? His emotional memory?"

"I know it sounds crazy, but just now, right before I called you, I was down in the cellar, filling the tunnel. I was putting the dirt in, and everything seemed to be going fine and then, and then it was like the dirt wouldn't stay—like it wasn't staying where I was putting it."

"Where was it going?"

"Out. All of a sudden, it started to fly back out at me—I mean really flying. At my face. All over. It was like it was being blown out by something really powerful, really angry. Something that didn't want the dirt there. And then, then I felt someone grab the other end of the shovel. He yanked on it, like he wanted to take it from me, and I started to pull it back, but then I realized I was acting just like, just like . . ."

"Just like Gram."

My hands began to tremble.

"Shit," Beth said. "Wow." She roped her fingers through

mine. "You look tired. How about spending the night with us? I'll run in and get your things—you can wait in the car."

I didn't answer. I just held onto Beth's hand and watched the facade of Harden House. Was something evil hiding behind those innocent, weathered clapboards? Cars rumbled past, music blared from an open window, two little girls argued with each other about a lost shoe, and the setting sun spread twilight over the neighborhood. Harden House watched me back.

I turned to Beth. "I thought you had some big mucky-muck gala tonight?"

"Russ got us out of it."

"I thought Russ loved that stuff?"

Beth let go of my hand and shrugged. "You want me to go in?"

I hesitated, then said, "I'll go with you."

"I don't know if that's such a great idea . . ."

"It's the getting back up on the horse thing," I told her with more confidence than I felt. "If I don't go back in now, I'm afraid I'll never be able to get myself to walk in there again." I opened the car door and dropped down to the driveway. I started toward the house.

Beth followed me to the back door. We stood silently staring through the window into the kitchen. "Looks pretty harmless to me," she finally said.

"It does, doesn't it?" I agreed, but neither of us moved.

"Unless, of course, the woman with the iron teeth is hiding in there—then we'll really have something to worry about."

I was beginning to feel foolish, to wonder what had in fact happened in the cellar, what was real and what I might have imagined. "Maybe it was the woman with the iron teeth who was pulling on my shovel," I suggested, trying to show Beth that I was maintaining my sense of humor. "Maybe she finally wants that dental work."

Beth walked into the kitchen and surveyed the room with exaggerated thoroughness, then held the door open. "I think the coast's clear," she said.

"So this parapsychologist guy really says doing renovations upsets the ghosts?" Beth asked, flipping through the pages of Holzer's book.

"He claims they get dislodged by all the activity. Wakes them up, I guess," I said. We were sitting in the west parlor, drinking tea and eating cookies.

"Nasty shock."

"I guess. The ghost doesn't know where he is—he's confused, lost, has no clue he's in a different time. So he thinks the people in the 'now' are where he is—or was—and that they're messing with his space and his things."

"He doesn't know he's dead?" Beth appeared to be growing more interested, more believing.

As Beth's acceptance increased, I felt mine diminishing, and I remembered that this was the pattern we had followed in our last conversation on the subject. "How can anyone know they're dead?"

Beth snapped the book closed and tapped the cover with her fingernail. "But the reason he's a ghost in the first place is because something bad happened to him, right? Isn't that what you said? He's a ghost because he was murdered or something?"

" 'Caught in a web of his unresolved emotions at the time of his physical death.' " It sounded like such nonsense.

"So he's got a score to settle?" There were two bright circles of color on her cheeks are she leaned toward me. "He's wants revenge?"

"Or he's just trying to get a job finished."

"Like digging the tunnel?"

I didn't answer.

"This actually makes sense," Beth said, her voice rising with excitement. "A runaway slave, who was hiding in the house and digging a tunnel to get farther away, was killed by some anti-abolitionists, and his unhappy, restless spirit, which has been sleeping in the cellar for all these years, was finally awakened by the construction! This could be the answer to the question you asked the other day about why now and not before. This could be the answer to a lot of things."

"I doubt it."

"Don't you see? This is why he killed Gram! He thought she was trying to stop him from digging his tunnel, trying to keep him a slave. And that policewoman—he messed with the stairs so no one else would be able to get down and bother him!"

"I don't think so."

"Well, then why'd you run out of the house and need me to pick you up?"

"It sounds so ridiculous when you put it into words."

"You've got a better explanation?"

"The stair broke because the house is old," I said. "Gram took too many blood-pressure pills."

"Or she was scared to death."

I slumped in my chair. "Maybe I did get the Dotty Aunt Hortense gene. Maybe I've been imagining it all."

"Well," Beth said with mock seriousness, "that's always a possibility."

I smiled weakly. "I'm tired. Tired and hungry and all wrung out—I don't know what I think about anything anymore."

"Well then how about Trina? Maybe there aren't any ghosts and you aren't losing your mind. Maybe it's like the cops think: Gram caught Trina stealing the bracelet so Trina killed her and then broke the stairs to keep the police from finding something incriminating in the cellar."

"That's ridiculous," I snapped. "Listen to what you're saying. It makes even less sense than what you were saying before and has nothing to do with the dirt. And anyway, the cops don't know about the bracelet."

"Don't you think you should tell them? You might be withholding important evidence."

"It's not relevant."

"You obviously didn't see Trina's face the first time she noticed that bracelet hanging out of Gram's jewelry box."

"That doesn't mean anything."

"You've got to face the fact that Trina's an ex-drug addict without a lot of options."

"She's got SafeHaven." And possible access to cocaine.

"My point exactly."

I was too weary to argue, to play my usual role in our ongoing liberal vs. conservative debate. "I'd rather believe in ghosts."

Beth took my remark as a concession to her superior logic and nodded graciously. "So where does that leave us?"

"Damned if I know." But as I said the words, I was overcome by that creepy, shivery feeling that someone was watching me. That sixth sense that tells you someone else is in the room. I swung around in panic. Michael was leaning against the doorjamb; he looked tired, but not devastated. I closed my eyes in relief.

"Damned if you know what?" he asked.

I jumped up. "How's your mom?" I came around the desk toward him, then stopped, not knowing what to do:

hug him? shake his hand? wave? I stood awkwardly behind Beth's chair.

"Good," he said. "Much better than they expected. The doctor gave me the usual 'the next 24 to 48 hours will tell the tale,' but I think she's going to pull through just fine."

I decided to give him a hug. "I'm so happy," I said, pulling away quickly.

"Me too," he said.

Beth stood and picked up the cups from the desk. "I'm happy too, Michael. It's great news. I'm just going to go make us another pot of tea."

I waved him into Beth's chair when she left the room. "Sit," I said. "You look exhausted."

He sat. "So do you."

"A fine pair." I settled into the chair next to his. "Tough day all around, I guess."

He leaned over and touched my thigh lightly; I felt a tingle outlining the place where his fingers had been. "Did something else happen?" he asked.

"Later," I said. "Tell me about your mother."

He explained that the operation had run an hour shorter than expected, which cut down considerably on the trauma, and his mother had come through it remarkably well. She had been awake and lucid when he left the hospital, ordering him to go home and get some sleep and not to show his face in her room until tomorrow.

"She sounds pretty tough."

"Oh, she's one tough old bird, all right." Michael ran his fingers through his scraggly hair, which was in desperate need of a good cut. "But I'm going to stay with her all day tomorrow—no matter what she says." My face must have registered disappointment at his words, because he added, "But I'm here now to get going on closing up that tunnel."

He seemed to notice the dirt on my clothes for the first time. "Have you been digging?"

I nodded.

"And that's why you had a bad day?"

"Part of it."

He leaned back in his chair and lifted an ankle to his knee. "Then I think it's your turn to—"

A scream pierced the air, high and thin and full of terror. Before either of us could move, Beth stumbled into the parlor. She was holding her right arm stiffly in front of her. It was bleeding profusely.

I ran to the doorway and grabbed her before she could fall. "Beth, honey, what happened? Are you okay?"

"The knife," she gasped, her face an ashy gray. "It cut me."

Michael ripped his jacket off and twisted it around Beth's arm, trying to staunch the flow of blood, but there was so much of it, more and more pulsing out with each beat of her heart. I raced to the bathroom for towels, and when I returned, he was leading Beth to the chair. He replaced his bloody jacket with a towel and twisted again. "Breathe deep," he told her. "Breathe deep and try to stay calm."

I dialed 911, begged them to come right away, then knelt down next to Beth's chair. "Just hang in there, honey, the ambulance will be here in a minute."

She looked at me as if she hadn't heard me talking to the dispatcher. "The knife attacked me." The sentence began as a murmur and ended as a wail. "It leapt out of the rack and came after me. It slashed my arm as if it knew I was there—as if it could see me!"

I wrapped my arms around her and glanced over her head at Michael. He looked as concerned as I felt. "Don't worry about it now, honey," I said, trying to calm her. "You're probably in shock. Let's get you to a hospital and then we can talk about what happened."

"No!" Beth screamed, her voice laced with hysteria. "You don't understand. You're not listening to me. The knife came at me out of nowhere. It wasn't being held by anyone!"

It took a few moments before I understood what she was saying. "You mean . . . ?" I began, then stopped. "You don't mean?"

"It was your ghost," she said in a raspy whisper. "It had to be."

CHAPTER TWENTY-TWO

The plastic chairs in the emergency room were lined up in haphazard rows facing a television set mounted near the ceiling. Although there was no way any normal-sized person could reach the "on" button, and there didn't appear to be a remote control anywhere, the TV was turned on and it was loud. The show was about a trio of young couples—all of whom fought a lot and looked alike—and it featured one of the worst laugh tracks I'd ever heard. Michael and I were waiting for the surgeon to finish suturing Beth's arm.

The ambulance had brought Beth to the hospital; Michael and I had followed in his truck. After a quick preliminary examination, the doctor had assured me Beth was going to be fine: she was just going to need a lot of stitches. He said I could sit with her in the curtained cubicle, which I did for a while, but I left when they started sewing. I had seen enough gore for one day. Russ was on his way.

There were only three other people in the waiting room: a father and his son, who seemed far too lively and rambunctious to be very sick; and an old man who was asleep in the front row, oblivious to the fake laughter blaring from the TV over his head. Michael and I sat in the back.

"Do you think it really could've been a ghost?" I asked, keeping my voice low so no one but Michael would hear my question. "Does any of this make any sense to you?" On the drive to the hospital, I had told him everything that had happened since he left Harden House last night.

"We live, we die," Michael said. "I don't think it's deep,

and I don't think we're special to anyone but ourselves. I don't believe in an eternal soul or a personal God or any of the shit they tried to stuff down my throat when I was a kid."

"Doth the gentleman protest too much?"

He stretched his arm across the back of my chair. "Yesterday, I would've told you there was no way a ghost was wandering around that house."

"And today?"

"I don't know," he said. "After what just happened, I've got to tell you, I'm not all that sure anymore."

"Me either." I lay my head on his shoulder and stared at the TV, but even though the show was clearly pegged to the intelligence level of an eight-year-old, I couldn't follow it.

"I keep running through it," Michael said, "and there seem to be only three possibilities." He held up three fingers and ticked them off as he spoke. "One, someone came into the kitchen, tried to sever Beth's arm, then ran away; two, Beth tried to sever her own arm; or three, the ghost did it. Number one is clearly the most rational explanation—except for the fact that Beth didn't see anyone going in or out of the house, and neither did either of us—and, as I can't imagine Beth inflicting that kind of injury on herself, that leaves number three."

"I'll take number four."

"What's number four?"

"Damned if I know."

"Seems like this is where I came in."

For a moment I was confused, then I remembered: just a couple of hours earlier, Michael had come into the west parlor as I was telling Beth that I'd be damned if I knew what it all meant. "Circles," I said. "We're just going around in circles."

We both stared at the television screen, and I could tell Michael didn't understand what was happening on the show any better than I did.

"But why would the ghost go after Beth?" I asked. "I can almost see why he might want to hurt Gram—if he actually is a runaway slave and she was filling in the tunnel he was digging to escape—and it's the same with the stair. He might have pulled it apart to keep people away from his tunnel, but why attack Beth in the kitchen? How did she threaten him?"

"You've got to remember we're just seeing one side of the story—what it looks like to us may not be what it looks like to him."

I sat up and stared at Michael, astonished by his words. "You say that as if you really believe it."

He shrugged. "Like I told you before, just because I don't believe in something doesn't mean I don't want to talk about it."

I put my head back on his shoulder, relieved that a man as sensible and grounded as Michael Ennen could be thinking the same insane thoughts that I was. "I've got this feeling that it's all somehow wrapped up with Sarah Harden. The man was calling out to her, asking her to help his brothers . . ." I let my words trail off, afraid I was going too far.

But Michael didn't seem to think so. "Maybe Sarah was more active in the Underground Railroad than anyone in your family ever knew. It makes sense if her father was a big abolitionist that she might have been one too."

"I keep wondering if she was ever able to save the brothers."

It was a clear conversation stopper, and we watched the young father valiantly trying to distract his squirming son with the bright-colored ads in an old *Time* magazine. The little boy ripped the magazine from his father's hand. "Who's this?" he demanded, pointing his pudgy finger at the enlarged, blurry photograph on the cover. It was a picture of James Byrd, the black man who had been dragged to his death on the back fender of a white supremacist's car. "I don't remember his name," the father said, "but a very bad thing happened to him. Very, very bad." He quickly opened the magazine and showed his son an advertisement for a Lexus SUV. "Isn't this a pretty car?" he asked. The little boy wiggled out of his arms and began to jump on a nearby chair.

"From the way you've described him," Michael said, "the runaway slave in your dream doesn't sound like the vengeful type, so maybe Sarah was never able to do anything to help his brothers. Maybe that's why he's still hanging around."

"According to Hans Holzer—the guy who wrote that book we were talking about the other day—tragic death is the most common reason a person becomes a ghost in the first place. He says the ghost's caught by the violence of his death, unable to 'move on.' So from that perspective, the revenge motive doesn't work. He wouldn't know if she saved his brothers or not because it happened later." I couldn't believe I was using Holzer's theories to buttress my argument as if he were a reliable source.

"Maybe it's like you were saying the other night, maybe the ghost's so confused about what's happening to him—where he is in time and space, who we are—that he doesn't know what he's doing, that he doesn't know he's hurting people."

"The guy I saw digging looked like he knew what he was doing. He looked mad enough to annihilate the entire white race."

"It could've been frustration."

I thought about the fury that filled every muscle of the man's massive body, the anger in every movement. I slumped in my chair. "If we follow that logic chain, our next step is to go down there and explain it all to him—that's supposed to be the only way to free him and let him move on." I wasn't going into the cellar to talk to that man, even if it did bring him the freedom that had eluded him for his entire life—and for his entire afterlife. He scared the shit out of me.

Michael put his arm around me and drew me close. "We don't have to figure this all out tonight," he said, brushing my hair back from my forehead.

"Sarah," I mumbled into his shirt. "Somehow it all goes back to Sarah Harden."

June 2, 1868

The weather has been most pleasant, and every day this week I have walked through the apple orchard, smelling the new fruit hiding within the elbows and fingers of the gnarled trees, holding Silas' hand in mine. I tell him of my days, but not of my heart, for I am afraid to be as open as I might be. Silas does not seem to know of Levi, as perhaps he would not, having died months before the babe was born, and I do not wish to remind him of the boy, as then I shall have to tell him it was I who lost his child.

Instead, this afternoon I told Silas about my recent discovery that Nancy Wallace, nee Southwick, was correct when she told me so many years ago that George Elliot was a woman. Silas was no more surprised in my imagination than he would have been in life. "More is possible than you might think," he told me kindly. "Perhaps you, too, could become a famous writer."

I started to laugh at his silliness, but then, right before my eyes, Silas began to change! He grew more solid, more opaque, most real. At first, I was suffused with happiness, believing my husband was returning to me, but then I saw that Silas' features were taking on a hardness I did not remember in life, and I knew something was not right.

And it was not, for the voice that spoke from Silas' mouth did not belong to my husband. "Much more would be possible if men like your father allowed it to be so," the man who would be Silas spat, his eyes icy cold. "Your wonderful Papa may think he has stopped me, but he has not! Nor, as God is my witness, shall he stop my brothers!"

I cried out in alarm, reaching to take Silas' hand. But there was no one there. I was standing alone amidst the neat rows of apple trees.

June 3, 1868

All week, Caleb has been watching me with a worried countenance. "Are you ill, Sister?" he asked just this morning. "You are pale and seem disturbed by the slightest of noises."

This was perhaps the longest speech Caleb had made since my arrival, and I was touched by his concern. I assured him I was fit, although I know I am not.

June 4, 1868

I have come to the difficult decision that I must cease my conversations with Silas. It shall be extremely painful for me to be alone again, but it is for the best. I fear I am making myself mad, for I am beginning to believe that Silas is actually, really and truly, here with me, that he is still alive, even though I know not who, or what, he may be.

I shall also admit to you, dear diary, that sometimes I believe Levi is with me also, right here at Harden House! And at this thought I become most distraught, for if I believe Silas is with me, and I know Silas to be dead, what does that portend for my sweet baby?

June 5, 1868

I wake in the darkest hours of the night to the distant scrape of metal against metal, of stone against stone. The sounds come from deep within the house and can be none other than Silas digging his tunnel.

I tell no one, for these are not the sounds made by a man who is at peace; these are the sounds made by a man full of hatred and vengeance. A man to be feared.

Michael and I drove back from the hospital in silence. It was a thoughtful, tired silence, not quite comfortable, but not really uncomfortable either, tinged with a tightness, a subtle tension that was both nervous and nice. We weren't discussing it, but we both knew he was spending the night. There was no way I was staying alone after what had happened to Beth, and Michael had once told me his studio apartment in Brighton was barely big enough for him and the cockroaches.

Russ had arrived at the hospital just as the nurse was helping Beth to the waiting room. He looked terrible, worse than I had ever seen him: unshaven and red-eyed and clearly very upset. He blustered until the doctor came out and assured him that Beth was perfectly fine. Twenty-seven stitches, but a clean cut that would heal quickly, a scar that would fade with time.

Then there was some problem with the insurance. Michael and I sat with Beth while Russ argued with a weary administrator. Beth had allowed her husband to bundle her into the blanket he had brought with him—why, I wasn't really clear—without any of her usual wisecracking. She was pale and looked depleted, perhaps still a little scared. And who could blame her? I put my arm around her, and she rested her head on my shoulder.

Russ finally told us to leave, that it was going to take longer than he had anticipated. The administrator was saying something about being sorry and canceled subscriptions, but Russ waved him into silence.

"Bureaucracy," he muttered to me. "Fucking bureaucrats."

I had never heard Russ swear like that before and decided it was best for us to take our leave. I kissed Beth and told her I'd call in a couple of hours. She nodded absently and closed her eyes.

Michael pulled the truck into the driveway behind Beth's Range Rover. Although I had more reason to be afraid now, I wasn't as frightened as I had been earlier, sitting in the Rover with Beth. I was either worn down by all that had happened or had acquired a protective numbness as a result of it. Either way, it was a relief to look at the house and just see home.

Michael cleared his throat. "I'll come in with you."

"Thanks." I jumped down from the truck, but waited for him to come around to my side before I started toward the house.

As we approached the back door, I took Michael's hand, but when we got inside, I gasped and dropped it. I had forgotten about the blood. It was on the countertop and on the wall behind the sink and all over the refrigerator door. It was on the floor, a wide trail of rusty brown leading across the kitchen to the dining room, and I knew, although I couldn't see it from where I stood, into the west parlor.

Michael gently led me toward the east parlor. "You sit

in here, and I'll clean it up."

I dropped into the old chesterfield, but shook my head. "You sit, too," I said, then added, "Please." But before he could, the telephone rang.

"Stay," Michael ordered. "I'll get it." He returned in a minute with the portable phone from the kitchen. "For you. A Mr. Dannow's office."

Dannow started speaking as soon as I said hello. "Just got off the phone with Steve Corr."

"Steve Corr?"

"The lieutenant detective. Lexington police. Wouldn't tell me much, but confirmed what you said."

"Confirmed what I said?" I was having trouble following him.

"About the black girl, the junkie. That's who they like."

"Ex-junkie."

"You've got to tell them about the missing bracelet."

"Trina didn't steal the bracelet."

"Doesn't matter. Still looks bad."

"I don't want to make it look bad for her."

"Yes you do. They like you too. Just not as much."

"Trina didn't kill Gram."

"The toxicology report is still pending and they don't have any solid evidence against either of you—yet. Just lots of suspicion—and the bracelet would add weight to the other side. You think about it over the weekend. I'm meeting with Steve first thing Monday morning."

"I doubt I'll change my mind."

"What if I told you I was going to need a 10,000 dollar retainer if Lexington goes after you?"

"Ten thousand dollars?"

"Like I said, they haven't got any evidence, so I wouldn't lose any sleep over it just yet." Dannow's voice was a bit slower and more kind. "I just want you to understand what you might be up against." He promised to call Monday after he spoke with Corr and hung up.

I put the phone on the coffee table and looked up at Michael, who had been watching me closely throughout the conversation.

He sat down on the chesterfield and took my hand. "That was the lawyer?"

"He wants me to make Trina look bad so that I look good."

"You already look good."

I smiled wanly. "Oh yeah." I glanced down at my T-shirt and jeans, at the dirt that still outlined my fingernails. "I'm looking real good."

Michael put his arm around me and pulled me to him. "You poor kid," he said. "You're having one hell of a time."

"Hey, I'm older than you are," I said, wanting diversion, needing diversion. I leaned back and batted my eyelashes at him in exaggerated coquettishness. "Robbing the cradle, Gram would say."

"Your grandmother wouldn't have minded a bit." Gram had never been shy about her opinions, and Michael was well aware of her schemes for the two of us. "She'd be thrilled if she could see us now."

"Maybe she can," I continued to tease, then dropped my head into my hands at my double entendre. "What does it all mean?" I mumbled. "What could it possibly mean?"

Michael raised my chin until I was looking at him. "Maybe we're not supposed to know—and that's why it's so confusing."

But I didn't want to be confused. I didn't want to think about the impossible being possible or missing bracelets or murder suspects or anything that wasn't directly related to Michael Ennen and what it felt like to touch him, to be touched by him. I reached up and pressed my hand to his cheek, then I kissed him. It was a long kiss, deep and dark and swirling. It made me think of chocolate, of losing myself, of swimming in thick, rich candy. When it was over I knew I was going to make love to this man, that he was going to make love to me.

I stood and took his hand. I led him up the stairs and into my bedroom.

"I've imagined being here with you like this," Michael said gruffly, and I realized that I had imagined it too. He pressed his lips to the soft spot at the base of my throat, and I moaned. "Let's go slow," he said. "Real slow."

When Michael and I finally fell asleep the clock was moving toward three. I didn't want the night to end, but exhaustion overcame me, and I fell into that deep, delicious sleep of the truly contented. I was so relaxed, so weighted by the luxurious heaviness of slumber, that I knew I must be dreaming when I heard his voice.

"Sarah." The voice was deep and filled with pain. "I can't find you."

He stood at the foot of my bed, his skin the color of milk chocolate, his cheekbones high, his eyes full of intelligence and anguish. He had a bewildered gentleness—almost a boyishness—about him, and he seemed to be lost. He was, and wasn't, the man I had seen in my dreams.

"I've lost my charm bag," he told me, pointing at the open neck of his shirt. "I don't know where I am."

I looked over at Michael, but he was out cold. So I sat up, pulling the sheet with me to cover my nakedness. "You're still at Harden House."

"But then where are you?"

"I'm at Harden House, too."

He shook his head sadly. "You and I are not in the same place anymore. I want us to leave for Kansas Territory, I'm ready to go now, but I don't know how to find you. Tell me where you are," he pleaded. "Tell me so I can come get you."

"I have your charm bag," I said.

He appeared puzzled, as if remembering but not remembering, grasping at something that didn't make sense. "I gave it to you?" he asked, and as he spoke, something cold fell over his features. Something that scared me.

"I think you gave it to Sarah," I told him, despite the dread growing within me. I was remembering and not remembering too, reaching toward the knowledge of a fleeting fragment, but not able to catch it. I wanted to know. And I wanted him to know.

"You are Sarah," he insisted, his jaw tightening, his eyes flashing steely and hard.

I looked down at Michael, hoping for help, but there was none. I took a deep breath. "I think you gave your charm bag to Sarah right before you died."

"Died?" His question rumbled low in the back of his throat.

"Yes," I whispered through my fear.

"I am not dead!" he bellowed at me, every muscle of his body, every emotion of his soul, fueled with fury. "I'm as alive as you are!"

I scuttled backward on the bed, away from him, afraid of him, of what he might do to me. Then, slowly, tentatively, I reached my hand out to touch this man who had come searching for Sarah, and had, instead, found his own death.

But my fingers closed on nothing. He was gone.

CHAPTER TWENTY-THREE

June 7, 1868

Caleb has been trying to cheer me, bringing me stalks of the fresh asparagus he knows I love and even attempting conversation at dinner. Yesterday he gave me a copy of a new novel by Louisa May Alcott, who lives right here in Concord. It is called Little Women, *and we chuckled over how Papa would disapprove. It did feel nice to smile, and I am touched by Caleb's kindness, yet none of it makes much of a difference.*

At luncheon today, Caleb told me he had something to show me that would please me. Although I appreciate his attempt to lighten my load, I find it difficult to even feign curiosity for I cannot imagine there is anything left on this earth that could bring joy to my frozen heart.

I tell Caleb I must rest before his mystery is unveiled.

June 7, 1868 (evening)

Oh, my dear diary, my hand trembles so as I write to you of my most wonderful news. I do not know where to begin, just as I did not know where to begin when I had my sad story to tell. So I shall start at the beginning, just as I did then, but, oh, my dearest, dearest diary, the end of this story is so gloriously different from the end of the tale I told you before.

Remember I spoke of Caleb's mystery, the mystery I did not believe could bring me joy? Well, Caleb knew of what he spoke, and he revealed to me the most wonderful secret there could be. You must bear with me, for in my delirium, I get ahead of myself.

After my nap, I came into the west parlor, where Caleb sat behind Papa's desk. I hate to be within the walls of that room, even the smallest whiff of its dusty scent brings forth memories I only wish to suppress, so I refused my brother's offer to sit in the leather wing chair and quickly agreed to accompany him on a trip to the old carriage house, never guessing what awaited me.

The carriage house is out beyond the barn, and although I do remember farm hands sleeping there during harvest time and seasonal machinery being stored there, I do not remember it ever being used for carriages. Still, it was always called the carriage house. Please bear with me again, dear diary, for now my folly is not that I get ahead of myself, but that I digress. Please forgive this silly, silly, happy woman.

I don't think I have ever seen Caleb so skittish; one moment he was grave and somber and the next he was all aflutter. A quiet, sickly boy, coddled by our mother and belittled by our father, Caleb has grown into a quiet, solemn man. But as we walked across the lawn and around the barn, he practically danced with impatience, and his face was flushed with excitement. Then he abruptly sobered and said, "I want you to prepare yourself, dear sister. What I have to show you may be very upsetting."

Despite the dullness of my emotions, I was pleased to see Caleb so cheerful. "Upsetting?" I asked, a touch of chiding in my voice. "You appear rather light-hearted to be showing your sister something that might upset her."

He stopped walking and grabbed my shoulders. His grip was tight on the sleeves of my dress, his fingers pressing into the flesh of my arms. "Sarah, I have done something that would horrify many," he told me. "I have defied our father, schemed and told many untruths, even to you, but I do not believe I have done wrong." He raised his chin and his eyes blazed deep into mine; it was as if the brother I had always known was no more, as if

Caleb had become someone else entirely, someone driven and passionate, almost frenzied. "I dare say you shall ultimately agree with me," he continued, "but my actions may well result in as much calamity as joy for us all."

His intensity scared me. "Calamity?" I repeated. "Brother, what have you done?"

Caleb's countenance shifted again, and he smiled awkwardly. "Perhaps it is best if we discover the joy before we worry about the calamity," he said, then led me through the open door of the carriage house.

A flight of rickety stairs hugged the left side of the large room, leading to a loft that had been made into a warren of tiny bedchambers for the hired help. Caleb motioned me to follow him. We climbed the stairs in silence, the pounding of the blood in my ears the only sound of which I was aware. For comfort, I had placed Silas' charm bag into the pocket of my skirt, and as I climbed, I pressed it between my fingers, for an alarming mixture of fear and jubilation was filling my chest. Although I did not know what I would find at the top of the stairs, a part of me suspected, and I was terrified by the hope that rose within me. I wanted so much for the impossible to be possible.

When we reached the landing, Caleb turned to me. "There is someone I want you to meet." His eyes were both bright with anticipation and hooded with apprehension. "But he is unaccustomed to strangers. Actually, he isn't accustomed to anyone but Minna and me, and he is quite young, younger and smaller than one might expect for his—"

"He?" I interrupted, my heart pounding so loudly I could barely hear myself speak. I grabbed Caleb's arms, as much to grab his attention as to steady myself so I would remain erect. "Who is he?" I couldn't bear to think what I was thinking. I couldn't bear to think it and have it not be true.

Caleb did not answer me. He knocked lightly at the door to his left and pushed it open. The room was larger than I expected, brighter, and filled with familiar furniture and toys. The old brass bed from our nursery stood under a row of narrow windows, and a small boy sat upon it; he was holding a book on his lap and appeared to be reading, although he seemed far too young to read The Last of the Mohicans. *When he saw Caleb, he jumped up with a broad smile, but when he saw me, he paled and scrambled under the bed, trying to hide himself.*

"There's nothing to fear, Ulysses," Caleb said softly, crouching down by the bed. "This lady is my sister. She's come a long way to meet you."

The little boy peered out from under the blanket, and there was something in his large brown eyes that tore a hole through the center of my being.

"Ulysses?" I whispered to my brother, my eyes never leaving the boy's face.

Caleb gently pulled Ulysses upright and placed his hands protectively on the boy's shoulders. "It is your own Levi."

June 16, 1868

It has been over a week since I last wrote, a week full of wonder and great happiness the like of which I have not known since those few precious winter days with Silas nearly nine years ago. That which I have longed for, dreamed for and prayed for, but never truly believed would transpire, has come to pass. My Levi has come back to me. My own boy. My heart.

My dear brother was unable to give up the tiny babe to the bleakness of the Negro foundling home. Instead of leaving his nephew in that sad warren of little rooms as Papa had ordered, Caleb kept him, finding a Negro woman to care for him and hiding him in the carriage house for eight long years. In all that time, no one but Caleb and Minna knew of Levi, now Ulysses, for fear of our father's fury. But Minna and Caleb cared for him well, doing as best they could with so little, and although Levi—Ulysses—is small for his age and in great need of both food and learning, he is a wonderful child, slightly bewildered, but full of warmth and intelligence. He reminds me of his father.

Caleb says that he wanted to write me of Levi while I was in Ohio, that he could only imagine the depth of my pain, but he is a cautious man and decided it would be best for Levi—for Ulysses—if I did not know. He feared that upon my return the child's presence would be revealed, and he did not trust what Papa might do under those circumstances. So Caleb remained silent, maintained his secret and watched over the growth of his nephew. And as much pain as these eight years have caused me, I do not fault my dear brother. Nay, I dare say he has done the right thing.

Caleb has apologized many times over for waiting so long after my return to tell me of Ulysses. At first, I could not fathom how he could do such a thing, but gradually, over the past week, I have come to know and understand my brother's mind. Caleb, still, remains our father's son, and although he was unable to give his nephew up to a foundling home, he was also unable to imagine the son of a Negro slave being reared as a Harden, which is what he knew I would do. Caleb feared Papa's wrath, even from the grave, and it took a full month for him to gather his courage. He says it was my deep unhappiness that finally gave him the strength to stand up against the dead man. I understand and forgive anything my brother has done, for he has saved the life of my son, and perhaps, saved my own too.

As Caleb had feared, and has now come to accept, Levi—Ulysses—is to be a Harden. Caleb had changed Levi's name when he was but weeks old, in the hope that the child would be safer without the appellation that brought such wrath to Papa's heart. I have decided that his name shall remain Ulysses to avoid confusion, though he will always be Levi in my heart.

My boy is now to be known as Ulysses Person Harden, the six-year-old scion of my tragically brief marriage in Ohio to George Washington Harden, a very distant cousin, who died of diphtheria within a year of our wedding day. Or so goes the story. Ulysses is the height of a six-year-old and very fair. With time, no one in Lexington shall remember that neither my marriage nor my child were spoken of before my return. It is a sign of the Lord's great benevolence that I had made no social calls since my return.

It is true that for the past week I have thought little of my husband, as I have been lost in the glory that is my son: talking with him, touching him, watching him, seeing what a fine boy he has grown into. Ulysses, although still quite shy, seems to be growing more comfortable with me, his own mama. He has not yet asked about his papa.

It gratifies me to know that it is Silas' child who shall carry on the Harden name. May Ulysses grow strong and have many children. May Silas finally be allowed to rest in peace.

June 20, 1868

Just as I had begun to hope Silas might find solace in having the last laugh on Papa, I learned this cannot be the case. I heard digging again last night, and it was the same digging I had heard before. Although I am loath to admit it, even to you, dear diary, I know these sounds are not my imagination at work; they are Silas, returned from the grave.

June 30, 1868

I am certain that Silas is still here, although I am not at all certain he is alive as we understand it. I think that perhaps my husband is frozen in time, lost and confused, and that he knows not what he does. I fear he is caught by the terrible injury that was done to him, and that he shall not rest until that wrong has been avenged.

I cannot believe that a merciful God would allow such a good man to spend all of eternity in this state, and I keep this thought with me when I feel myself sliding into despair.

July 2, 1868

In the cellar today, I stood before Mama's canning cupboard, clutching Silas' charm bag and trying to cheer him. I told him of all his son does: the lessons Ulysses learns, the books he reads, how fine he grows. But this does not seem to please my husband, it does not gladden his heart, and I fear his anger and frustration are far too easy to understand, far too easy to share. How could I ever have been so foolish as to think otherwise?

Silas believes his blood has, once again, been lost to my father, that as it has always been and will continue always to be, the white man has won. And I wonder who am I, the mother of his white child, to tell him differently?

As I cannot contradict the truth of these facts, I instead vow to raise Ulysses to be a compassionate white man, to respect and honor those whose skin is of any color. But Silas is indifferent to my promises, and sometimes I wonder if he understands that I am the young woman he married, that Ulysses is his son, that he is no longer among the living.

October 12, 1868

Silas came to me in a dream last night, and I now have no doubt that he is a different man from the one I knew. He is changed, bitter and unforgiving, and the harsh set of his face frightened me in a manner Silas never could have done while he was alive. He demanded to know where his brothers were, and I only wished I had good news to share, but I did not. Though the Vigilance Committee still searches, there has been no word, and Clara Garrison informed me just yesterday that she fears there never shall be. I could not tell Silas this, so I said nothing.

Silas misinterpreted my silence. "You are filling my tunnel," he thundered, "and you must stop immediately! You are replacing the dirt in the day while I sleep, undoing what I do every night! You wish to keep my brothers enslaved!"

"Oh no, my darling," I cried. "I would never do such a thing."

"Why should I believe the words of a white woman, when I see the truth of your acts before my eyes?"

"But I am not a white woman," I protested. "I'm your wife, Sarah, Ulysses'—Levi's—mother. All I've ever wanted is for your brothers to reach Canada. That, and for you to be with me."

He said nothing, but I could see from the cold gleam in his eyes that the man standing before me did not believe my words, that he saw only the color of my skin, not the color of my heart.

October 15, 1868

Silas came again last night, and the depth of his wrath knows no bounds. He smashed his heavy shovel into my chiffonier with such force that the rocker sitting next to it pitched and rolled. His face was mottled with fury as he shouted of his brothers, swearing that anyone—man or woman, black or white—who stood in the way of their freedom would die at his hand. He raged on about dirt and women filling his tunnel and other things I could not understand.

He did not appear to see me, and for that I was grateful. Although I am certain that the dear man I married would never lash out in hatred, never hurt a living creature without a prevailing reason, this man is vengeful and beyond compassion. I know not what this man will do.

My heart is broken, for now I am certain my husband is not at peace and never shall be. My dearest Silas is as enslaved in death as he was in life.

Perhaps more so.

CHAPTER TWENTY-FOUR

When I woke up in the morning, Michael was gone, but he had left a note on the pillow. "Didn't want to wake you. Did some clean-up downstairs and now off to the hospital. Will be back later to finish the tunnel and do anything else you'd like me to do." I smiled. I could think of a few things I'd like him to do. I reached my arms over my head in the self-satisfied stretch of an overfed cat basking in the sun, focused on the sensual ache of my muscles, on the gentle throbbing between my legs, on how good Michael had made me feel, would make me feel again and again . . .

Then I remembered my dream.

The man had arrived in the night, lost and lonely and confused; he left steely-eyed with anger and vengeance. He had arrived looking for Sarah; he left knowing he would never find her.

I reached for the phone and dialed Beth's number. "How are you feeling?" I asked when she said hello.

"Where are you?"

"Home."

"Alone?"

"Yes."

"Aren't you scared?"

I didn't want to talk about being scared. "You haven't told me how you are."

She sighed in resignation. "I'm fine. It doesn't even hurt much, and I slept great for a change—the upside of this thing's the good meds."

"I didn't sleep all that well—I had a weird dream."

There was a long silence. "About the ghost?"

I rolled onto my back and stared at the crack on the ceiling. "He was young, good-looking, and he was searching for Sarah. He couldn't find her. He was confused. He didn't know where he was."

"For Christ's sake, Lee, are you trying to tell me that some nice, little lost boy tried to kill me with a kitchen knife? Don't forget I'm sitting here with twenty-seven stitches in my arm."

"He wasn't so nice by the end of the dream—when I pretty much told him he was dead."

"He didn't know?"

"I don't think so."

"So you are scared?"

I still didn't want to think about how scared I was or wasn't, so I changed the subject to a topic I knew Beth would find irresistible. "I have something to tell you."

"Do you think you should get out of there?"

"I'm on my way to work."

"Do you want to come here when you're done?"

"I've got to finish the tunnel."

"Don't be stupid, Lee."

"I promised Michael."

There was a long pause. "Is that the something you have to tell me?" Beth asked.

"Perhaps."

"He spent the night?"

"He spent the night."

"You must be feeling good," she said with a leer in her voice. It was nice to know that no matter what happened, Beth would always be Beth.

"Much better," I had to admit.

"So he's meeting you there when you get done with work? He's going to finish the tunnel?"

"Maybe. Probably later. After dinner. I want to take it slow."

"You're not going to go into the cellar alone." It was a command.

"The cement guy's coming first thing tomorrow morning—it's got to get done."

"Why can't you wait for Michael? Why can't he just do it himself?"

"His mother just had open-heart surgery, Beth. I think he's a little busy today."

"Well, then why can't he do it when he comes over later?"

"I don't know for sure that he is coming over. It depends on his mother."

"I don't like this."

"Don't worry," I said. "It's under control."

She told me Russ had been by earlier to pick up her car—which was a good thing, as I had forgotten it was parked behind mine—then queried me on exactly how long I would be at work and how long I anticipated being home before Michael came over. I told her to take it easy and hung up.

I showered, dressed and ate breakfast. But before I left for SafeHaven, I went into the cellar. I tried not to think about what I was doing, or what my actions might imply about my beliefs, as I lay the tattered charm bag on the ground at the mouth of the tunnel. Maybe if he found it there, he wouldn't be as angry. Or better yet, maybe he'd go away.

There was an aura of festivity at SafeHaven when I arrived. Saturdays are visiting days for the juniors and seniors, and a swarm of small children raced through the narrow hallway. Their mothers sat in the front parlor, smiling indulgently. When you only see your child for a few hours a week, you're loath to discipline them. This was the good and bad news for these children, who lived with grandparents and aunts and in foster homes, whose past, present and future were embedded in shaky ground. I watched them with a twinge of sadness. They appeared so normal, so carefree, like any bunch of kids that you'd see at any middle-class daycare center.

I looked around for Trina, but didn't see her. Saturday mornings were difficult for her under the best of circumstances—she grieved for her lost little girl more than she ever let on—but today, with her restriction and impending expulsion, was sure to be her own personal hell. If Kiah decided to kick Trina out of the program, she was going straight to prison. Do not pass go. Do not collect two hundred dollars. I climbed the back stairs to the second floor landing and called out to her, but there was no answer, so I went on up to my office.

What a dump, as they say in the movies. Or, more correctly, what a disaster. In the week and a half since Gram had died, the mail and the memos and the faxes and the telephone messages had piled up. Not to mention the emails that were sure to be cluttering up my own little niche of cyberspace. I was determined to keep my mind away from Harden House and all it conjured; I was determined to stay focused on what was before me. As I looked at the piles leaking into each other—leaking onto the floor in one case—I figured if there ever was a task capable of holding ghosts at bay, this was it. But I needed to see Trina before I got started. I wanted to make sure she was okay and commiserate with her about the police's stupidity. If Dannow was talking about a 10,000 dollar retainer for me—and it was clear I wasn't really a suspect—I couldn't imagine what Trina's situation would be if the police started taking this more seriously. Poison and broken stairs and missing bracelets. Shit.

I went back down the stairs to check the dorm room. Only seniors were allowed in the dorm during the day, and although I suspected Trina had lost this privilege, I couldn't imagine where else she might be. But the dorm room was hushed, completely still, all the blankets pulled taut around their thin mattresses, neat hospital corners trying to initiate neat lives. If not for the personal mementos displayed on the night tables, it could have been an army barracks. Basic training for life.

I walked through the narrow pathway between the double row of cots to the window that faced the street and thought about the women I knew who had slept in these beds: Jenna, Deborah, Anthia, Holly, Sarita, Melanie, Carmen, Willow, Blondell, Gwen, Freddie, Susan, so many others. What had become of them once they returned to the street? I'd heard Freddie was assistant manager at the Burger King on Columbus Ave., that Willow was staying clean but having trouble getting her sons back from DES, that Anthia was using again, as was Holly, and that Susan had gone to live with her mother in Seattle. There had been no word on the others.

"All you need is love," was written in tiny block letters under the window ledge. Was that all they needed? I didn't think so. With or without love, most of those women could probably be found right where they had begun, doing what they had been doing, pretty much unaffected by their time in this room. To live in poverty is to live on the edge: trying to survive the dreariness, to make sense out of the chaos, to stay alive. I understood all too well why the women went back to drugs: it was a way to navigate through their world, perhaps not the safest or the wisest choice, but a valid choice nonetheless. I wondered if it was going to be Trina's choice, which made me wonder if I was getting worn down by the hopelessness of cycles, burning out. No, I reminded myself, Trina still had a chance. The cycle didn't win every time. Jenna and Deborah and Sarita were probably doing just fine.

Only one night table was completely bare, and I knew it was Trina's. She had once told me she hated all those Virgin Marys and stuffed animals and rosary beads. "I've only got me to count on," she had said. Probably a better bet than love.

I sat down on her bed and tried to imagine what it was like to be Trina, what she went through every day just to survive. But I knew it was impossible for me to truly understand: I checked the *Boston Globe* Metro/Region section every morning to make sure no one I knew from SafeHaven had been killed or hurt or arrested while I was safely asleep in Lexington. Trina didn't need to read the paper; this was where she lived.

I looked down and saw something sticking off the bottom shelf of her night table. It was a book. *Jackie By Josie*. One of the books Gram had given her. Who would've thought this was the kind of book Trina would like? I recognized that my surprise was a confirmation of my previous thoughts: what did I really know of Trina? What the *Boston Globe* told me? The small glimpses Trina had allowed?

I picked up the book. A hard cover, fairly new, still carrying that spicy, slightly funky bookstore smell. It looked cheerful, sort of silly, fun. Trina reading a light book just for the joy of reading. A sign of hope. I opened the book absently, then froze. A rough cavity had been gouged from the pages, about an inch and a half square. Inside the cavity, carefully coiled within the small square, was Gram's emerald-and-diamond bracelet.

"What are you doing in here?" Trina demanded. She was standing in the doorway, glaring at me.

I jerked my head up as her words cracked the silence, and for a moment, I felt guilty, as if it was I who had been caught red-handed, then I just felt sad. I scooped the bracelet out of the book and stared at it twinkling in my palm. I held it out toward her.

"You have no right to mess with my things."

"What's this doing here?" I asked, my voice surprisingly calm.

"I'm not throwing down for this." Trina marched into the dorm and stood at the foot of the cot, her jaw jutting forward in anger. "I didn't steal it."

I felt a flicker of hope. Perhaps there was another explanation. "Then how did it get in your book?"

She crossed her arms and pursed her lips together. "I don't know."

I thought about Lionnel being arrested for fencing stolen goods, about Trina getting caught trying to pass him something from the window, and my hope dimmed. I waited.

"Well," she said, back-stepping a bit, "I know how it got in the book—I put it there—but I don't know how I got it in the first place."

"I don't understand," I said, but I was afraid I did.

"Please, you have to believe me," she begged, her eyes glistening with unshed tears. "It's not what you think."

I wanted to believe her, to believe my friend, the woman I had defended to Kiah and Blais, the woman who had commiserated with me yesterday about handsome men, but who had assured me—and correctly so—that Michael was an exception. And part of me did believe her, but another part held Gram's bracelet. It was difficult to deny the weight of the evidence in my hand.

She stared at my hand. "What are you going to do?"

"I don't know, Trina. I honestly don't know." I could almost hear my illusions—delusions?—shattering around me.

"I'll go to prison if you tell."

I looked at the young woman standing before me: such potential, such waste. Kiah always said Gram and I were too trusting, and it appeared that, once again, Kiah was right.

"Please, I can't go to prison, and I can't crawl the street."

"Did Gram know?"

"I told you, I didn't steal the bracelet. Clara didn't know anything—there was nothing to know."

I couldn't believe Trina was standing in front of me, denying that which was so patently obvious to us both. How stupid did she think I was? "Did you do anything to her?"

"Do anything to her?" Trina repeated, clearly confused by the question, then her eyes turned icy cold. "Oh, I catch it now. You want to know if I did anything to Clara. You want to know if I killed your grandmother." Then she began to laugh, a harsh, bitter laugh filled with self-righteous indignation. "Always the same," she said. "You're all the fucking same."

This was getting beyond believable. "Don't give me that sanctimonious shit about how hard it is to be black," I cried. "I gave you—we all gave you—every chance, every break, because you're black." I raised the fist that held the bracelet and was astonished to find myself shaking it at her. "It was in your book, Trina, on your night table, so don't give me any crap about how this is about race."

Trina wasn't laughing anymore. Her mouth was set in a thin line of fury and her eyes blazed with such fierceness that it crossed my mind she might actually pose a physical threat. "It's always about race."

"Well, I'm not buying it." I stood up and brushed past her. "You're trying to guilt-trip the wrong person." I walked out of the dorm, up the stairs and into my office.

I shut the door and jammed my chair under the knob. Then I picked up the phone and called the Lexington police.

Trina knew from experience that it didn't take long to get funky in the hold, and she could smell herself turning already. This shit was coming down the same way it had come down with Hendrika. Yeah, she had done wrong then, lots and lots wrong, plenty she wished she could take back and do over again, and she had done some wrong now. But neither time did she do what they were accusing her of doing.

And just like with Hendrika, the man was gonna hang it on her all the same. She knew there was no point in telling him her story or trying to buck him in any manner 'cause he was gonna win in the end. He always won in the end.

She was done, done with the changes, done with the plans. She was done with it all. All's that ever happened when she made plans was that she got herself disappointed.

No plans. No disappointments. She was done.

CHAPTER TWENTY-FIVE

Once again, I left SafeHaven without cleaning my desk. Although there was nothing forcing me out the door, I knew I was going to be useless after watching Trina handcuffed and put in a cruiser. Kiah assured me I had done the right thing. She hugged me and told me that no matter how hard you try, some people just can't be helped. But it didn't make me feel any better. I was a squealer. A snitch. A shit.

I reminded myself that Trina had lied to me, stolen from Gram, and tried to hide her guilt by raising the false specter of racism, but she was my friend—had been my friend—and I felt bad about turning the final screw in her coffin. Although I also recognized that it was Trina, not me, who had turned all the others. The facts were the facts, and no matter how much I detested them, they were impossible to refute. How could I have misread her so completely? How could I have been so blatantly and startlingly wrong about her?

As I drove through Lexington Center, a headache furiously pounded behind my eyes. The bright spring day was a piercing contrast to the darkness that filled my soul, and the intense sunlight made my headache worse. The short drive from the Common to Harden House seemed to take forever, as if the pain in my head was consigning me to slow motion. I also had the nagging suspicion that there was no aspirin in the cabinet at home, that I had finished a bottle the day after the funeral and written it down on a list somewhere. Of late, I hadn't been attentive to the details of ordinary life.

At first, I was relieved to see Beth's Rover in the driveway. She was sure to have aspirin in her purse, and I needed someone to talk to. But then I realized that my discovery proved Beth had been right about Trina: it verified her distrust and racism, snickered at my knee-jerk liberal assumptions. My heart sank. There was no way I could avoid telling her, and Beth's smug satisfaction at her vindication was not going to be pretty to watch.

I dragged myself into the house, and for the first time since I discovered the bracelet coiled in Trina's book, I thought about the ghost and wondered if he had found the charm bag. But I was almost too tired to care, too worn down by the day's events to be concerned with something so amorphous. I thought about Michael and my spirits lightened a bit, but not enough to alleviate the pain of Trina's defection or the pounding in my head.

I called out for Beth, and when she didn't answer, I made a beeline for the kitchen cabinet where Gram kept the medicine and vitamin pills. There was no aspirin, no Tylenol, no Advil. Just as I had suspected, nothing for my headache. I yelled Beth's name again. Still no answer, but her purse lay on the table. Beth was about as open a person as you could find anywhere—she never bothered to close the bathroom door, and once, when a younger cousin had thrown up on me, she had literally given me the shirt off her back—so I didn't hesitate to rummage through her purse. I found a small bottle of aspirin and was so agitated as I pulled it out from the bottom of the bag that Beth's comb, lipstick and a letter from BankBoston fell to the floor. I swallowed the pills with a large gulp of water, then kneeled down to scoop up Beth's scattered possessions.

As I returned the lipstick and comb to the purse, the letter fell open. A sociology professor had once told my class that if you were a naturally nosy person you had a good chance of becoming a top-notch sociologist. I don't know about top-notch, but I do have a master's degree. I read the letter. It didn't make any sense, so I read it again. I double-checked the addressee: Russ and Beth Conyers, holders of mortgage #354-985-2 on property at 17 Patriot's Way, Wellesley, Massachusetts. It was a foreclosure notice from a vice president at the bank. He apologized for the inconvenience—inconvenience?—but declared June 15 to be the last possible date by which the balance due could be paid, an amount totaling $362,893.37. If said balance was not received by that date, the house would become the possession of the bank and all occupants and their personal effects were to be vacated from the premises at that time.

I dropped into a kitchen chair and stared at the letter in my hand. Slowly, as if out of a thick fog, I became aware of sounds coming from the cellar. The scrape of metal against stone. Of dirt falling to the earth. The sound of digging. The sound of my nightmare. The sound of Gram's final efforts. I leapt from the chair, the letter still clutched in my damp palm. The sound of Beth. Why would Beth be digging?

I looked down at the BankBoston letterhead. A ghost in the cellar was more plausible than Beth and Russ's mortgage being foreclosed, than Beth digging. Tales of spirits and phantoms had long been part of the human narrative, but Russ had all that Microsoft stock and a thriving second career as a dentist, for God's sake. Beth had twenty-seven stitches in her arm. It was clear I didn't know what was plausible and what was not. Both. Neither. One of each.

I stuffed the letter back into Beth's purse, unable to process its meaning, unable to process the meaning of anything that was happening around me. When I turned toward the cellar entrance, the sounds ceased, and I approached the open door slowly, listening, hearing nothing. Then, stepping carefully around the broken tread, I went down into the shadowy darkness.

The musty odor threw me back into my first nightmare, the first time I had seen the man, and I pressed my hands to the damp fieldstones for support. I imagined I smelled his sweat, saw once again the fury and hatred in his movements. Then I remembered my dream from last night: he was barely a man, on the cusp of adulthood; he just wanted to find Sarah, to find himself. I continued down and crossed slowly to the rough-cut opening that led to the old cellar. He had not been happy when I had told him he would never find her.

But it wasn't him. It was Beth. Her back was to me, and she was kneeling in front of a thick trunk of electrical wires that hung from a metal box in the far corner of the room. I was filled with a blinding relief tinged with a touch of disappointment. Beth was holding wire cutters in her right hand; her left hand was bandaged from wrist to elbow. A shovel lay off to the side.

"Hey," I called, puzzled.

Beth whirled around, her eyes wild and her color high. "What are you doing here?" she demanded. "I thought you were at work."

For a moment, I couldn't remember why I was there, what had happened at SafeHaven or what had brought me down the stairs. When I did remember, I didn't want to tell Beth about Trina or how the sound of digging had scared me, so I shrugged and said, "Left early."

"You told me this morning you'd be there all day."

"I lied," I joked.

But Beth wasn't laughing. "Why? What'd you think you'd catch me doing?"

This conversation didn't make any more sense than ghosts or foreclosure notices. "What are you doing?"

Her eyes narrowed and her voice was coated with disdain. "As if you didn't know," she spat at me.

"I don't."

"The sump pump," Beth explained calmly, but sweat broke out above her upper lip. "I wanted to make sure it worked in case it rained."

"Sump pump," I repeated. Beth had often helped Gram during electrical emergencies—she had even come over to Richie's and my apartment in Brookline late one night and rewired the fuse box—but it was late May. Heavy rains came in April.

"I heard a forecast."

The sun was out.

"They said there was a threat of thunderstorms," she insisted, although I hadn't contradicted her. "I heard it on NPR."

I looked at the long coils of wire snaking from the electrical box, across the dirt floor, and into a large puddle in front of the tunnel opening. If she was installing the sump pump, why were the wires leading to the water instead of to the pump? It was dangerous. Anyone who accidentally stepped in the puddle would get electrocuted . . .

I looked back at Beth, and there was a gleam in her eye that reminded me of the mean little girl she had been, of how she had reveled in frightening me into tears. There had been no forecast of thunderstorms today.

"You . . . ?" I started, but was unable to finish my thought, my accusation. "You . . . ?"

Beth picked up the shovel. "I had no choice," she said. "You've got to believe me. I didn't mean to do it, but I didn't know what else to do."

I backed slowly away, not wanting to startle her. What was she saying? What did she mean? I caught sight of a wooden spool that had once held electrical wire on the ground to my right. There was a hammer and a couple of screwdrivers on a sawhorse to my left. I could trip her with the spool, smash her head with the hammer, drive the screwdriver into her neck.

What was I thinking? This was Beth, my dearest cousin, the sister I had never had. Beth, who right at this moment was standing before me, a shovel held menacingly in her hands. The muscles in her biceps bulged, and I knew even with twenty-seven stitches that she was capable of doing me serious injury with a single, strategically placed blow of that shovel. And I believed that she might. This wasn't happening.

Except that it *was* happening. "They're going to take my house," Beth cried. "Don't you see? Don't you understand? That would destroy us. Me, Russ, Zach. All of us!"

Beth's pathetic justifications were an admission of guilt. Nothing was as I believed it to be; no one was who I believed they were. I didn't understand. I did understand.

"It was Russ and his God damn precious stock market. And now it's all gone—every last penny of it. The son of a bitch thought he was so smart with his high-tech options and his short selling, but he was stupid, and he lost it all!" Beth clutched the shovel as if it were a lifeline; her knuckles were white on the handle. "Someone had to save the family. I just did what I had to do. You understand, don't you, Lee? You see how it happened? How I had no choice?"

Russ with his eyes glued to his computer, his cell phone in his pocket, the *Wall Street Journal* by his side. It had never occurred to me that there was any chance he might lose. Nor had it occurred to me that Beth was capable of such madness, such self-delusion. It was obvious I didn't know Beth at all, that I didn't know much of anything. I had been played the fool for the second time in as many hours. "I understand," I tried to assure her, but I could hear the waver in my voice. I took a deep breath, striving to make my tone smooth, sympathetic. "It must have been awful," I added. "Just terrible."

"It was. It is." Beth loosened her grip on the shovel and allowed it to hang at her side. "Can you find it in your heart to forgive me?"

I swallowed the bile that rose in my throat. Forgive her for murdering our grandmother? It wasn't likely. I nodded. "Sure," I lied. "Sure I can." But even as I was trying to grasp Beth's revelations, trying to devise a plan to get out of the cellar alive, it dawned on me that Trina hadn't made a fool of me—I had made a fool of myself. Beth had somehow set Trina up, planted the bracelet, implicated her in more than just theft. Trina had done nothing but been on the receiving end, just as she had said—and I hadn't believed her.

A flicker of my understanding must have flashed across my face, because Beth let out an inhuman roar and raised the shovel. "I have to have Harden House!" she bellowed. "I need the money. You have no right to it! It was always mine! Always!"

I ducked and kicked the wooden spool at her. It shot out from my foot and whacked Beth in the legs. She stumbled forward, and as she fell the shovel clattered to the ground. I turned and ran.

I started up the stairs, not knowing what I was going to do, where I was going to go, how I was going to get away. Beth was in far better shape than I, faster and stronger, and I knew from the way she had fallen that she hadn't been hurt by the spool, just startled and slowed for a moment. I leapt over the broken tread and launched myself across the kitchen and toward the back door. I could hear Beth yelling as she came up the stairs.

She'd be on me in seconds. I swung my head in a wild arc. There was no way I could make it to my car and drive away. Nowhere to hide out there in the bright sunlight. Nowhere to run. Her feet pounded up the steps. My only hope was to outsmart her.

Instead of going outside as Beth would expect, I pushed the back door open, allowed the screen door to slam, then turned back inside and sped toward the front of the house, hoping Beth would assume I had run out into the yard. Without conscious awareness of where I was going, I slid into the entryway and slowly, softly, approached the main stairway. I climbed to the first landing and stood as quietly as I could before the hidden door of the safe room.

I willed my ragged breath silent, my body completely still, and listened intently, not breathing, as Beth roared from the cellar, across the kitchen and out the back door. I pressed my fingers to the hinges hidden by the stairway's carved panels and waited. When I heard her circle to the rear of the house, I pushed the fake panel and jumped into the safe room. My ankle twisted under me as I fell to the rotting floor, which was farther below the opening than I had remembered. Ignoring the pain, I stood on my toes and pulled the panel shut. It was dark and hot and horribly close, but I was hidden. I was safe. For the moment.

The room was just ten feet by four feet, perhaps less, the claustrophobic crush of its walls only slightly eased by its height, which rose through the attic. I crouched in the east corner, which seemed to have the greatest number of intact floorboards, shivering in the sweltering heat. I had always wondered what it felt like to be a runaway slave, hidden in the safe room, terrified and without recourse, without the ability to act, just waiting, waiting, only waiting, as the hunters prowled overhead.

Now I knew.

I could see whole families crowded together in this tiny space, hear the mothers soothing their fretting babies, feel the men straining to be strong, smell the sweat and the fear. Theirs and my own. It seemed not only possible, but probable, that the souls of these men and women still hovered nearby. I felt the weight of their history, of all that pointless hatred, all the hope and all the suffering, wrap around me. As close as the walls.

And I hadn't believed Trina. She who doesn't learn from history is doomed to repeat it.

As I sat there, berating myself and waiting for Beth to come or to go, to find me or to give up the search, waiting to discover if I was going to live or die, it occurred to me that Beth could have set up the ghost the same way she set up Trina. Did her revelations mean that my ghost was no more real than my assumptions about her? Michael had speculated that Beth could have stabbed herself, but at the time neither one of us considered it plausible. I was discovering that plausibility was much more complicated than I had ever imagined.

I heard her reenter the house, screaming my name. I heard her pound up the stairs, not more than an inch from where I cowered. I heard her circling the upstairs bedrooms, racing down the back stairs. Then there was silence. Nothing. I held my breath. Had she gone outside again? Had she given up?

Suddenly I was rocked by a powerful smash to the stud just above my shoulder. I cringed and pulled my legs tighter to my chest. The wall of the east parlor was violently pounded again. The next crash came at the level of my head. Beth had not been fooled.

"You think I'm stupid?" Beth thundered. "You think I couldn't guess where you'd hide? You with your tedious Harden family obsession, always sucking up to Gram. 'The Colonel, the Congressman,' " she intoned with a sing-songy whine. "Always thinking you were so smart and ed-u-ca-ted. The fair-haired girl." Another blast to the wall shook my entire body. "Well, who's the smart one now?"

I jumped to a stand and looked around. There was nowhere to go. Beth was right: I was trapped. Stupidly, stupidly trapped. What had I been thinking?

Then Beth began to laugh, and the sound was so clear, so close, it was as if she were in the room with me. She continued to laugh as she crossed through the entryway and climbed the stairs. "Ally-ally in free," she called out cheerfully, in imitation of our childhood games. "Loser gets fed to the woman with the iron teeth!"

I smashed my foot hard into one of the rotted floorboards, and it broke under my shoe. I hit the one next to it, and it did the same. Just as Beth yanked open the fake panel and leered down at me, I kicked another board out of the way and jumped down into the cellar.

I landed hard again, on the same ankle I had twisted in the safe room, and I crumpled atop a pile of dirt. For a moment I couldn't catch my breath, and when I did, I began to cough. I grabbed my foot, rocking in pain, choking as I expelled the dirt in my lungs, not at all certain I was going to be able to walk.

Again the fiendish snicker. This time from above. "Perfect," she screeched. "Just perfect!"

I stared up at Beth, barely able to recognize the twisted

face that flashed its teeth at me. She held the shovel and was looking down at me from the same position I had looked down on the dying man in my dream. Did this mean I had been seeing into the future, not into the past? That Harden House wasn't haunted? That I was foreseeing my own death?

I tried to stand, but my ankle resisted the weight, and I collapsed to the ground again. I was lying beneath the mouth of the tunnel, on the same spot where the man had been digging, the same spot where Gram had died.

Beth's footfalls were buoyant and joyful as she came down the stairs toward me. But suddenly it wasn't Beth who I feared the most. From somewhere behind my head, I heard the sound of metal scraping against metal, manacle against stone. The sound of digging.

CHAPTER TWENTY-SIX

I lay motionless on the dirt, my eyes squeezed shut, my fists clenched, the pain in my ankle dwarfed by my fear. He was back and she was coming. I needed a plan, a way out, but my mind refused to cooperate. The synapses wouldn't fire; they were anesthetized, numb. He was back and she was coming. A single word scratched at the skin of my terror. Escape. If I did not escape, I would surely die.

There were three exits: the safe room, the cellar stairs and the tunnel. I opened my eyes and stared up at the shattered remnants of the safe room, at the splintered floorboards swinging precariously over my head, ominous and threatening. No exit. Beth was advancing down the stairs toward me; I could hear her footfalls coming closer and closer, feel her insanity obstructing my way. No exit. And the tunnel was collapsed in on itself, filled with one-hundred-fifty years of dirt and roots and leaves. No exit.

Adrenaline pumped its way through the mush of my mind, and I thrust myself up on my hands and frantically scanned the shadowy room. A weapon. A tool. A technique. Something. Anything. There had to be another answer. I was not going to die here. Not in the lair of the woman with the iron teeth. Not in the place I feared more than any other.

The empty electrical spool lay where I had pushed it. A screwdriver and hammer lay on the sawhorse. Cobwebs, fieldstone, dirt—and the sound of digging. Had someone lain inside the tunnel for all these years? Had he now emerged?

Then the scraping noise stopped. I didn't want to look. I didn't want to know. Ghosts weren't real. There was no such thing. Ghosts didn't exist. They were infeasible, unworkable, impossible. I twisted my head to the east wall. To my great relief, no one was there. Just the tunnel's gaping mouth, dirt dripping from its lower lip. Mocking me.

Beth's feet hit the floor. I heard her cross to the opening between the cellars and threw myself at the sawhorse. I grabbed the screwdriver just as she stepped over the threshold and into the room; she had the shovel jauntily cocked under her good arm. Using every bit of strength I possessed, I pulled myself to a stand, hiding the screwdriver behind my back. I tried not to wince as I put weight on both feet. I didn't want Beth to know I was injured. To think she possessed an additional advantage.

"Hurt your foot?" Her voice was coated with concern, but the menacing casualness with which she held the shovel said all there was to say. "Perhaps it's my turn to drive you to the emergency room."

"I'm fine, thank you." I had to stall for time, and false pleasantries were all that came to mind.

"I put liquid cocaine in her milk that day at lunch," Beth said conversationally, as if she were telling me how she liked her coffee.

I had no idea what she was talking about. She could have been speaking in tongues. Maybe she was.

"I read in a book on poisons that milk slows down the absorption process," she continued.

It still wasn't registering. "Absorption process?"

"That's why the police never considered me a suspect," she said proudly. "That's why I left right after lunch. I knew no one but Gram would drink the milk."

"Milk." Now I understood. Beth was speaking English,

and her words and their implication were all too clear. She had read a book about poison. Dentists used liquid cocaine for surgical procedures. Gram was the only one in the house who drank milk. "Russ," I faltered, then tried again. "You got the cocaine from Russ."

Beth smiled. A teacher with a slow pupil who had finally caught on. "You might say I 'borrowed' the keys to the drug cabinet in his office."

I didn't know what was worse, that Beth had killed Gram or that she had planned it so thoroughly. Then another sick link, another insane piece of a lunatic's puzzle, smacked me between the eyes. "And because it was a street drug, it made Trina look even guiltier." This was beyond belief, beyond understanding, beyond anything I had ever imagined could happen in my world.

"Dumb luck," Beth admitted with a self-deprecating wave of her shovel. "I admit I wanted to set Trina up—that's why I put Gram's bracelet in her backpack—but I've got to be truthful with you here, the cocaine connection was just a lucky break."

". . . Got to be truthful with you here . . ." Beth's words echoed through my brain. *" . . . Just a lucky break."* She was a madwoman, far crazier and more deadly than I had ever imagined. This was much more than Dotty Aunt Hortense. This was true danger. My eyes involuntarily darted around the room.

Like a lion at the kill, Beth smelled my fear. Keeping her eyes on me, she assumed the stance of a fighter, holding the shovel in front of her as both barrier and weapon. She began to dance a wide circle around me, as if in a boxing ring, her back to the wall. Her eyes were an inky black, almost completely dilated; they never left mine. "I'm sorry it had to come to this," she said in a soft, sorrowful voice, as if she actually believed what she was saying. "If Gram hadn't changed her will, this never would've happened, but she did what she did, it was her decision, and it's beyond me to undo what's she's done." Beth's self-delusion was unfathomable. Did she really believe Gram was responsible for her own death?

I gripped the screwdriver and turned as she circled, keeping pace with her every movement, holding her in my sights, biting my lip against the thunderbolts of pain shooting up my leg.

"I'll give you the house," I offered, finally understanding that Beth was capable of anything. Of everything. The terror that filled me as I watched her slow, crazed circuit, was stunning. I wondered how long a person could live with such fear. "I'll sign it over to you tomorrow," I pleaded. "However you want it. Whatever you want."

Beth paused under the safe room's dangling floorboards. She pursed her lips in a gruesome mockery of serious consideration, then shook her head. "Too late now," she said with a resigned sigh. "If only Gram had done that in the first place this—" She froze. All color drained from her face.

I turned and followed her gaze. I had thought the fear that filled me was the greatest a human being could experience and still survive, but now I knew it had been just a prelude. I clung to the sawhorse as if it could save me from being drowned by the terror that towered before me.

He was real.

As real as I. As real as Beth, and most likely, even more dangerous.

He stood in front of the tunnel, throwing a long and solid shadow over the earthen floor. Shirtless, he was taller and thicker, stronger, more ominous, than I remembered.

He had a ragged cast on his leg, a shovel in his powerful hands, and he stared at Beth with a loathing that could easily precede murder.

I tore my eyes from him and looked at Beth. If she didn't see him, maybe he wasn't there. Maybe this was just another one of my nightmares. But if it was a dream, Beth was having the same dream as I.

"Who?" she stammered. "What the hell . . . ?"

I couldn't answer. I couldn't speak. My world was listing so far off kilter, I could barely stand. Beth had killed Gram. Ghosts were real.

The ghost raised his shovel and started toward Beth, who stood completely paralyzed with incomprehension and disbelief, or maybe, in this case, belief. His muscles rippled as he moved closer to her, molten iron steeled with hatred. He wasn't ephemeral, and he wasn't transitory: there was nothing ghost-like about him. He was a man, an angry man bent on destruction. And it was clear he could accomplish it with ease.

For the most fleeting of moments, I thought I should just stand back and let him kill Beth. She surely deserved it. But I couldn't. "No!" I cried. "Stop!"

Again, it was as if time had slowed to half-time. The ghost, the man, halted in his course toward Beth, and slowly, with the grim tediousness of inevitability, turned toward me. Every muscle and sinew of his being radiated a deep, all-consuming hatred, and when the searing enmity of his gaze fell on me, I knew I was dead.

"Please," I croaked, although I had no idea what I was pleading for. My life, I supposed. "Look," I pointed to the charm bag that lay where I had left it for him this morning. "I brought you your charm bag."

His expression softened, and he mouthed the word,

"Sarah," although no sound came from his lips.

Just as in my dream, he believed I was Sarah Harden. And from the expression on his face, it was apparent he loved Sarah and would never allow anyone to hurt her. For the second time in as many minutes, I thought about how easy it would be to just let him kill Beth, but I said, "Don't hurt her. Please."

He picked up the tattered charm bag and placed it around his neck.

"You're not where you think you are," I said softly. "This isn't what it seems."

"Sarah," he mouthed soundlessly.

"What?" Beth whispered hoarsely. "What's he saying?"

I ignored her and spoke to the ghost. "You're lost," I said. "Lost in time because of what happened to you. What the anti-abolitionists did to you."

He shook his head. It was obvious that he could hear me, and that he didn't understand a thing I was saying.

I tried again. "When they killed you, right after you called out for Sarah to help you, to help your brothers, you got stuck. Stuck in time because your death was so awful, so needless. So wrong."

"What the hell's going on here?" Beth demanded, sounding like herself once again.

He ignored her too, looking at me as if we were the only two in the room. "Sarah?" And this time his silent word was clearly a question.

"No," I said as gently as I could, although I wasn't at all certain I should admit I wasn't his missing love. "I'm not Sarah, I'm her great-great-great-granddaughter."

His bewilderment transposed into stupefaction, and I was afraid.

I took a deep breath and said, "Sarah's been gone a hundred years." Now that I had begun, the truth seemed the only course, and the fact that he was finally going to hear it gave me courage. "You were probably killed about forty years before that, probably right before the war began. The war between the north and south—the Civil War. The north ended up winning and all the slaves were freed when it was over."

He was listening carefully, not moving toward Beth or me, apparently caught between believing and not believing.

"After the war, they changed the constitution and slavery was abolished everywhere in the country," I continued. "So, you see, now you don't need to finish your tunnel. Your brothers have been free for a long time—as have their children's children." But even as I spoke the words, I thought of Trina and wondered how free his brother's children's children really were.

I saw the gleam of comprehension, of recognition, cross his face, the realization that I was confirming something he already knew, but had been unwilling to acknowledge. This flash was followed quickly by anger.

"Don't be angry," I said, staring into his hauntingly familiar eyes. "Don't be afraid. It's okay to put it down, to let it go, to be with Sarah. Go to her, to your brothers. You'll finally be a free man."

Before he could respond, I caught the glint of flashing metal out of the corner of my eye. Beth. I turned toward the movement and raised my screwdriver in a futile effort to ward off her shovel.

Beth swung the shovel at my forehead, but instead of connecting with my head, it dropped to the ground at her feet. Her face was a mask of complete bafflement as she stared, stupefied, at her empty hands. A deep rumble came from above, and before she could raise her eyes, the floorboards that had been hanging over her head crashed to the ground in deluge of lumber and mortar and nails. Beth crumpled into a motionless heap.

I dropped down next to her, the screwdriver clattering uselessly from my fingers. "Beth!" I cried, already forgetting what she had become, remembering only who she had been. I frantically pulled the splintered boards from her face and groped for the pulse in her wrist. It was faint and skittish, but it was there.

Weak with relief, I swung around toward the man. But I found myself staring directly into the yawning mouth of the tunnel. He was gone.

CHAPTER TWENTY-SEVEN

The rest of the weekend was a nightmare, and I don't know what I would have done without Michael. Fragments of thoughts and images swirled through my brain: the light of understanding in the eyes of the man to whom I had just explained his own death, the melancholy face of Sarah Harden staring out from an old photograph, Gram wrestling with no one, a vial of liquid cocaine, a tattered red charm bag. I couldn't sleep and couldn't eat, and I got into talking jags that Michael and Raymond Langley and even my mother tolerated with infinite patience.

Beth hadn't been hurt as badly as I had feared, not nearly as badly as her self-inflicted knife wound of the previous day. So after a quick visit to the emergency room for a tetanus shot and a few bandages, I had the privilege of watching Langley place handcuffs on her wrists and put her into the back seat of his car. It was the second time in a single day I had watched someone I loved being cuffed and taken down to the police station. Trina was released as soon as the Lexington police informed their Boston counterparts that someone else had confessed to the theft of the bracelet and the murder of Clara Barrett. She went back to SafeHaven, but refused to speak to me.

I didn't tell the police or my mother about the man who had saved my life—the ghost who had saved my life. Only Michael knew what had really happened. He held me as we discussed it late into the night and was still holding me when the sun rose. Neither he nor I came up with any answers, just lots more questions, but I was grateful for his presence.

My nights had been turned into days and days into nights, and when the ringing phone woke me, I guessed it was late afternoon from the angle of the sun and the sweat running between my shoulders blades. But I didn't know which day. Monday or Tuesday? Michael wasn't in the bed, but I could hear hammering somewhere beneath me. Fixing the floor of the safe room I had demolished. I picked up the phone. It was Ms. Tosatti at Cary Library. The boxes my grandmother had given the library had been found, and Nancy Winsten said I was welcome to them.

"You found Gram's boxes?" I asked, although that was exactly what she had just told me.

"I'm on my way out, but if you stop at the reference desk someone will help you." She thanked me and hung up before I could thank her. I had the feeling she had been hoping to reach a machine.

I lay back on the pillow, thankful for any crust of good news, but so weary it felt as if I hadn't slept at all. I knew that the boxes might hold some clues about my ghost, but the idea of getting up and driving the quarter mile to the library was overwhelming. Beth had killed Gram. Poisoned her. On purpose. I couldn't stop thinking about it, yet I couldn't quite grasp it. It eluded all logic, yet made its own demented kind of sense. Beth had killed Gram. Trina had done nothing wrong. I had misjudged everyone—including the ghost. The ghost. Another impossible concept with its own frightening consistency.

I dragged myself from bed and went downstairs to find Michael. He was in the cellar, and I leaned into the safe room's hidden doorway to call down Ms. Tosatti's news. He told me I should take a shower and go pick up the boxes. He was worried about me, concerned I wasn't handling the mounting stress very well, that I was withdrawing, hiding. I knew what he really wanted was for me to get cleaned up and out of the house. It seemed easier to do as he suggested than to argue, so I did.

When I got to the library, Ms. Tosatti had already left for the day, but the librarian behind the reference desk knew exactly where the cartons were. She even got a high school kid shelving books to carry them to the car for me and patted my shoulder encouragingly as we left the building.

The kid didn't say anything, but he kept throwing furtive glances in my direction, then turning quickly when I met his eye. Murder was a rarity in Lexington, and everyone in town must know by now what had happened at Harden House—or at least know as much as anyone would ever know. It occurred to me that a granddaughter killing her grandmother was pretty rare anywhere, that anyone who read a newspaper or watched television must be aware of what Beth had done. I supposed I was going to have to accept my fifteen minutes of macabre fame, but I pretended I didn't notice the boy's stares.

When I got home, I set the cartons next to the ones Michael had brought up from the cellar less than two weeks before. I sat on the couch and watched the boxes at my feet as if I believed they might suddenly stand up and walk away or start spitting snakes. The sound of hammering in the cellar reverberated through the floor boards, and I pressed my damp palms to my jeans. Hammering, not shoveling, I reminded myself. Michael working on the safe room floor, not a ghost digging a tunnel.

Inspecting the contents of the cartons seemed less scary than thinking about the ghost, so I knelt down and began rummaging. As Gram had said, there didn't appear to be anything that was all that sexy. Mostly illegible letters and equally illegible account books, but there was a recipe book—called a receipt book—that had belonged to Charlotte Harden and a few family photos. It was amazing to think that Gram had let this stuff go without going through it. Gram before and after Tubman Park.

I was well into the second box when I found a small, leather-bound book filled with a tiny, neat script. A journal of some sort. Apparently quite old. *"August 28, 1858,"* I read. *"Today is my seventeenth birthday . . ."* My eyes raced down the page, and I gasped when I saw the words, *"I am Sarah Abigail Harden, daughter of Stanton Elijah Harden and Charlotte Abbott Harden . . ."* Sarah Harden had written a diary. A diary which might contain everything I had longed to know—and everything I didn't want to.

I sat back down on the couch and looked at the small book in my hands. Pulled and repelled. Frightened and enthralled. Could this tell me if Sarah had ever been able to help the black man's brothers? Who her husband had been, and what had happened to him? If the ghost I believed I had seen had anything to do with actual events at Harden House?

There was nothing to do but read it, and once I began, I didn't stop until I had finished. I read about Lewis Campbell and Wendell Parker and the Buffrum-Chase Ball. I read about Sarah's hopes and dreams and how everything had changed when a runaway slave named Silas Person appeared at the door of Harden House. I read about why the root closet—canning cupboard—was so small and what the east and west parlors had been used for. At one point, Michael came upstairs for a beer, and although I wanted more than anything to tell him what I had found, I couldn't bear to stop reading long enough to explain. I blew him a kiss, and he returned to the cellar.

I read about the charm bag and why there were mounds of dirt on the cellar floor. I read of the tortured decisions Sarah was called upon to make, of their disastrous results. I read of the hypocrisy of the Colonel, the great abolitionist of whom we were all so proud. And yes, I learned about Sarah's inability to help Silas' brothers and who her husband had been. I remained surprisingly calm until the end of the diary, and then my hands began to tremble and it was difficult to follow the words. But I read on.

"Michael!" I yelled down the cellar stairs as soon as I had read the final page. Within seconds, he came bounding into the kitchen.

"What?" he demanded, grabbing me by the shoulders. "What's wrong?"

I handed him the diary. Without a word—wonderful man that he is—he sat down and began to read. I didn't interrupt him. I paced silently around the house, trying to understand the ramifications of all Sarah had written. I walked through the east parlor and into the west. Silas. Sarah. Ulysses. The Colonel. The bloodlines that crossed in my veins. I was proud to be descended from Silas and Sarah, proud of the risks they had been willing to take for love and for fairness. I was ashamed of the Colonel. And ashamed of myself.

Silas Person, my ghost and my great-great-great-grandfather, who had been killed by my great-great-great-great grandfather. Silas Person, who had come north in search of freedom and instead found both love and death. Silas Person, dead almost one-hundred-fifty years, who had saved my life two days ago.

I climbed the stairs and peered into the open door of the safe room, reliving the dream in which I had stood on this spot and looked down through this opening and saw a man bleeding to death on the floor. Silas Person had bled to death. He had been on that ground below. What I had seen had actually taken place. *"Silas still waits for his brothers. He digs his tunnel by night and sleeps by day, just as he did before Papa killed him."* I had seen him do that, heard him do that. *"Silas is as enslaved in death as he was in life."* I had seen this, too.

Michael finally closed the diary and looked up at me. "Do you think this could be true?"

"What else could it be?"

"It's amazing. Even without the metaphysical stuff—which I can't even begin to think about."

"Me either."

Michael reverently opened the diary. "Listen to this: '*Silas believes his blood has, once again, been lost to my father, that as it has always been and will continue to always be, the white man has won.*' "

"After I go apologize to Trina, will you help me get him out?"

"What if he isn't there?"

"He's there."

Dinner had just ended when I arrived at SafeHaven. Trina was in the kitchen washing dishes with a woman named Lorelei, and she appeared neither surprised nor pleased to see me. Kiah had recommended I wait another couple of days before approaching Trina, but after reading Sarah's diary, I couldn't wait any longer.

"Trina, could we go talk somewhere privately? Kiah's office maybe?"

She shrugged and kept washing.

"Please?"

Trina shrugged again.

Lorelei turned and gave me a cool up-and-down.

"Trina," I said, "I know you have every right to be furious, every right not to talk to me, but I've come to apologize, and I'm just asking for you to hear me out."

She didn't respond, but I detected a slight relaxing of the stiffness in her spine.

"I know I didn't hear you out, and that I'm asking a lot for you to do for me what I didn't do for you, but that's one of the things I came to apologize for—although not nearly the most important."

Trina peeled the stained yellow gloves from her hands and handed them to Lorelei—who scowled at me—then, without looking up, she marched across the hallway and into Kiah's office. I followed slowly.

When I closed the door and turned into the room, I saw Trina had seated herself at Kiah's desk. The principal and the recalcitrant student. How apt. I sat in the chair across from her, but found I was tongue tied, just like the bad girl I was.

"What'd you do about the inspection?"

I hadn't expected her to speak, and she caught me off guard. For a moment, I had no idea what she was talking about. "Oh, the inspection," I finally stammered. "It was supposed to be on Wednesday."

She eyed me as if I were a not-too-bright child, which was exactly the way I was acting.

"We cancelled it—or Michael did. Gram's just going to have to wait for Phase II."

Trina nodded. "So the way it came down with Clara was pretty different from how you had it all pictured."

"I guess you had a better take on Beth than I did."

"Seems that way."

I tried to smile. "Are you going to let me apologize or just sit there and rub it in?"

"It's a free country," Trina said, but her eyes said she didn't believe that for a second.

"Look Trina, I'm sorry. Really sorry. I was a shit. I wouldn't listen, I didn't believe you, I fell for the old stereotype, just like you said I would—like you said we all would."

Trina was playing nonchalantly with a paperweight on Kiah's desk, but I could tell from the tilt of her head that she was listening.

"You were right about how we're all racist—even when we don't think we are. I see it now, and, well, I'm just sorry. Sorry for doubting you. Sorry I was wrong. Sorry about everything. I was a lousy friend."

Trina twirled the paperweight around. "We're not friends."

"I know." I swallowed my disappointment, the self-inflicted pain, and added, "It's no good when the white man always wins."

"No good!" she said. "Ha!"

I reached into my purse and pulled out Gram's emerald-and-diamond bracelet. I placed it in front of her. "I want you to have this."

Trina eyed the bracelet.

"I know Gram would want you to have it, too."

She raised her eyes. "Your grandmother was a hot-shit lady, and I liked her a lot, but I don't have any attachments to this bracelet. I'm not the kind of folk who can afford to have feelings about jewelry."

"I want you to have it anyway. It's yours. You can do whatever you want with it."

"I'm just gonna sell it."

"Take it to a legitimate jeweler," I said before I realized how condescending my advice sounded. "You'll get a lot more money that way," I finished lamely.

Her eyes narrowed. "You trying to buy me off? Is that why you're doing this? To get yourself off the hook?"

"No," I said. "I don't think anything's going to get me off the hook."

"Then I'll take it." A ghost of a smile crossed her face as she scooped up the bracelet and left the room. A moment later, she poked her head back in the doorway and said, "Thanks."

Michael was still working in the safe room when I returned. Neither of us said anything as we headed down the narrow stairs into the cellar. Silently, we picked up the shovels and began removing dirt from the tunnel we had worked so hard to fill, the tunnel which had at first held hope, then sorrow and hatred, and now might become the repository of dignity restored.

There was no sign of Silas, but I spoke to him anyway. "Mr. Person, I'm your great-great-great granddaughter," I explained as I worked. "I can't do anything about the Colonel's betrayal or any of the awful things that happened to you, but I can get you out from under this damn house."

I could feel Michael watching me, but I didn't stop shoveling or talking. "Don't think your blood's been lost to the Colonel—it hasn't. It's been mingled with his, and the fact that I'm here right now is proof that you've survived. But you deserve more than just to survive in me, you need to be with the woman you love, to be at peace—to be free. So, if it's okay with you, I'm going to take you to Sarah. You can spend the rest of your days with her, as her husband, as Ulysses' father, as the patriarch of this family."

I took Silas' silence as consent.

That night, Michael and I dug until we couldn't lift our arms any more, then in the morning, we worked on hands and knees with tiny gardening tools. By late afternoon, we found what we were searching for, and a few months later, I stood in the Old Burying Ground as a headstone was placed over the newest grave in the Harden family plot. The chiseled letters read:

SILAS PERSON

1839–1859

LOVING HUSBAND OF SARAH,
LOVING FATHER OF ULYSSES

MAY HE FINALLY FIND
THE FREEDOM HE SOUGHT

LEXINGTON MINUTEMAN

On Wednesday, October 13, Harden House, owned by Lee Seymour, granddaughter of the late Clara Barrett, and located at 15 Hancock Street, was inducted into the Harriet Tubman Network to Freedom National Park and designated an official station of the Underground Railroad. Harden House boasts both a concealed "safe room" in which slaves were hidden and a tunnel beneath the house for the use of the runaways. To date, Tubman Park, which stretches from Louisiana to upstate New York, consists of 87 sites which represent points of interest along the route taken by slaves before and during the Civil War.

But our own Harden House is famous for more than participation in the Underground Railroad: it is the site of the so-called "Grandma Killing" (*Lexington Minuteman*, May 6, May 21) and is said to be haunted by the ghost of a runaway slave, Silas Person, who was killed in the cellar by Colonel Stanton Harden, the very abolitionist who was sheltering him. Human bones were indeed recently found under the house (*Lexington Minuteman*, May 28), and these bones were exhumed and reinterred in the Harden family plot in the Old Burying Ground by Ms. Seymour, the great-great-great granddaughter of Mr. Person and the great-great-great-great granddaughter of Colonel Harden.

The original diary of Sarah Harden, daughter of the Colonel and wife of Mr. Person, has been graciously donated to Cary Library by Ms. Seymour. A contract has been signed with a major publishing house to publish the diary sometime next year, and there has been considerable interest in the story from film companies.

The Hancock Street house is currently unoccupied. When asked, Ms. Seymour, who resides in Brookline with her fiancé, Michael Ennen, said that the memories were too painful. Tours of Harden House are held daily, on the hour, between 11:00 a.m. and 3:00 p.m. More information on both Harden House and Tubman Park can be found at the Lexington Visitors Center opposite the Minuteman statue.

Descendants of Silas Person

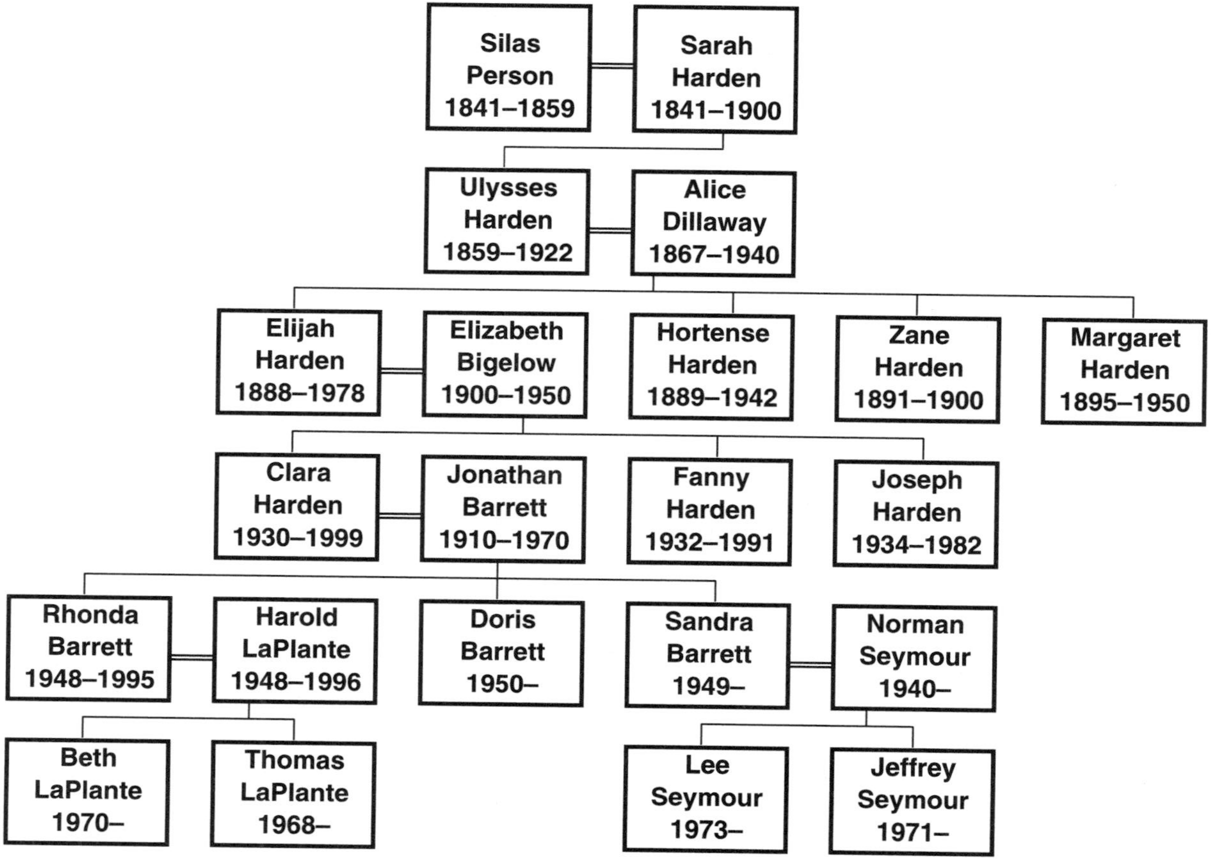